MY ONE A

Without a bit of trepidat... her bedroom. She looked ... ivory décor with wonder, as though it was the ... had seen the room. And in truth, it did look a bit different. There were candles lit on the dresser and bedside table, and the rumpled bedclothes had been put to rights and were turned back invitingly. She finally turned to Martin with a look that was part surprise and part bewilderment.

He led her over to the bed and instructed her to get in. "You *are* going to sleep tonight," he said quietly. He removed her ivory silk robe and watched her as she slid under the covers. He carefully folded the delicate garment and laid it across the peach boudoir chair by the vanity table. And then his intentions became plain as he stretched out next to her on top of the covers.

"Go to sleep, Ceylon," he said in that same quiet, sexy voice. "I'm just going to lie here with you until you nod off. We both know that you can sleep if you're relaxed, and sometimes it helps to have someone lying down with you," he said easily.

And sometimes it drives you right out of your mind, too! Ceylon rose up on her elbows and was about to protest when Martin snaked a long, muscular arm around her waist and pulled her next to him.

"Don't talk. Don't think. Just sleep," he murmured encouragingly.

Ceylon's mouth closed tightly and she lay there as brittle and stiff as a sheet of ice. She looked around at the dimly lit room, inhaled the fragrance of the scented candles, and felt the warmth of Martin's big body beside her. And before she could formulate another coherent thought, her eyes closed and she melted against his heat, beginning the first real sleep she'd had in months.

BOOK YOUR PLACE ON OUR WEBSITE AND MAKE THE ARABESQUE ROMANCE CONNECTION!

We've created a customized website just for our very special Arabesque readers, where you can get the inside scoop on everything that's going on with Arabesque romance novels.

When you come online, you'll have the exciting opportunity to:

- View covers of upcoming books

- Learn about our future publishing schedule (listed by publication month and author)

- Find out when your favorite authors will be visiting a city near you

- Search for and order backlist books

- Check out author bios and background information

- Send e-mail to your favorite authors

- Join us in weekly chats with authors, readers and other guests

- Get writing guidelines

- AND MUCH MORE!

Visit our website at
http://www.arabesquebooks.com

MY ONE AND ONLY LOVE

Melanie Schuster

ARABESQUE

BET BOOKS

BET Publications, LLC
http://www.bet.com
http://www.arabesquebooks.com

ARABESQUE BOOKS are published by

BET Publications, LLC
c/o BET BOOKS
One BET Plaza
1900 W Place NE
Washington, DC 20018-1211

All Kensington Titles, Imprints, and Distributed Lines are available at special quantity discounts for bulk purchases for sales promotions, premiums, fund-raising, and educational or institutional use. Special book excerpts or customized printings can also be created to fit specific needs. For details, write or phone the office of the Kensington special sales manager: Kensington Publishing Corp., 850 Third Avenue, New York, NY 10022, attn: Special Sales Department, Phone: 1-800-221-2647.

First Printing: August 2003
10 9 8 7 6 5 4 3

Printed in the United States of America

*Dedicated to Chandra Taylor
the most wonderful editor in the world,
for her patience,
perseverance, and most of all
for believing in me.
Thank you from the bottom of my heart.*

Acknowledgments

With each book published, I feel more and more richly blessed and more privileged to know that so many wonderful people are on my side.

First, to my family as always for their loving support, especially my mother for her continued and very vocal enthusiasm! Thanks, Ma!

To my dearest friend, Joyce, who knows better than many what real love is all about. This is your year, girl. And thank you for getting that new phone!

To my fabulous friends in the state of Florida, a shout out to all of you!

A special thank you to LaShanda Ross; Shonnie, you keep me sane and entertained.

To my SBC friends who continue to warm me with their support, including Angela Riley, December Whitfield, Bethany Brown, Tolerance Moore, Margaret Jones, Chris Klatt, Tina Johnson, Rebecca Kern, Steve Hale, Barbara Harrison, Jeremy Brand, and the always charming Eric Hanskett. And to Trina Johnson, a special thank you; you know why!

And a special thank you to Tony Howard for his continued support.

Once again, thanks to the gallant and gregarious men of the SCFM. If you want it done right the first time, call a steelworker.

And as always to Jamil, my anchor and my wings; none of this would mean as much without you in my life. You always know the right words to say, you always make me feel like the most special person in the world and, best of all, and you always make me laugh. I truly treasure you.

Prologue

A classic Marvin Gaye tune floated over the ballroom where the wedding reception was being held. The tall man observed that the jazz band was taking a break, which accounted for both the recorded music and the woman standing in front of him. The woman was a well-known singer; now she was looking at him as though he were something especially good to eat, something exotic.

He had barely noticed her gaze when she floated into his arms like that was where she belonged. He was about to tell her that he didn't dance but it was too late; they were already moving onto the edge of the dance floor like they had done it many, many times before.

She felt so good that he couldn't remember why he had declared a moratorium on dancing. Her full, rounded body flowed into his arms and the warm seduction of her scent enveloped him. The skin of her bared back was moist and luscious; he wanted to stroke her all over, all night. She was tall enough so that he could fully appreciate every womanly part of her lush frame pressed against his. Incredibly, her entrancing hazel eyes were locked on his face as though she had never beheld anything so sexy in her life. Which was, of course, impossible.

He was lost in the silken sensation that was her, drawing her closer until he felt her unmistakable heat. Mesmerized, he bent his head; he had to taste her just once, to make sure she was real. Suddenly, the music changed and someone tapped her shoulder to remind her that the band was coming back out.

"Has anyone ever explained bad timing to you?" she murmured to her unwelcome chaperone as she felt her partner's body step away from hers.

She turned back to say something to the tall, gorgeous man who had just captured her heart. But he was gone . . .

Chapter One

"Well missy, you know it's a good thing your part is over today. Because God on His throne knows I couldn't have taken that costume up one more time." The words of censure were accompanied by a stern look over a pair of bifocals that, as usual, were dangerously close to the end of Mattie Donovan's nose. Her pointed remark, as well as her look of disapproval, were directed at Ceylon Simmons. The two women were in the makeup trailer on the movie set where Ceylon had spent the last eight weeks. During that time, Mattie, the wardrobe mistress, had taken Ceylon under her capable wing, coddling her and fussing over her so much that she sometimes wanted to scream. But she never did, knowing that Mattie was just showing her love.

And Ceylon had to admit Mattie was right. She had lost a considerable amount of weight during the course of the shoot, and only Mattie's magic had made this fact indiscernible to the camera's implacable eye. Ceylon looked at her reflection in the merciless mirrors of the makeup area and repressed a shudder. *Damn. All I need is a wreath and a casket and I could be playing the dearly departed.* She did not express this irreverent thought aloud, fearing Mattie's wrath. But she did try to soothe the older woman's fears.

"Oh come on now, Mattie. I didn't lose that much! Besides, when you've got hips like battleships, you have to toss some ballast every once in a while or you'll sink! Compared to the *real* actresses in Hollywood, I'm still an ocean liner," Ceylon teased.

Mattie wasn't buying it. She rolled her eyes impatiently as Ceylon continued to try to get a chuckle out of her.

"Looky here, Moms—I still have a majestic prow," Ceylon said, pushing her full bosom out proudly, "and a serious bulkhead," she added, poking out her rounded behind.

Mattie smiled in spite of herself, but Ceylon was not fooling her. Ceylon Simmons had always been a full figured, voluptuous woman with curves to spare. She was too firm and shapely to have ever been called fat, and men who knew her were mad for her lush frame. There was an extremely popular song about a big beautiful woman that was rumored to be about Ceylon, and the rumors were true. From the top of her head with its short, silky, golden brown curls, to the bottom of her shapely, sexy feet, Ceylon was 5'9" of café au lait beauty with mischievous hazel eyes and adorable dimples. Or she had been until a few months before. Now she was virtually a shadow of her former self and she had everyone worried.

Ceylon tried to distract Mattie from her lecture by giving her a small gift. She retied the sash of her cotton robe and patted the pocket to make sure the box was still there. "Mattie, sweetheart, you have been an absolute angel to me and I will never forget you for it. You helped me in so many ways, and I wanted you to have a very tiny token of my love and appreciation. Don't even think of saying no, you hear me?" She ended sternly, as she could see the word forming on the older woman's lips.

As Mattie opened the small box, she gasped. It contained a pair of citrine earrings that she had often seen Ceylon wearing. They were large oval cabochons in a yellow gold setting with European back clasps. Mattie's eyes filled with tears and her pale Irish complexion took on a bright red color. She opened her mouth to protest and was again silenced by Ceylon.

"None of that, now. You know I don't have much since . . . well, I always loved these earrings and if you don't think it's tacky to give a gift that isn't out of the store, I'd be so happy if you would wear them to remember me by," Ceylon said softly.

Mattie threw her arms around Ceylon's waist and hugged her hard. "Oh, you sweet child! I would be honored to have these. On one condition—when you get back home please start eating properly! I'm not going to be there to look after you anymore," she reminded Ceylon acerbically.

Finally, Mattie left her alone in the trailer, and Ceylon sank down into a makeup chair with a sigh that was not of gratitude or relief. She felt odd—cold, clammy, and hot all at once. Assuring herself it was the hot lights in the trailer that made her feel so wiped out, she quickly removed her makeup and combed her hair. A hot shower was waiting for her back at the little cottage she'd been living in during the filming. It wasn't home, but it was nice. The small town in the southwestern part of Michigan had been a tranquil and pleasant location. The people were warm, friendly, unobtrusive, and respectful of a person's privacy. That fact, coupled with a super team of people with whom she worked, had made the past few weeks more than bearable. But there was no denying that she was tired.

Ceylon slipped on jeans and a sweater and prepared to leave the trailer for the last time. She had to pause by the door to collect herself. Even the cool spring air of Michigan was not enough to keep the weird feeling from settling over her. Soon, she told herself, she would be back in the small cottage where she could shower and relax. Her icky, clammy feeling persisted, though, and the nausea that had been sim-

mering under the surface of her consciousness began its inexorable bubble to the top.

Finally, she stepped outside the trailer. She was happy to
see Bennie and Clay Deveraux, her closest friends and the executive producers of the movie. For one thing, she loved them
dearly. For another, it would give her an excuse to stop walking for a minute. Her feet had suddenly turned into heavy
weights, which reminded her of when she had been swimming for a long time and tried to clamber onto the poolside
with her legs feeling like wet logs. But her relief was short-
lived as everyone on location ringed the trailer and yelled
"Surprise!" Bennie had decided to give her friend a party to
celebrate the wrap of her first starring role.

Ceylon smiled gamely and was kept busy for a few minutes greeting her fellow actors, the crew, and the support
staff. She was by far the most popular person on the set because of her warmth and genuine friendliness. And she was
funny when she was feeling good. Right then she was as far
from being well as it is possible to be and remain upright.
She was happy that Clay was busy with the babies—his
eagle eyes missed nothing and he would have known for
sure that she wasn't well.

Clay held the hand of Martin Andrew, one of his 18-month-
old twin boys and cradled the other, Malcolm Adonis, to his
shoulder. Bennie was occupied with Clayton III, her ram-
bunctious two and a half-year-old. The little boy's face lit up
when he saw his beloved 'Sweetie,' as he called Ceylon.
Ceylon seized the opportunity to stoop down to his level for
a kiss; a posture that she hoped fervently would give her
more stability. She leaned over for his kiss and faintly heard
a piercing shriek as her lips caressed the pine-strewn path of
the set. Blissful, silent blackness enveloped her and the nausea at last vanished in its grip.

*　*　*

Slowly coming back to consciousness, Ceylon felt nothing but embarrassment. It was bad enough that she had fainted, but to have passed out cold in front of the whole crew, her best friend, and her best friend's husband was particularly galling, especially since she was currently in their employ.

"Well, *this* is a swell way to show my gratitude," she bluffed. "Here you write this wonderful part for me and I fall out on my chubby behind in front of the whole crew. If I were you, I wouldn't speak to me again," she added, hastily pushing herself into a seated position. *Oh God, I don't even want to know how they managed to get me in here,* she thought worriedly.

Unfortunately, the thought of her large frame being hauled over the shoulder of an unsuspecting grip or gaffer made her smile, which did not reassure Bennie in the least. Her phenomenal talent as well as her friendship with Bennie had gotten her the role in the first place.

Bennie sat on the floor next to the couch where Ceylon was lying and held her hand. She didn't bother to hide her concern and the anxiety in her voice.

"Ceylon, I knew you were pushing yourself too hard. I don't care what you say; you've been doing too much for too long now. You need a break and a break is what you're going to have," she said in a manner that showed she would not tolerate any nonsense.

Ceylon tried to stand up, rather hurriedly. It was so shaming to be sitting there. Even though Bennie and Clay knew the truth of her situation, she still felt as though she needed to play Superwoman. Ignoring the slight lightheadedness that was still plaguing her, she tried to be upbeat.

"Girl, you know I'm fine! I just have to be the center of attention, that's all," she said with a winning smile that fooled no one.

Bennie and Clay's movie, *Idlewild*, was the first endeavor

for their new production company. After years of working in other media, the couple decided to try their hand at moviemaking. Bennie wrote a screenplay about the heyday of Idlewild, Michigan, a black resort area that reigned supreme from the 1930s to the 1960s. Clay was looking for an avenue into films and jumped at the chance to produce this one. It looked to be the start of an exciting, fulfilling venture for the two of them. But all the success in the world was not worth her friend's health, which is exactly what Bennie told Ceylon.

"Ceylon, no one could keep up with the pace you have set yourself. I understand, we *all* understand why you're doing it, but this is too much. Now if you don't get some rest, some real rest, I'm . . . I'm going to get someone else to work on the soundtrack," Bennie said flatly.

She would have done no such thing, but she had to make Ceylon see that she meant business. She raised one slender hand to forestall the barrage that Ceylon was about to let fly.

"I mean it! You're going to take an entire month off and relax or I will get some MTV diva to do that soundtrack. And Bump says if that's what it takes to get you to cool your heels, so be it." Bennie was standing by the time she finished speaking, and Ceylon had to believe she was serious from the flame in her almost-black eyes.

Bill "Bump" Williams, the legendary jazz composer and musician, was Bennie's godfather, as well as Clay's stepfather after his marriage to Clay's mother, Lillian. He gave Ceylon her start in the business and she knew that he meant every single word of his threat.

Ceylon turned big puppy eyes to Clay, hoping for some support, but saw that it was fruitless. His usually smiling face was set in stern, unyielding lines as he crossed the small living room to put his arms around Bennie. It was obvious that they were united, and his next words confirmed that theory.

"Listen, Ceylon, I hate to play policeman here, but it's obvious that you aren't taking care of yourself. The looping doesn't start for a few weeks and you're going to use that time to recuperate. And Bump says that until he is sure you are 100% ready to work, you're not putting one foot in his studio."

Finally she gave in. She flopped dramatically on the sofa and sighed deeply. "Oh all right," she conceded wearily. "If you're all going to gang up on me, I don't have a choice, now do I? I wish y'all would sit down; it's like being in the Land of the Giants," she added querulously. That much was true, as Bennie was 6'1" and Clay about 6'7" and both of them seemed to loom over her.

Bennie sat down next to Ceylon and took both her hands. "Ceylon, cut it out," she said softly. "For almost a year you've been working like a sharecropper and we all know why. I don't know you why you continue to punish yourself this way, but it has to stop, do you hear me? We appreciate all the effort you've put into *Idlewild*. You know we couldn't have done it without you. But you're on the verge of a breakdown and it can't continue. Since your part has been committed to film and there's nothing for you to do until the looping starts, you need to take a vacation."

Ceylon immediately began to protest, but was silenced by Clay. His deep voice cut across anything that she tried to say.

"Ceylon, look at yourself in the mirror. I know I'm not supposed to comment on this, but you look terrible! You're exhausted and you deserve some time to yourself away from the camera, the press, and anything else that adds tension to your life. You need to unwind and relax, and Bennie and I know the perfect place for you to do just that."

Ceylon felt hot tears coming to her eyes. She knew that what Clay said was true; she didn't have to look in a mirror to know she was worn out. Her normally flawless complexion was splotchy, there were dark circles under her huge hazel eyes, and her cheekbones protruded in a manner that would have elated her in other circumstances. She looked like hell and she knew it. They were right; she needed to get away, if only for a few days. But in her present situation, she did not know if it would be possible.

Bennie saw the look of uncertainty warring with the pure need on her friend's face. She hugged her fiercely and told her not to worry.

"You know that Clay's family has a vacation home on St. Simon's Island back in Georgia. No one'll bother you because no one will know you're there. It's quiet and peaceful and beautiful, and it's just what you need. You're going down there tonight and you're going stay there until you feel like coming back. The house is all ready for you; there's food in the refrigerator and a rental car waiting for you. Take as long as you need to rest and relax and you'll be back to your old self in a couple of weeks, you'll see."

Ceylon couldn't get words past the huge lump in her throat. Bennie had always been a special friend, and Clay was equally dear to her. She knew they wanted the best for her, but she wasn't so optimistic that she thought she could get back to her old self in a few weeks. She would try, though, for their sake.

She managed a watery smile and said, "Okay, you're on. St. Simon's Island, here I come."

From where the woman sat, the tall, golden man was the best looking thing in the restaurant. His long, glossy black hair was pulled into a ponytail, which gave him a mysterious, sexy air. He had heavy lidded eyes with long eyelashes, and had to be at least 6'6" or 6'7", judging by the length of his legs. And even though he was dressed in a casual linen blazer and jeans, he looked like an aristocrat. Although she could only see part of him through the abundant foliage of the eatery, this man looked more than interesting—he looked *collectible*. And enticing. As she whispered to her girlfriend, she strolled across the dining room of the quaint Key West eatery and boldly approached the man.

"I was wondering if you'd like to buy me a drink," she purred. As the man slowly turned to look her full in the face, the purr turned into a choking sound. The man wore a patch on his left eye and a jagged scar ran down his left cheek, barely missing the thick moustache that topped his unsmiling mouth.

The woman turned bright red and continued to sputter, finally saying something about mistaking him for someone else. The man looked at her with no expression whatsoever on his brutally handsome face. Finally, he nodded and rose to leave. It was little consolation to the mortified woman that he was indeed every bit as tall as she suspected. With a careless toss of his left hand, he threw some bills on his table and departed, all without saying one word.

The eagle-eyed server immediately moved in to scoop up his extremely generous tip, shaking his head at the scene he had just witnessed.

"Ummph, Miss Thang, you sho' picked the wrong man to act a fool with. That was Martin *Dev-er-aux* and he got more money than *God*, honey. You sho' blew that one actin' hinckty." And with two snaps and a twist, he vanished, leaving her to slink back to her friend.

The pleasant-faced woman who greeted Ceylon was the soul of hospitality. She was short, plump, and dressed casually but with femininity in a summer yellow linen skirt set. "Hello, Miss Simmons! I'm Jackie Torrence, and I manage the house for the Deveraux family. Everything is ready for you. Let me just show you around a bit and I'll be off," she said cheerfully.

Ceylon returned her greeting with one of her own and tried to get her bearings. Ever since she left Michigan it was the same thing. Someone chauffeured her to the airport. Two delightful ladies from the rental car agency met her plane and drove her out to the house, one following the other to ferry her coworker back to the dealership. And now someone who looked like everyone's grandma greeted her at the door of a lovely summer home. Bennie and Clay certainly knew how to do things right, Ceylon mused.

Jackie, as she insisted on being called, led Ceylon into the charming house. Jackie talked almost non-stop, but it was a kind of relief for Ceylon, weary though she was.

"You know, this place was little more than a fishing shack when Lillian and Big Clay bought it," she said, referencing Clay's parents. "And bit by bit they just added on to it and kept improving it until it's one of the nicest places on the island! They could sell it for a mint, but the family just keeps it for vacations and holidays and what not," she prattled as she led Ceylon into the kitchen.

"Here's the kitchen. It's a nice one with a double oven range and a big ol' work island, too, if you've a mind to do any cooking. And the refrigerator is completely stocked," she added over her shoulder as they stepped through the French doors onto the deck.

Despite her weariness, Ceylon had to smile. The house was so much a reflection of Clay's mother, Lillian Deveraux. It was lovely, surrounded by a carefully tended herb garden as well as a brilliant array of wildflowers. There were light and shady areas in the huge backyard, the shade provided by live oak trees dripping with Spanish moss. Best of all, there was a huge hammock waiting for someone to curl up and read, as well as a variety of comfortable looking twig porch furniture on the deck itself.

Jackie caught Ceylon's sigh of approval and gave her a smile of her own. "It's lovely, isn't it? So restful. Lillian has done such a beautiful job with this area. But wait until you see the rest!" She led Ceylon back into the spacious house and toured the rooms. Lillian had indeed made it a place of refuge and hospitality. The house evolved over the years from a rustic fishing lodge into a spacious, elegant home. Not that it was fancy—it was just perfect.

There were pickled pine floors throughout, and the center-piece of the house was the huge great room, which also served as an entertainment area with a television hidden in a country French armoire. The big, cushiony sofa was slipcovered in sturdy washable duck so that the many Deveraux grand-children could play with abandon and not ruin anything. But even among the casual, crisply striped cotton covers, there were Lillian's special touches; a flotilla of flowered throw pillows, family photographs and colorful prints of vintage sheet music and advertising art on the walls, and her colorful Majolica plate collection in the dining room. Everywhere Ceylon looked, from the screened in porches at opposite ends of the house, to the homey looking bedrooms, she saw an oasis of comfort and charm.

Ceylon thanked Jackie sincerely for the tour. "I feel right at home already. And thank you also for the maps and sight-seeing information. That was extra thoughtful of you."

Jackie brushed off her thanks. "You just rest and enjoy yourself while you're here. And maybe later, when you feel up to it, we can have lunch and maybe you'll sign one of your CDs for me. I'm a huge fan of yours so this is a big, big thrill for me," she confessed. Before Ceylon could get em-barrassed, Jackie left, bidding her a charming good-bye.

Two days later, and Ceylon still felt about as tired as she was when she first arrived. She took walks on the beach, drove around the island a bit, and busied herself with tend-ing Lillian's herbs and flowers. At the moment, she was pre-tending to watch a movie on the DVD player. She really wasn't paying it any attention, though. She was just too numb. So numb that it was minutes before she realized that the movie had played through.

"So much for *Casablanca*," she muttered. She felt slightly idiotic for having spaced out for the whole movie, but it seemed like spacing out was all she was able to do lately.

She decided to clean the already spotless kitchen to keep her mind occupied. Rearranging the cupboards and cleaning the double oven would at least keep her busy for a while, she reasoned.

The silence on St. Simon's was a little unsettling to Ceylon. She grew up in Detroit and lived most recently in Los Angeles. She was used to any number of city noises, but the velvety quiet took some getting used to. So when she heard twigs snapping outside and the unmistakable sound of a man's footsteps, she didn't hesitate. Ignoring the adrenaline that surged through her body, she armed herself with the cordless phone and the Louisville slugger that a Deveraux child had left in one of the bedrooms. She thought about turning off the kitchen light, but before she could chastise herself for not thinking of it first, the knob in the back door began to turn.

Ceylon quickly positioned herself at the side of the frame in order to handle the prowler. She had risen up on her toes with the bat clutched in her right hand when the door slowly inched open. Her heart pounded like a piston as she prepared to knock the crap out of whoever was invading the house. The light from the kitchen illuminated the very tall figure of the unknown man, and gave enough light to let her see an eye patch over a scarred face. She gasped as she stopped the bat in its lethal arc, then sighed in disgust.

"Oh, it's *you*. Why would you come creeping up here in the middle of the darned night without letting a person know you're coming? You almost got popped in the head, you know." She carefully leaned the bat in the corner by the door and looked past Martin to his beautiful Akita, Satchel.

"Hello, baby," she crooned to the big dog.

With one sheepish glance at his master, Satchel immediately went to Ceylon so that she could scratch his head and talk baby talk to him. Martin surveyed the scene with equal parts amusement and bemusement. Satchel had always been a one-man dog until his brother married Benita. Anytime he was around Bennie, Satchel turned into a big baby, and Ceylon had the same effect on him, the traitor.

While Ceylon was engrossed with the big dog, Martin eyed her warily. He wasn't so much concerned with why she was at his family's lodge, but what was wrong with her. She had all but ignored him for one thing, and she looked terrible for another. She appeared thin and tired, which was contrary to all he knew about Ceylon. Admittedly he did not know a lot about her. He did know that she normally flirted with him outrageously whenever she saw him, and he couldn't help but wonder why she was so underwhelmed to see him. He was not vain by any means, but Ceylon made no secret of the fact that she was interested. Over the years they encountered each other many times and she was always sweetly flirtatious, but certainly not at the moment. Tonight she acted like he was invisible, for reasons he couldn't fathom.

Once Ceylon and Satchel's love fest was over, she informed Martin that she was busy cleaning the oven, and he could have any room he desired. She'd barely finished speaking when she returned to the kitchen without a backward glance. Martin was truly mystified. He looked at his watch and decided it was too late to call Bennie and Clay; he didn't want to wake his nephews. But the next morning, he planned to get some answers from somewhere.

In the meantime, he followed her into the kitchen, where he could see that she was quite serious about her cleaning duties. All manner of supplies were neatly arranged about the stove and she was on her knees scrubbing away like a charwoman. Martin cast one look at her rounded derriere pointed up in the air and tilted his head to one side. Nope, there was no doubt about it; Ceylon was way too skinny. He thought about her nice, firm, voluptuous fanny of yore and mentally contrasted it with the poor imitation that moved back and forth with every thrust of her arms. Something had happened to her, and he would find out what it was soon or his name wasn't Martin Mercier Deveraux. In the meantime, though, he decided to try to act as normal as possible.

"Didn't mean to scare you," he apologized in the deep, gravelly voice that had so often sent chills through Ceylon. "I've been down in the Keys on the boat for a few days and I decided to stop over here to put in that outdoor shower that Bennie and Mom have been wanting."

Ceylon barely paused in her toils as he spoke. "Martin, you certainly don't owe me an explanation. This is your family's house, after all. There's plenty of room for all three of us, so there isn't a problem, is there?"

She finally stopped scrubbing and sat back on her heels to look him directly in the face. There was a smudge on one of her cheeks and she was not wearing a speck of makeup, which made Martin conclude again that something was amiss. He'd seen her in a variety of guises, from ballroom fancy to play clothes, and had never seen her looking as haggard as she did this afternoon, even after babysitting his active nephews for a day. No, this woman had troubles. Plus, the normal soft glow that appeared in her eyes when she looked at him was absent. It was as though a light had gone out.

Before he could delicately probe for answers, though, Ceylon resumed speaking. "I don't mean to be rude, but I'd like to get this finished. If you're hungry, there's some stuff in the refrigerator." Without another word, she went back to scrubbing the already clean oven as though her hope of parole rested on the results.

Martin continued to stand in the doorway and watch her for a moment before going to get his things from his SUV. Bennie and Clay would be getting a call first thing in the morning, and he hoped they had some good answers for his questions.

Chapter Two

The next morning, Ceylon thought it would be prudent to leave the house for a while. She had never been uncomfortable around Martin, but she wasn't up to answering questions. And with that keen lawyer's mind of his, Martin was bound to be more than a bit curious as to why she was staying in his family's home. She stood for a moment, staring out at the cool, hazy dawn as she sipped a cup of coffee. It was the last of the pot she made an hour earlier, but it was still delicious. One thing her grandfather had taught her to do was how to make a great pot of coffee.

Ceylon sighed and leaned over the sink to observe more of the quiet dawn unfolding outside the kitchen window. Everything was so fragrant and moist with fresh expectation; it was more like a new beginning than a new morning. And that's what she needed desperately, a new beginning. Against her considerable will, Ceylon felt her throat constricting into the usual discomfort that proceeded a spate of tears. *Stop it, stop it, stop it! This gets you nowhere, so just cut it out,* she told herself fiercely. Sniffing loudly, she wiped her eyes roughly with the back of her free hand and then stifled a shriek as something cold and wet touched the back of her knee.

"Satchel, you scared me to death! Don't ever sneak up on a black woman first thing in the morning! Evil as I am, I could have thrown this hot coffee at you and made you eat the cup. You wouldn't like that, now would you?" she said fondly.

As dogs do, Satchel reacted to the sound of her voice and not the words and was panting happily as he waited for her to produce some food and a lovely ear scratching, two things he always associated with her.

"Okay, okay," Ceylon sighed as she filled his dish with food and his bowl with water. "How about a little walk after breakfast? We can go down on the beach and exercise our youthful figures. Well, *one* of us can. The other one will just be avoiding an interrogation," she acknowledged.

Without giving her unflattering dungarees and sweatshirt a thought, Ceylon fetched a baseball cap and a pair of sunglasses while Satchel wolfed down his food. She hastily made another pot of coffee for Martin and then slipped out the back with Satchel. It might not have been an escape, but a reprieve was just that—a reprieve. At least she would have time enough to come up with a plausible story for Martin while she and Satchel took their constitutional.

"And if all else fails, I can just faint. Nothing scares a man more than a woman passing out on him," she said with satisfaction.

As he decided to do the night before, Martin phoned his sister-in-law to get to the bottom of the Ceylon enigma. Whatever caused her to lose weight and look as tensed as a cello string had to be something fairly tumultuous; of this he was sure. The Ceylon he knew, albeit from a distance, was the most sparkling, effervescent woman he had ever encountered. Nothing stopped her natural merriment and sweet nature from enveloping everyone in her orbit, and no one knew that better than Martin. He had been swept up in her scented eddy more than once.

As he drank a cup of the coffee from the fragrant pot she had thoughtfully left in the kitchen, he recalled their first meeting. She was nowhere to be found, even at this ungodly hour. Apparently, she and Satchel, the lovesick turncoat, had gone off somewhere. He knew she was safe with the big dog near her side. He sipped the coffee appreciatively—he had no idea that Ceylon was in any way domestic. She was inextricably locked in his mind as a sensual, stunning force of nature. At least that's the way he remembered meeting her.

It was at the wedding reception for his oldest brother, Clay, and his beautiful bride Benita. Martin surprised everyone by not only showing up, but by standing up for his brother as best man. The reception was lovely, as those things go; however, Martin couldn't wait to leave the festivities. He had far surpassed his annual quota of family gatherings and was just about to make his customary early escape. Suddenly, an arresting scent like Casablanca lilies and rainwater seduced his nostrils. He felt a pleasant warmth against him and looked down into sparkling hazel eyes with a lush fringe of lashes top and bottom.

Even Martin knew this was the Ceylon Simmons who had sung so beautifully during the wedding. Ceylon Simmons, who was the Next Big Thing in the music industry and a dear friend of his new sister-in-law. He knew who she was, all right; he just didn't know what she was doing in front of him. He didn't have long to wonder as she stepped into his arms.

"Dance with me, Martin," she murmured in her incredible voice.

She was only speaking and it still sounded like music. Before he knew what came over him, he was on the dance floor with his arms around Ceylon. She was wearing a shimmering dress that bared her back. She felt absolutely fantastic in his arms. In the short time that they danced she got to him, got him where he lived. It was those eyes, he decided.

She never took her eyes away from his face. She stared into his soul as though he was a work of art and she an eager collector. To this day, he could remember exactly how warm and supple she was in his arms. He could still smell her incredible scent and feel the bounty of her ripe, lush body pressed against his own. Their dance was over much too quickly. As her fragrant body left his arms, something like a chill descended over him, something sad and lonely.

A tremor passed through Martin as he remembered the unique sensations that Ceylon created in him. *If only . . . nope. Forget about it and make the call.* Martin set the coffee cup down and glanced at the clock. Surely he could call his brother's house without risking the wrath of a mother whose little ones have been awakened. Bennie's cheerful greeting bore out his theory.

"Martin, we've been up since seven! Your nephews aren't particularly interested in sleeping when there are so many other things to do, like seeing how many things they can flush down the toilet. We've been up and quite busy around here, believe me. Are you still in Key West?"

"Actually, Benita, I'm in St. Simons. I decided to put in that outdoor shower you wanted, so I stopped here on my way back to Atlanta. And you can pretty much imagine what transpired after that," he said dryly.

"Ohh," sighed Bennie. "I see what you mean. Well, how is Ceylon doing? I know she must have been surprised to see you and Satchel," she added with a smile in her voice.

Martin decided to get right to the point. "Benita, what in the Sam Hill is wrong with her? What's happened to her? She looks terrible! She barely spoke to me last night. Not to have a big head or anything, but she was always pretty flirty with me. What the hell is going on? And why is she here anyway?"

Martin could almost see the expression on Bennie's face as he listened to her deep sigh. It took her a couple of seconds to reply, but she apparently decided that this was something Martin needed to know.

"Okay, Martin. This isn't exactly confidential information, since it was all over the papers, but be careful with how you use what I'm going to tell you. Ceylon is very fragile when it comes to this stuff." Bennie paused to chastise a child before continuing. "Trey, if you do that again, something very unpleasant is going to happen. To *you*, that's who! Go play with your daddy, *please*!

"Martin, Ceylon is completely broke. Her income taxes haven't been paid in about five years and the IRS is after every single penny. She refused to file bankruptcy and she's been working like a maniac to pay back everything she owes. She just finished the picture we're making and she passed out from sheer exhaustion, so we insisted that she come to St. Simons to recuperate. And that's all there is."

Martin disagreed, however. True, he didn't know Ceylon that well, but he couldn't believe that she was reckless enough to just go her merry way without paying her taxes. And with the kind of money that she was earning, it seemed impossible that she was broke. For some reason, he was deeply disappointed. He never thought of Ceylon as being a flake before, but apparently she was, big time. He said as much to Bennie, only to get his ears pinned back.

"Now, Martin, don't go jumping to conclusions. Ceylon had no idea that her affairs were in such disarray. She is *not* flaky, not at all. She's a very responsible person and she actually lives quite frugally. Her biggest indulgence was buying a new piece of jewelry after every CD was pressed and every concert tour ended, and I'm not talking the Hope diamond here. She just loves nice jewelry. The thing is she has a lot of sorry-ass relatives who think of her as the National Bank of Ceylon. These people have their hands out so much that it's beyond scandalous, and for some reason, she simply can't turn her back on them, something for which I have prayed fervently. They're terrible people. Just awful.

"Anyway, Ceylon's business manager was quite the little thief. He was the one who didn't pay her taxes and who managed over the last year of his employment to move her money from her banks into his and clean her out nicely. Then he disappeared, leaving her holding a very empty bag. She found out when a check that she wrote to a charity for a rather large sum bounced . . . and kept on bouncing. That's when it all came to light," Bennie said sadly.

"I can't give you all the details, because she hasn't given them all to me. She didn't come to Clay and me when this happened, or to Renee or my brother Andrew, which is too bad. We'd do anything to help her. But she was too proud and tried to handle it all on her own and she's about at the end of her rope. This has been a terrible time for her, Martin, and she hasn't had anyone that she felt she could turn to because she was so ashamed."

Martin was the one who was ashamed when Bennie finished cataloging the things that had befallen Ceylon. No wonder the poor woman looked like hell. Still, he had to ask Bennie one more question.

"Did she try to have this business manager found? You know that I have some detectives that can find a gray grain of sand on a white sand beach if I ask them to," he said. And he was speaking the utter truth—he had a friend who made Nemesis look like a lightweight.

"Umm, no, Martin, she didn't," admitted Bennie.

Martin frowned. He was about to go off again when Bennie explained.

"Despite what he did to her, she couldn't bring herself to go after him, Martin. She loves him in spite of what he did."

"Well, Bennie, I hate to sound crass, but she deserves what she gets. Any woman who lets a man treat her like that is a damned fool. What the hell was she doing letting her lover run her business?" he growled. Once again, he was deeply disappointed in Ceylon.

"Wrong, Martin. He wasn't her lover—he was her *brother*."

At the same time Martin got off the telephone with Bennie, Ceylon decided that it was time to head back. She was probably just exaggerating Martin's interest in her presence on St. Simon's; after all, he had never been interested in her, period. She snorted inelegantly, and the ever-alert Satchel took that to mean 'time to go'. He galloped to her side and she shrugged. It was as good a time as any, and besides, she had another project to tackle. Having cleaned the ovens, rearranged the cupboards, and generally overhauled the entire kitchen, Ceylon was ready to take on the dining room. True, there was a cleaning service on the island that made periodic visits to the house when it was unoccupied, but how thorough were they? Ceylon had no idea and she needed something to keep her busy, anyway. She needed to be too busy to think about that damnably gorgeous Martin Deveraux.

There was a time when the mere sight of him would warm her from head to toe, like taking a slow sip of Courvoisier on a cold night. More than once she had been so on fire for him that she had been tempted to the brink of madness, but he had always been a perfect, proper gentleman. He had always made his disinterest obvious, except for a couple of glorious moments that were forever locked in her memory.

Like the time in Atlanta when her friend Renee had a traumatic experience at a gala held in a posh hotel. Martin had quickly taken them to his sister's house, where Renee was staying. After Ceylon had gotten her comfortable and helped calm her fears, she had herself been trembling from anxiety. To her utter amazement, Martin had not only been a pillar of strength and comfort, he had been extraordinarily sweet with her and passionately tender, too.

Ceylon couldn't help it; she sighed and closed her eyes as she remembered that night. She had come downstairs to the family room where Martin had put on some soft music and was pretending to read. He had opened his arms to her and she had cuddled into his side while he gave her warmth, comfort, and reassurance. And he gave her some absolutely fantastic kisses, too. Her eyes popped open and she fanned herself lightly at the surge of heat that had arisen with the memory. He was one sexy man, Martin Deveraux was, and he had no more interest in her than the man in the moon. Which was just as well because the last thing she wanted or needed in her life was some kind of romantic entanglement. *Please. I'd rather wear a breadcrumb suit into a cage full of hungry birds.*

She finally arrived back at the house after their ramble along the beach. Satchel was happy to see his master, who was sitting in a big Adirondack chair on the deck of the cottage. He rose from his seat when Ceylon came into view. All the Deveraux men had lovely manners; their mother Lillian had seen to that personally. Ceylon was not quite as thrilled as the loyal Satchel; if Martin were going to put her through the third degree, she would have to make other living arrangements. She just was not up to answering a bunch of questions, no matter how well-intentioned. She was pleasantly relieved when all Martin did was compliment her coffee.

"I'm glad you like it. I can make some more if you'd like. Well, I have a project to get after, so if you'll excuse me . . ." her voice trailed off as she quickly went into the house.

Martin resumed his seat and raised an eyebrow at Satchel. "Don't give me that look," he warned. "I'm not the one, buddy. Saving damsels in distress is not my schtick. So don't even think about it," he said firmly.

Satchel looked disappointed in the extreme. With a sharp, short bark, he abandoned his master and went in search of Ceylon. Martin was amazed. "I'll be damned. We haven't been here a day and she's already got my dog wrapped around her little finger."

He'd always suspected that Ceylon was a dangerous woman and now he was quite sure.

After an hour or so mostly spent with his laptop and on the telephone, keeping abreast of developments at The Deveraux Group, Martin went inside and was greeted by chaos. Ceylon had taken everything out of the oak sideboard and arranged the items in neat stacks on the kitchen counters. She also managed to take down the vertical blinds and the muslin curtains as well as roll up the floral area rug. She was dragging the rug out to the kitchen when she encountered Martin.

"What, may I ask, are you up to?" he inquired mildly, although even to his male eye it was plain to see that she was on a cleaning tear.

"Well, I'm going to put this rug out so I can beat it before I send it out to be cleaned. And I'm putting the curtains in the wash and I'm going to hose down these blinds after I wash the walls in here. Could you excuse me? I'm on a mission," she said cheerfully.

Martin grunted and took the rug away from her. After he placed it on the clothesline to her specifications, he looked at her retreating figure as she went back into the house. Against his better judgment, he followed her into the dining room. She was carefully removing his mother's prized Majolica plates from the walls. The bottom row was easy enough for her to reach, but she needed a step stool for the next row. Seeing her looking around vainly for something on which to stand, he offered his assistance.

"Here, let me," he said gruffly. As he reached for the plates, he was reminded of another time when Ceylon needed a hand.

It was during a New Year's Eve party at Clay and Bennie's home in Atlanta. Ceylon was a frequent holiday guest, so he was used to seeing her there. It was close to midnight and he had wandered into the kitchen on the pretense of getting ice; in actuality, he just wanted out of the living room when the inevitable midnight kissing began. Ever since the accident that had left him looking like Frankenstein's darker brother, he was uncomfortable with that kind of thing. But instead of solitude, he found Ceylon, teetering on the edge of a small stool as she tried to get something from the very top of the cabinet.

"Ceylon, be careful! Here, let me get it for you," Martin chastised in his deep voice.

Ceylon immediately pointed to the crystal canapé tray she was seeking and smiled sweetly when he placed it on the counter. Still on the stool, she turned to face him.

"Thank you, Martin. And now I need something else," she said softly. Before he could react, Ceylon wrapped her arms around his neck and kissed him like her lips had been created simply to please him. She sighed in sheer bliss as his arms went around her waist and they held onto each other for what seemed like hours, kissing like lovers reunited after a separation of years.

Her lips were soft and sweet and as delicious as everything else about her. Ceylon's stance on the stool brought her body to his in a way that was arousing in the extreme. She smelled wonderful and her mouth was like paradise. She kissed him for what seemed like hours and finally pulled away long enough to murmur, "Happy New Year, Martin." Then he pulled her right back into his arms . . .

Martin suddenly realized that he was perspiring a bit, remembering that night. This was just what he didn't need. He didn't need to torture himself with desire for a woman, especially not this woman. He knew better than anyone that those days were over for him. In the first place, there was no way in hell that he was going to get so involved with another human being. In the second place, there was no way that he could ever have Ceylon and he was too old to be mooning around after impossible dreams. Jerking the last plates off the wall with unseemly haste, he handed them over to Ceylon and growled something about going into town. And then he got out of the house before she could utter a sound. He didn't bother to whistle for Satchel; he needed to get out of there in a big hurry. He jumped into his Lincoln Navigator and took off like he was being chased by the devil—a soft, sultry devil with passion fruit lips, silken skin, and a smile that could cause a nuclear meltdown.

Ceylon was so occupied with her endeavors that she really didn't notice his absence. Using an old tennis racket as a rug beater, she whaled the tar out of the floral rug to Satchel's utter amazement. At first he thought it was some kind of prey to be conquered. He wasn't sure how the rug was attacking his friend, but if that's what it took to quell it, he was all for it. He bravely attacked the fringe with his strong white teeth, snarling viciously at the flat thing that was apparently trying to savage Ceylon.

"Whoa, whoa, Satchel! It's okay, boy! I'm just getting some dust out of the rug before we send it to the cleaners, okay? It's not hurting me, really it's not," Ceylon assured him.

Satchel sat back on his haunches and watched carefully. But when Ceylon took up the racket again, it was his cue. Obviously the flat creature wasn't dead yet and there was no way he would let it harm her in any way. This time he got quite a chunk of it in his strong jaws and the growls that issued from his throat were fearsome.

Ceylon stopped whacking immediately and gave up, seeing as how Satchel was too well-trained to trust her judgment in the matter.

"Okay, you win. No rug beating. To tell you the truth, it was more to exorcise demons than dust mites. But that'll be our secret. Wanna wash some walls?" she asked brightly.

He agreed immediately and they tackled the dining room walls with a solution of sudsy ammonia and vinegar. Satchel disliked the smell of it very much and made his displeasure known by several loud sneezes. Ceylon laughed at his expression of disgust and suggested that he take a nap on the deck.

"This won't take very long and then we can hang the curtains out," she promised.

And it really didn't take very long for her to wash down all the walls, the woodwork and the windows. Of course, with the walls so sparkling clean, the floors looked a little dull, and so she went down on her knees to apply a stripping solution. While the solution did its job, she hung the muslin curtains out on the line, smiling as she anticipated the wonderful smell they would have when she re-hung them in the house. Then she scrubbed the stripping solution up and applied floor wax. She would buff the floors later that afternoon, she decided as she polished the oak sideboard.

Ceylon carefully hand washed the Majolica plates and was just replacing them on the walls when Martin finally returned. Everything was back in place with the exception of the floral rug, which she had picked up by a local cleaner. The dining room was now sparkling—there was no other way to describe it. Every surface was polished, buffed, and gleaming from her care and there was the kind of lovely fresh smell all over the house that can come only from sun-dried linens. Martin was both impressed and a little frightened. How had she gotten so much done in one afternoon? And why was she not exhausted?

Ceylon moved to the living room and stripped the duck slipcovers off the chairs in order to launder them. All the walls and tables were already divested of all pictures, photographs, and bibelots, giving it a stark, impersonal feel. It was obvious that Ceylon's cleaning frenzy had not abated in the slightest. Other than a preoccupied and disinterested "hello" when Martin came in, she hadn't even looked his way. For some odd reason, this was intensely annoying to him.

He asked if she would like to get something to eat, and she assured him that she had eaten already. Martin found that hard to believe, since there were no smells of cooking lingering in the air and her rental car was parked exactly where it was when he left. Moodily, he rummaged in the refrigerator and saw a Saran-wrapped bowl containing a green salad as well as half a pear similarly attired in the green wrap. That rabbit food was hardly a meal! If that's what she had been living on, no wonder she looked so emaciated.

He headed back to the living room to confront her and stopped himself. It wasn't his business, after all. Concern over her eating habits was the first step in being sucked into the role of dragon slayer. And as he had told Satchel, rescuing fair maidens was not his job. Whatever problems Ceylon Simmons had were hers to deal with. He had a shower to install and that was the end of his role here as far as he was concerned.

Chapter Three

After an evening spent in near silence, Martin finally went to bed. Ceylon was so occupied with consigning every washable item in the living room to the laundry that she barely acknowledged his presence, which continued to irritate him mightily. It wasn't as though he wanted to have lingering conversation with her, get to know the real woman behind the public persona or any of that claptrap; it just seemed like the polite thing to do. But politeness did not appear to be her aim; she was determined to set some kind of Guinness Record for housecleaning, for some unknowable reason. With a gruff goodnight, Martin went into the bedroom he had selected and prepared for bed.

Sometime later, Ceylon finally wound down her efforts in the living room, more out of deference for Martin's slumber rather than exhaustion. It was ironic, but this so-called vacation had given her tremendous energy instead of lulling her into relaxation. She needed to keep busy all day and all night if possible. If she could just keep her mind occupied with the mundane she wouldn't drift off into the abyss of pain that had become her life. Every time she thought about what her life was like a mere year ago . . .

The tears she could hold back during the day were once again forcing themselves into her eyes. Dashing them away she went into her bathroom and had a long, hot, and much-deserved shower. *Goodness, I must have smelled like a nanny goat! No wonder Martin kept out of my way*, she snickered. She frowned slightly at the bottle of shower gel from the discount store. Once nothing but Algemarin, Badedas, and fragranced gels that matched her perfume were permitted to touch her skin. But that was then and this was now. It would get her clean, it didn't smell too badly, and, most importantly, it was cheap. Ceylon had a budget to live on and it did not encompass frivolities like expensive bath gels.

Thoroughly cleaned from head to toe and sleek from a heavy application of Curel lotion in lieu of her usual Lancôme, Ceylon donned a pair of sweats and an oversized T-shirt. She learned the hard way that there was no point in trying to sleep when sleep would only elude her. Arming herself with the necessary equipment for a manicure, she went into the living room and opened the big armoire, which held the TV and DVD player.

"Well, what shall we space out on tonight? *To Sleep With Anger*, *The Piano Lesson*, *Eve's Bayou*?" she murmured to herself.

Eve's Bayou was the winner and she slid the disc into the DVD player, turning the sound down as she did so. She sat on the floor in front of the television and proceeded to remove her nail polish, laughing quietly as she did so. A year ago, Ceylon had her nails done weekly by a wonderful technician in Beverly Hills. The woman didn't do anything Ceylon couldn't have done herself, but it was a nice little luxury. And like all of Ceylon's other luxuries, it was no more.

"Good thing I kept my beauty license up," she said under her breath. "I might be back to frying hair before this is all over."

She began to restore her nails to beauty, even though they

had not been destroyed by her labor. She had taken the pre-
caution of wearing gloves during her toils so that her pretty
hands would be protected. As she shaped, buffed, and polished her nails, Ceylon tried to ignore the little voice in her
head, the one that said she should have looked out for her
money the way she looked out for her stupid hands.

Ceylon really did watch the movie, but it might not have
been the best choice. The beautiful, haunting film with its
complicated family dynamic just cut too close to the bone
for her to really enjoy it. She took it out and replaced it with
The Matrix, which she enjoyed until she got to the part
where the main character, Morpheus, was betrayed by someone close to him.

"Oh, please, there has got to be something to watch that
does not involve that theme!" she muttered. "Let's see;
Blade . . . nope, his mother turns on him. *The Godfather* . . .
goodness no! Everybody turns on everybody in that one . . .
Rush Hour . . . nope, that old guy was a big traitor . . . what's
with that, is treachery the central motif in all modern
movies? *Dang.*"

She was about to give up and turn the television off in
disgust when she found *Made in Heaven* and *Who am I This
Time?*, two little known films that were positive, uplifting,
and did not involve any kind of Machiavellian twists. She
breathed a sigh of relief. It wouldn't be much longer before
she could start making cleaning noises again and in the
meantime, here was something to keep her from crying. She
could make it through another night.

The smell of coffee and the sound of Ceylon conversing
with Satchel awakened Martin the next morning. Her voice
drifted through his window, which faced the side of the
house where the deck lay.

"It was just a suggestion; you needn't look so offended.
It's just that as long as I'm washing these cushions, I thought

you might like a little bath, too. I'm not saying that you stink, or anything," she said coaxingly.

That brought Martin to his feet and he looked out of his window to see Ceylon in a now-familiar pose, arm deep in a sudsy pail of water as she scrubbed the cushions she had removed from the deck furniture. Satchel regarded her with suspicion from a safe distance for a moment and then trotted over to give her a lick on the cheek. All was apparently forgiven. Once again, Ceylon managed to amaze Martin. The very mention of water was enough to make Satchel head for the hills, and Ceylon had him giving her kisses. She was the kind of woman who met her fate in the bonfires of old Salem; Martin was willing to bet his life on that.

After showering and dressing in his worst jeans and a long sleeved flannel shirt that had seen better days, Martin's first act was to call Bennie. He could hear his nephews singing "Jingle Bells" in the background, which caused him to point out the fact that it was June and not December.

Bennie sighed happily. "Yes, but it's their favorite song right now. It's a choice between the 'Barney' theme song, the 'Veggie Tales' theme song, or this. I'm actually kind of happy with this," she admitted. "So, what's new on St. Simon's?" she wanted to know.

Martin blew out a long breath before answering. "Bennie, she's definitely not herself. She's barely said ten words to me the whole time I've been here. All she does is clean," he said in the same way he would have announced that she had been roping goats or something equally unsuitable.

"And I don't mean dusting and vacuuming," he added grumpily. "She's taken apart three rooms and done everything but use a toothpick to go in the cracks of the floor. And I'm not too sure that she isn't doing that, too."

Bennie tried not to let her amusement show. "Well, that's Ceylon," Bennie suggested. "Whenever she's upset about something, she cleans like a maniac. Try to distract her. Get her to cook for you. She loves to cook."

Martin was amazed. "She can cook? Cook real food?" For some reason, he never associated anything normal with Ceylon. He always thought of her in terms of her star status, someone who was completely unacquainted with anything as lowly as a kitchen. He had to admit, though, the woman could scour like it was the only way she could escape the fires of hell.

"Martin, Ceylon is a fabulous cook and she doesn't get to do it too often. Get her to make you some gumbo or some lasagna. You'll transcend all reality when you taste her cooking, trust me. Just ask her to fix you something, she'll be thrilled," Bennie assured him. "And it might help her to get her mind off her troubles. Speaking of troubles, two of your nephews just sped past me butt naked. I think I should find out why," she said reflectively. She bid him a hasty good-bye and was gone before Martin could ask her any more questions.

Clay, dressed for the office, had a naked toddler under each arm as he came into the breakfast room where Bennie had been talking to Martin. "I don't know why these children can't seem to stay in their clothes, but I'm running late. I hate to do this to you, but here you go," he said ruefully as he handed the squirming, laughing boys over to her.

After a quick, sweet kiss, Bennie informed Clay that Martin had called about Ceylon. "He was really worried about her. He's concerned about her well-being and wants to help her."

Clay raised an eyebrow as Bennie related their conversation. "You know, this could be just what Ceylon needs right now," he said slowly. "Maybe what both of them need. God knows they've both suffered enough to deserve something good in their lives. This could be just what the doctor ordered."

Bennie adjusted her grip on their wiggly sons and agreed

fervently. "Let's just hope they realize it," she agreed as she and the boys kissed him good-bye.

Martin made his appearance in the kitchen just as Ceylon entered from the yard, carefully removing her sneakers and slipping on a pair of thongs near the back door. Despite his pose of disinterest, Martin could not help noticing her feet, which were long, slender, and nicely shaped with a high, feminine arch. The toes were polished in a soft rosy pink that was extremely attractive on such sexy feet. He tore his eyes away and forced himself to look into her face. She again wore no makeup, but looked fresh and lovely all the same. He realized for the first time that those long, fringy lashes were real; he had always assumed they were part of her Hollywood makeup gear.

"Good morning, Martin. Would you like some coffee?" she asked politely.

There it was again. She was using that stiff, disinterested tone of voice that grated on his last nerve. Reminding himself that he was at the house to put in a shower and not deal with stuck-up divas, he regrouped.

"Nope, I'm fine. I'm going into town to get the shower fixtures. Do you need anything?" he asked, a bit shocked that he bothered to ask. Ceylon surprised him with a request.

"May I go with you? I've depleted your mother's cleaning supplies something awful and I'm afraid I need more. Would you mind if I tagged along?" she asked nicely.

Martin was too bemused to do anything but nod. He did have some more of Ceylon's excellent coffee while she got ready to go.

She quickly showered and dressed in peach drawstring pants and a matching linen shirt, both of which were too big for her. Everything she owned was too big since her weight loss, but there was really nothing she could do about it. She actually had to roll the pants up at the bottom into a cuff to avoid stepping on the hem. Ceylon stared at her reflection in the mirror. She looked like a little girl in her mother's clothes.

"My butt must have been the size of a Volvo," she muttered. "Yikes."

Her short, silky hair air dried by the time she swiped a coat of mascara on and a bit of lip gloss, although she wasn't sure why she was bothering. Martin certainly wouldn't pay any attention to how she looked and Satchel couldn't have cared less as long as she kept the Iams dog food coming.

"I'm ready, Martin. Thank you for waiting," she said as she entered the kitchen. Martin gave a noncommittal grunt as he picked up his car keys and held the door open for her. Satchel, who knew when a ride was in the offing, was waiting by the Navigator. They rode in silence for a while, with Ceylon quietly appreciating the beauty of the spring morning on the island. Her beautiful eyes were hidden from view behind her black Chanel sunglasses and her pretty mouth was closed. He wasn't getting any conversation out of her this morning, it seemed. It didn't cross his mind that *he* could have started talking. He could not have admitted it for the world, but there was something intimidating about Ceylon.

A slow, wicked grin took over Martin's face. He knew that Ceylon liked jazz and favored old standards—he had heard her recordings at Clay and Bennie's often enough and had heard her perform with his stepfather. Lillian Deveraux had married the legendary Bill 'Bump' Williams, a jazz artist of impeccable taste and talent, and to see Ceylon with his orchestra was a treat indeed. That's why Martin took great glee in deliberately selecting a CD that would drive her right out of her genteel, sophisticated mind. In seconds, Eminem was blaring out of the speakers.

Martin waited for Ceylon's horrified reaction, but was

stunned when he took a surreptitious glance at her. Not only was she *not* recoiling in horror, she was quietly singing along and apparently knew every word by heart.

Martin's jaw dropped in amazement. "You *like* hip-hop?" The remark was quite unnecessary as the refined, ladylike Ceylon was jamming her butt off in the front seat of his vehicle.

"I love it! I'm not too crazy about gangsta rap, but the Goodie Mob, The Roots, Missy, Common; child, please! I meet a lot of these kids while I'm touring or at award shows and they're very nice people, not to mention very talented. This is a whole new form of art; energetic, poetic, exciting—what's not to like?" The CD selector did its little job and "Beautiful Skin" by the Goodie Mob came on. Ceylon was in heaven.

Martin, after his initial shock, was just happy to see her animated and relaxed for the first time since he had set foot on the island. This was more like the Ceylon he knew. That thought was quickly replaced by a disturbing thought; the Ceylon he knew could be very bad for his health in a lot of ways.

Just then she turned and smiled at him, her luscious lips bracketed by those irresistible dimples, and he felt something like pain somewhere deep inside.

"Martin, after we get the hardware and cleaning stuff, can we go to the grocery store? Suddenly I feel like cooking," she said happily.

Martin agreed immediately, but he had a question for her.

"Don't you worry about being seen when you're out in public? I mean, don't people recognize you and start pushing up on you and stuff?"

Ceylon laughed that idea off. "In the first place, I'm not Queen Latifah or Jill Scott or somebody really famous," she said modestly. "In the second place, nobody knows I'm down here, and no one's looking for me anyway. And in the third place, ta-da!"

Ceylon pulled a nondescript baseball cap out of her tote bag and covered her glossy hair. That, with the big black sunglasses actually transformed her into a nonentity, or as close as she could come to one.

"There you go; I'm totally incog-negro. Nobody will know it's me, even if anybody cares," she said merrily. "Now let's get to shopping. Suddenly I'm ravenous for some real food!"

They spent a pleasant hour going in and out of the shops on the main drag. Martin obligingly pushed the grocery cart as Ceylon selected the freshest of produce and the most appetizing looking meats for their dining pleasure. They were so absorbed in each other that neither of them noticed a small man who seemed to appear everywhere they went. Unobserved by anyone, he was able to trail along behind the couple and carry on a discreet conversation on his cell phone at the same time.

"Yeah, I'm positive. It's her. I'm absolutely sure. Just get your butt over here as fast as possible," he muttered.

Bennie meant it when she said Ceylon could cook, much to Martin's gratification. He could smell something appetizing floating out to him as he worked on the outdoor shower. It was a simple job, really, not much more than extending the waterlines from the laundry room into the back. He had already made a hole in the house to accommodate the extra piping and was proceeding with the next step when Ceylon came out bearing a tray with two glasses of iced tea and a plate of fresh baked cookies.

"I thought you could use a cold drink," she said, setting the tray down on the redwood table near his work area.

She took the opportunity to look over his tall frame once more. Martin was one beautiful man, in her estimation. She loved his towering height, the pale gold of his smooth skin, the strong angular features of his face and his shiny, thick black hair. She suspected that it would have a natural wave in it if it was shorter like the other men in his family, but he wore it in a long ponytail, which suited him. That, coupled with the patch on his eye, gave him a dashing, debonair look. Right now, though, there was something wrong with the picture before her. She tilted her head to one side to figure out what was jarring her consciousness. Suddenly, it struck her.

Here it was, a hot June afternoon in Georgia and Martin, who was working outdoors in the sun, was wearing a long-sleeved shirt; flannel, at that. His long legs were encased in worn-looking jeans and his feet were in deck shoes sans socks. His broad shoulders looked strong and muscular under the plaid flannel and they also looked hot. The perspiration pouring off Martin's forehead and down his neck told its own story. Why in the world was he working in that get-up?

"Martin, I think you need to take off that hot flannel shirt and wear a T-shirt, or nothing at all," Ceylon offered helpfully as she handed him a glass of tea. "You're going to get sunstroke out here in this heat."

Martin gratefully accepted the glass and drained it in about two gulps, wiping the moisture from his face afterwards. "I'm fine," he said gruffly.

Ceylon did not say a word; she merely handed him the other glass of tea from the tray and went inside the house. She returned in no time with a pitcher of ice tea and a large pair of kitchen shears. Carefully placing the pitcher on the tray, she turned to Martin with a glint in her eye.

"Take the stupid shirt off now or I'll cut it off your body. You're burning up out here. Who do you think you're fooling?" she asked rhetorically.

Martin paused with the glass halfway to his lips. Was she kidding? Nope, apparently not. She took a few steps closer to him, brandishing the scissors for effect. Martin also stepped back and raised his hands.

"Stop. Look, I'm fine. I always wear long sleeves. I'm used to it. I'm fine," he said warily.

Ceylon wasn't buying it, however. She laid the scissors down but kept coming towards Martin. "Look, at least roll up your sleeves or something," she said as she grasped his left wrist. "That way . . ."

Whatever she was going to say was lost as Martin jerked away from her so quickly that she lost her balance. He looked murderously at her and growled, "Leave it alone, Ceylon! I told you I was fine, just back off!"

Ceylon regained her balance and blinked her long lashes at Martin. Suddenly, she knew why he was being so difficult, and the simple explanation pained her very soul.

"Oh, Martin, it's the scars, isn't it? I'm so sorry, I didn't think! It's just that you looked so uncomfortable," she apologized as she darted a look at the obvious sweat patterns around his neck, down his back and under his arms. "Please forgive me, Martin, I seem to have made a bad situation worse. I-I, I apologize, really I do."

As always, Ceylon caught Martin completely off guard. She was the only person who ever dared use the word 'scar' in his presence. Everyone else tried to act as if they weren't there, which was almost as galling as having someone stare at them. But Ceylon had the intuition to realize the source of his discomfort and to apologize for overstepping her bounds. Martin was the one who felt humble in the face of her discomfort.

She was turning to go into the house when he reached out to her. "Ceylon, it's okay. I know you meant no harm. It's just that I've never gotten used to having people look at me. I'm so used to covering up that nobody ever asks if I'm too hot or something. They seem relieved that I have the discretion to do it. It's not a pretty sight, after all," he said honestly.

Ceylon did not take her eyes off his face once during this recital. She took him by the hand—his left hand, the one with the faint scars on the back—and made him sit down next to her on the cushioned loveseat.

"Martin, please tell me what happened. No one ever talks about your accident—not that they should, I don't mean it should be gossip or anything," she corrected herself hastily, "but I would like to know how it happened, if you don't mind telling me."

Martin looked into Ceylon's beautiful face and did not see one ounce of morbid curiosity or pity. He saw a woman who wanted to better understand his past and for once, he was willing to share a part of it. Before he began to speak, though, he removed the flannel shirt, and breathed a huge sigh of relief as his skin felt air for the first time that day. Ceylon did not look at his scarred arm; she looked instead at his South Park T-shirt that had been concealed by the flannel.

"A flannel shirt and a T-shirt? My God, you must have been burning up! Don't you feel better now?" she asked.

And yes, he did feel better. So much so that he was able to tell her the story that no one ever talked about. Turning toward her to compensate for the fact that she was on his sightless side, he began to speak.

Chapter Four

8 years earlier

Martin looked at his identical twin and smiled broadly. "Don't worry about when we'll catch up, bro; getting there is half the fun. We've only been married a year. There's plenty of time to start having babies," he said confidently.

Malcolm, the younger of the twins by five minutes, gave his brother a superior smile. "Well, you've got some catching up to do. Selena and I can't be the only ones producing grandchildren and Mama doesn't seem to think she's got enough. If you and Clay don't get busy, she might have to wait until Angelique gets married and who knows how long that will take," he laughed.

Since their baby sister was only nineteen, it did seem premature to be talking about marriage for her. She was still in her first year of college and was not thinking about anything close to marriage. And their older brother Clay appeared to be a permanent bachelor. Any mention of the taboo 'M' word brought a look of absolute dread to his face. So far, the only marrying Deveraux were Martin and Malcolm, and they were both extremely happy with their lots.

Malcolm married his college sweetheart while they were still in school, a move that many predicted would bring certain disaster. On the contrary, Malcolm and Selena were not only still married, but also the parents of three beautiful daughters. Malcolm finished his MBA in finance, and Selena was in the last year of her residency in obstetrics and gynecology.

Martin was a relative newlywed, having married Gayle Williams barely a year before. Gayle was a model with acting aspirations and while her talent was questionable, her beauty was obvious. She was tall, reed slender, and delicate with olive skin and jet black hair. She and Martin looked fabulous together and turned heads whenever they were in public, which was often. Gayle felt it was a good career move to see and be seen as much as possible. There were not too many affairs in Atlanta that Gayle missed, and she went to as many in Miami, New York and Chicago as she could.

Living in Atlanta could have put her in a perilous position as a model but Gayle fortunately had a husband who traveled often to the world's major cities. Gayle received plenty of exposure and work, to which Martin did not object in the least, as long as the majority of her time was spent with him. So far, the marriage was meeting all of his expectations, even though the courtship had been short and tempestuous.

Martin met Gayle when he was participating in a bachelor auction for one of his mother's charities. Lillian Deveraux never had trouble getting her tall, handsome sons to support her in whatever she was doing, especially when it meant that they would be exposed to beautiful, available women. Gayle had been modeling that night. Martin took one look at her and was smitten, and the rest was history. They were married three months later in a small ceremony in Gayle's hometown of New Orleans.

Martin made no secret of the fact that he was crazy about his beautiful wife. He spared no expense and suffered no hesitation in giving her anything and everything he thought she might like. She was always thrilled to receive the flow-

ers, jewelry, furs and whatever else he presented her with.
This was the kind of life to which she had no trouble becoming accustomed. But even so, there was some discontent deep within her.

Her modeling career was not taking off as she wanted. At 5'8", she just barely made the mark for print modeling, and she wasn't quite unique enough for runway modeling. Gayle was pretty, true enough, but not exceptional. Her eyes were a bit too close together and her teeth protruded just a bit too far for perfection. Her legs, while lovely, were not quite long enough to make her exceptional. And every year a new crop of girls came along, younger and fresher and possessing more of what the camera was looking for. After a couple of years of losing assignments to the Tyras and Naomis and their clones, Gayle felt that a wealthy husband would be a prudent hedge against anonymity. Martin came along just in time, but the hunger persisted.

Now, he was making it plain that he wanted a child. He was mad for his three little nieces and that affection was returned one hundredfold. Martin was a man made for home and family and she knew it in her heart. She had done everything possible to sidestep the issue, but there would be a day of reckoning soon. In the meantime, she had another very wealthy fish on the hook. A man many years her senior who lived in Bermuda wanted Gayle and wanted to give her the kind of life that she had a hankering for, with no strings like children attached. Gayle had been walking a tightrope for a long time, but Martin did not know any of this on the fateful night.

That night, as he laughed with his brother and got ready to go out on the town with his wife for an evening of dancing, Martin had no problems at all. The two men were at Malcolm's house waiting for Selena to get ready. Since Gayle was going to be late leaving a photo shoot, they were going to meet her at the trendy club that she favored. Martin and Malcolm had the kind of closeness that only twins share and were making ridiculous jokes at each other's expense and just generally having a good time while waiting for Selena.

Their good mood was broken by the unexpected appearance of their sister, Angelique. It was clear that Angelique was upset; she had been crying quite recently to judge by the redness of her swollen eyes. She was visibly startled to see Martin; she had come to talk to Malcolm and Selena.

"What's the matter, Angel? You can tell your brothers anything, you know that. Spill, it honey, you'll feel better," Martin said comfortingly.

Surprisingly, his words of comfort made it worse for her. She burst into tears all over again and would only shake her head from side to side. Malcolm went to get her a soft drink while Selena got her a cold cloth for her face. Once she and Martin were alone, Angelique gulped hard and finally unburdened herself.

"Marty, I saw Gayle at . . . at the clinic. The abortion clinic that's near the campus," she whispered. "And they called her name and she went up to be checked in, just like a patient."

The whisper became a whimper as Martin grabbed her upper arm in his big hand. The utter fury in his eyes would have cowed most people, but this was his baby sister Angelique and she felt that he had to know what she had seen. Simply put, she had accompanied a leery friend who was conducting research for a Human Sexuality class. Angelique knew that the woman she saw was her sister-in-law; there could have been no mistake at all. Gayle was a person that Angel loved and admired, so she was not likely to make a mistake of that magnitude. She had wrestled for hours about whether she should tell someone and came to the conclusion that Malcolm and Selena could help her decide. Unfortunately, when she arrived in obvious distress, there was Martin. When Malcolm and Selena came back to the living room,

Angelique was alone. Martin had taken off in a big hurry to get some answers. He did not get them that night.

The last thing Martin remembered from that evening was swerving to get out of the way of a car that had lost control and crossed the median. He did not remember the impact, or the car bursting into flames, or being dragged from the car. He did remember waking in the hospital, disoriented, in horrible pain and alone.

All he wanted was his wife. He wanted to see Gayle, to hear her words of consolation and love, to feel her hand in his and to know that everything would be the way it was. And that was the one thing he would never get.

All the time Martin was speaking, Ceylon's hand gently stroked his forearm with its fading scars. She didn't say a word, but her eyes never left his face. He shrugged and turned his gaze towards the beach that lay beyond the backyard.

"And that was it. She finally came to see me after I had been in the hospital for about a week. She claimed that she couldn't stand to see me in pain; she had been too hysterical to see me. And when she did make herself look at me, she turned green, stammered for a minute or two and ran out of the room. The next time I heard from her, it was through her lawyer. Something about her delicate constitution not being able to stomach being married to a gargoyle," Martin snorted. "Oh, and yeah, she did have an abortion. I don't know whether it was mine or the other guy's, but Angel was dead on the money."

"So you went through this all by yourself?" Ceylon murmured. "All the time you spent in the hospital, all the skin grafts, the therapy, everything, all alone? How awful for you."

Martin shrugged again. "Hey, I have a good family, you know that. It wasn't like I didn't have support from people who cared about me. And sometimes I *needed* to be alone, you know? Like Bennie needed to be alone after her accident," he reminded her.

Ceylon could remember quite vividly when Bennie had been in a terrible car accident in California that caused her to lose the child she was carrying. It would have been the first child for the couple. Martin had been a pillar of strength for Clay and for Bennie during that time, and his own tragedy was part of the reason why. What a horrible woman that exwife of his was! *What a bitch*, she thought savagely, but she did not say the words out loud.

She did not speak, but continued to stroke Martin's arm and really look at it. There were puckered lines and ultra smooth patches, the result of the intricate grafting that had taken place. It wasn't terribly discolored, but slight variations were visible. Altogether, it wasn't nearly as bad as Martin thought it was, but there was no way she could say that without putting his back up as well as sounding like an idiot. *Oh, I'm so sorry that you were married to a selfish, hateful bitch and you got burned up and all, but jeez, it's not that bad.*

Ceylon raised her head to find Martin looking at her expectantly. She knew she had to say something and said a quick silent prayer for guidance. "Martin, I'm so sorry that you had to suffer like that. I don't think there is anything I can say to make it any better for you. But . . . I have to tell you that I am glad you have these scars. Because if you didn't, it would mean that you died in that car crash. And that would have been a terrible loss. I'm glad, very glad, that you're here," she said softly. And before he could react, she pulled his head down to her and kissed him right on the long, jagged scar that seamed his face. It was a long, soft, sweet kiss, and he could feel it all the way through his body.

"Now, why don't you finish up this shower and knock off for the night. I've made a fabulous dinner and you are going to eat every single bite. And you didn't even taste my cookies that I slaved all afternoon to make," she scolded.

She jumped up from the settee and handed Martin the offending plate with a look that suggested he had better taste at least one or face her wrath. With a look of profound gratitude, he bit into one and praised it to the skies. And in truth, they were delicious; light, soft shortbread cookies with a delicate lemon flavor. Somehow order was restored to the afternoon.

It wasn't until she was alone in the house that Ceylon cried her heart out for Martin's pain.

Dinner that night was a festive affair, despite the emotional exchange of the afternoon. It was as though a dam had broken, at least for Martin. He felt curiously light inside after talking to Ceylon. She hadn't done anything but listen to him, but the mere fact that she didn't do a lot of prattling after he was done was a relief. She seemed to understand exactly what he had been feeling and still felt about the situation. And she hadn't slopped a lot of sympathy over him, either. She was just there for him, for which he was deeply grateful. And he was also grateful that Bennie had not lied about her ability to cook.

Ceylon made him a dinner that was both pretty to look at and a treat for the tongue. It wasn't fancy food, but it was expertly prepared and delicious. Crisp, golden brown crab cakes were accompanied by coleslaw, fresh asparagus, a deliciously piquant red pepper and lemon conserve, and amazingly, hot homemade rolls. Ceylon brushed away his praise, but she blushed with pleasure as he fell on this meal like he hadn't eaten in days. He couldn't stop raving about the rolls, which for Ceylon were the easiest parts of the meal.

"My grandfather was from down south and you know how southerners are about hot bread! My granny had a billion quick recipes; these are basically biscuits with a little yeast, that's all," she said modestly.

Martin raised an eyebrow at her disclaimer. *Biscuits my*

foot, there are restaurants in Atlanta that would kill to get her recipes. Everything was delectable from the nicely seasoned crab cakes to the delicately prepared conserve to the coleslaw that had an unusual fresh flavor instead of the sickening sweetness often found in the humble salad. He hadn't enjoyed a meal so much in a long time. His mother and sisters-in-law all set fine tables, but this meal was something special to Martin. The fact that his enjoyment had more to do with the cook than the cuisine did not escape him, either. He drank deeply from his glass of iced sassafras tea and moaned with contentment.

"Ceylon, you are amazing. A fine actress, comedienne, and singer who can appreciate hip-hop, wrap my dog around your little finger, and cook like a graduate of the Culinary Institute of America. What other talents are you hiding from me?" he teased.

Ceylon smiled sweetly and enjoyed the look of total relaxation on Martin's face. Nothing was nicer than preparing a good meal and sharing it with someone who could appreciate good cooking. *If only he could appreciate something else, like me!* But there was no sense in wishing for something that was not going to happen and would only cause more turmoil in her life. Without betraying the warm flush she felt from his words, she smiled again and assured him she was hiding nothing.

"I have nothing up my sleeve but a key lime pie. Want some?"

Martin assured her that he certainly did want some pie and as soon as possible. "I think this is where I'm supposed to say I'm too full and wait for later. Uh-uh. There hasn't been a Deveraux man yet who would turn down food. You can't fill us up and we all have a sweet tooth, so yes ma'am, I would love some pie."

He sprang to his feet to clear the table over Ceylon's protests and set out the dessert plates he found on the counter. Ceylon served him a large wedge of the luscious confection and herself a much smaller piece. She topped it with cream she had whipped herself with the merest hint of almond extract and a little confectioners' sugar. Martin was halfway through his slice when she sat down with the carafe of coffee that had brewed while they were eating.

"Damn, Ceylon. I lived in Key West and this is the best key lime pie I have ever eaten," he sighed happily.

It was sweet and citrus-y but with a distinct, subtle tang that gave it a sensual bite. The crisp cookie crust was obviously homemade and the addition of the real whipped cream made it a blissful experience in dining. Martin expressed this thought to Ceylon as she sipped a demitasse cup of rich black coffee with her pie.

"Ceylon, this was magnificent. Absolutely the best meal I have had in years."

Surprising them both, he leaned over and gave her a huge kiss on the cheek. The warm, molten beauty of her gaze was almost his undoing, but he rallied.

"Why don't you sit out on the deck while I clean up the kitchen?" he asked. "It's the least I can do to show my appreciation."

Ceylon immediately agreed with no protests. She had learned long ago that to graciously accept a man's largesse would insure that he did more things to please you. Nothing was more unsettling to a man than to have to argue with a woman about opening a door or washing the dishes or some other mundane thing. Ceylon learned from her granny how to be a graceful, grateful recipient. She and Satchel went outside to enjoy the warm, scented evening as Martin made short work of the dishes.

He soon joined them, sitting next to Ceylon on the glider. This time, he was more comfortable because he could sit to her left. He didn't have to try to turn his head to maintain eye contact with her as they talked. They chatted quietly with companionable silences until Martin asked her a direct question.

"Tell me about yourself, Ceylon."

Ceylon did not indicate by tone of voice or body language that this was an uncomfortable topic for her, but he noticed a distinct coolness in her eyes before she answered him.

"There's nothing to tell, really. I'm just what I seem to be, a chubby kid from the projects who got lucky. End of story," she said firmly.

Martin could tell that she had dug her heels in and was about to try another tactic when the whine of a night insect distracted him. "I think I'm going inside before I become bug chow. Are you coming, Ceylon?"

Ceylon breathed deeply; this was her chance to put some distance between them. He was just too desirable and she was too weak to resist. Besides, those questions were coming, she could just feel it.

"Thanks, Martin, but I think I'll stay out here for a while," she answered.

"Okay," he responded, "but watch out for the bats. They come out about this time."

The next sound Martin heard was the banging of the screen door as Ceylon beat him to the kitchen. He found her in there looking out the French doors with a worried expression on her face.

"What do you think God had in mind when he made bats?" she asked in all seriousness. "I mean, what do you suppose he was aiming for?"

Martin looked at her pretty, flushed face and started laughing. But she wasn't finished.

"Do you think he intended them to be party favors?" she continued. "Practical jokes? Something to make the ugly animals feel better? I know they eat bugs and all that, but he could have made, oh let's see now . . . *horses* eat bugs and people would have been a lot more receptive to the idea. Horses are tame and pretty, after all. People would even put up with horse . . . *leavings,* if the horse ate bugs, too, you know? There would be a horse-sized scooper in every garage if *horses* ate bugs.

"Now, *bats* eat lots of bugs and you don't see anyone celebrating that fact except science teachers and that poor little person at the zoo who gives the bat lecture. They're always *happy* to tell you just how many insects bats consume, as though that should make them more popular, more like a pal, a *chum,* a potential house pet. But it doesn't work, does it?" she asked rhetorically. "And you know why? Because," she lowered her voice to a conspiratorial whisper, "bats are *ugly.*"

By this time, Martin was holding his side and letting tears of laughter roll down his face. This was the kind of comedy Ceylon did in her act; simple, well thought out routines based on the absurdities of life. She was always ladylike and somewhat startled by some of the things she discussed, and always funny. She had a way of making the commonplace absurd and vice versa. Now, she was looking at Martin with huge, rounded eyes.

"It's true, the bat is not an attractive animal. It's not the cocker spaniel of the rodent world, you must admit that! It looks like one of God's helpers couldn't decide what to do with some spare parts," she said musingly. Then, in a perfect 'surfer dude' accent, she went on.

"Dude, like I've got this like rat thing, and these leftover wings, here. Like, suppose we like, stick the wings onto its little rat body. So now we've got this, like, flying mouse thing, dude! This is better than the time we put that duckbill on the gopher. That was bitchin', dude."

Ceylon concluded her spiel with the idea that the bat merely needed a publicist to extol its virtues or, failing that, a plastic surgeon to improve its appearance.

"Now, if we could get rid of the little snarly face and make it look like . . . oh, I don't know . . . a Teletubbie? Or a

Beanie Baby, maybe, then the bat might be on its way to getting some positive recognition. And endorsements," she said seriously.

Martin was laughing so hard now that Satchel looked concerned. He gave a short, worried bark, which helped Martin regain his composure. "Damn, Ceylon, if you can do that off the cuff, your act must be hilarious," he gasped.

Ceylon decided to put him on the spot. She looked at him leaning back in one of the kitchen chairs, still wiping his eyes and skewered him with a mock angry look.

"Are you telling me that you have never been to see me perform, Martin? I'm hurt. Hurt, I tell you! You should be ashamed of yourself," she added for good measure.

She bounced out of the kitchen, pretending great rage. Martin followed her into the great room, making a great show of contrition.

"Mea culpa, mea culpa. I can see that I have done myself a great disservice by missing your performances. And I have done you a similar disservice by not paying you the proper homage. Please forgive me," he added, kissing her hand.

Ceylon pretended to consider his apology and she settled onto the big striped sofa with its floral pillows. He sat next to her and draped a long arm around her shoulder.

"I'll tell you what, Ceylon. I not only promise to attend your next show, but I will come to see you at least once a month from now on if you will do one thing for me: tell me about yourself," he said in his deep, sexy voice. "Tell me everything about Ceylon."

Ceylon knew that resistance was futile. She hesitated as long as she could before turning to Martin and telling him everything he wanted to know.

Chapter Five

Twenty-five years earlier

Keeping still was very difficult for most small children, but not for Ceylon and especially not today. Today was Easter and her daddy was coming to get her, and she would spend all day with her mommy and her brothers and sisters. He said so, and mommy said so. She had repeated their promise to her grandparents many times, each time getting a carefully blank smile in return.

She sat in the front window so that she could watch the street to make sure they did not miss her. Clad in her Easter finery, she looked like a plump brown doll in a pink bonnet and coat with lace-trimmed white ankle socks and white patent leather Mary Janes on her tiny feet. She sat very still so she would not wrinkle the creation her grandmother made for her, and so she could rightfully claim to be a good girl when they came.

Sometime in the late afternoon, after refusing repeated coaxing from her grandmother to eat lunch, to eat dinner, to play with her Easter basket, anything to get her out of that window, Ceylon finally understood. They weren't coming. They had forgotten her, again. They didn't want her, again.

She slid off the piano bench and went into the living room where her grandparents were talking anxiously in hushed voices.

"I'm not going to wait for them no more. Nobody's comin' for me and I'm going to stay here with you. I'm going to take off my nice dress now," she said quietly.

When her grandmother asked if she needed some help, Ceylon shook her head no.

"I'm a big girl, Grandma. I can do it myself," she said in a dignified voice that belied the huge tears flowing silently down her perfect little face.

She was five years old.

Martin was aghast as he listened to Ceylon's quiet voice explain the circumstances of her childhood. Her mother had five children by two different husbands and when she became pregnant with Ceylon, it was just too much for her.

"She said five children were more than enough. She could afford to have another child because both she and my father had good jobs. She was just tired of mothering, as she put it. If my grandmother hadn't come to get me, I would have gone from the hospital to the foster care system," Ceylon admitted.

"She left you at the hospital?" Martin said hoarsely. "Why in the name of God did she do that?"

Ceylon looked him fully in the face for the first time since she started speaking. "Because the abortion didn't work. She wasn't kidding about not wanting another child. And I was stubborn, even in the womb," she said with a bitter, wry wit. "I didn't seem to understand that the tube was supposed to suck me out of there, I hung on for dear life, apparently. And here I am," she ended dryly.

Martin was dazed from the information he had just received. How could this vital, sweet woman come from an environment like that?

As if she could read his mind, Ceylon hastened to explain that her upbringing was actually quite nice. "My grandparents were wonderful to me. I had an old-fashioned, sheltered kind of childhood. They took me to the park, to the Ice Capades, to children's theater, to church; Granddaddy used to take me fishing. They gave me every bit of love they had, Martin, and there was a *lot* of it there. And I had my great-aunt Ruby and her husband Erroll and they treated me like I was a little princess, believe me!

"We lived in the projects, true enough. But I went to Catholic school, and Grandma could sew like a couturier so I always had the most beautiful clothes in the world. My grandparents were very old-school; they did not believe that women should work, which was a huge point of contention around the house. They didn't see the need for me to have a college education since I would get married and have babies. The best I could do was getting them to let me go to cosmetology school. I mean, I owed them everything, I owed them my very *life;* I wasn't going to disobey them. And I did get married the year after I graduated from high school. That was . . . interesting," she said with a twinkle in her eye.

Married? Ceylon? He had never heard of this and was immediately curious about her marriage.

Ceylon chuckled and said, "Well . . . he was a nice guy. He really was, although not nearly mature enough to be a husband. Running with his boys and hanging out was far more important to him than coming home at a decent hour. But he wasn't a horrible person, just a bad husband. For *me,* at any rate; he's re-married now and has two small children and he's a different person, he really is. If it hadn't been for his condition, we might still be married," she said teasingly.

"Condition?" repeated Martin. "What kind of condition did he have?" Surely Ceylon wasn't the kind of woman who would leave a man because of some impairment, he thought.

Ceylon fastened her big hazel eyes on Martin's questioning face and said slowly, "He had genital amnesia." At Martin's look of utter disbelief, she explained. "He couldn't seem to remember exactly which 'feminine attribute' was his exclusive province, so he felt the need to try a lot of them out. 'Oops, that ain't mine! Oops, sorry, thought I knew you! Aww, you mean this one ain't mine either . . .' I got tired of waiting for him to figure it out, so I had to let him go," she said saucily.

Martin tried not to laugh and was successful for about thirty seconds. His arm tightened around Ceylon as he gave her a huge hug.

"Ceylon, you are truly one of a kind! Your family, well your birth mother, has no idea what she missed out on, not raising you."

Ceylon basked in the warmth of his arms for a moment and then had to correct him. "Oh, we saw each other from time to time. Despite the fact that my parents had no interest in me, and I realized that when I was five, I was still drawn to my brothers and sisters. My father and mother divorced when I was quite small, so I saw virtually nothing of him, although my siblings saw him regularly. You know, I went to see him when he was ill, just before he died. I was in my twenties then and he kept saying, 'Where's that little girl? What happened to that little girl?' He didn't even remember my name, Martin. He had no idea who I was," she said sadly.

"It's hard on a child to know that you have five siblings and yet you don't get to live with them, you know? And they were grandchildren, too, so they did see my grandparents from time to time. I tried so hard to be loved by them, to be accepted! You know, despite the fact that I lived in the projects and they lived in a fancy brick house in a nice neighborhood, my brothers and sister put the 'O' in Ghett-o," Ceylon confessed.

She couldn't look at Martin as she explained. "Oh, they were serious thugs, even as kids. They would break up my toys, tear my clothes, and the things they did to me! Like playing hide and go seek in the park and running home and leaving me there when I was 'it,' locking me in the closet, locking me in the basement and turning off the lights, all that hateful kind of crap. Do you know to this day I'm afraid of the dark? I had too many ugly things done to me in dark places," she said quietly.

Suddenly she jumped up from the sofa. "Do you want some more pie? I'm having some," she said over her shoulder as she hurried into the kitchen.

Ceylon suddenly realized just how much she had told Martin and how strongly her childhood contrasted with his. He grew up in a happy upper-middle-class home with no drama, no abuse, no ghetto antics, and no weirdness, and she had just told him all—well *almost* all of her darkest secrets. She did not want to face him, but he was right on her heels as she went to fetch the pie that she really did not want. But as she served him another huge wedge, her heart was made easy by his next question.

"So tell me, Ceylon, how did you get started in show business?" Martin asked.

Finally Ceylon's face lit up. This was a story she did not mind telling at all.

After her marriage broke up, Ceylon was determined not to sit at home and wait for another Prince Charming to happen along and take over her care from her grandparents. With her cosmetology license in hand, she plied her trade as a stylist while she took classes to become an instructor in Cosmetology College. Her aim was to open her own beauty school after being a director for a local school. She couldn't do any worse than the haphazardly run schools that proliferated the area, she reasoned, and she could probably do a lot better.

She had a positive gift for teaching, she found. Her stu-

dents loved her as she made her lessons clear, concise and
practical. They also loved her sense of humor. Ceylon would
have her students laughing so hard that they did not realize
they were learning. Her favorite students were Renee Kemp
and Benita Cochran. These ladies had the funds to open a
posh day spa and were in school to get the credentials to do
it right. They were both college educated and very savvy, as
well as being genuinely nice, warm women. And they
thought Ceylon was the funniest person in the world. Renee
often dared her to go down to the comedy clubs on open mike
night, something that Ceylon would never do. It was bad
enough that she was a working woman, something her grandparents abhorred, but to be a comedienne? That was something nice women just did not pursue.

One day, though, Bennie heard Ceylon singing. Ceylon had
been born with perfect pitch and had sung all of her life,
mostly at church, of course. Bennie knew the real thing
when she heard it. Not only did her family own a string of
radio stations, but her godfather also happened to be Bill
'Bump' Williams, a jazz artist of the highest caliber, like
Duke Ellington, Count Basie and Miles Davis before him. So
Bennie managed through some clever chicanery to get
Ceylon and Bump at her house at the same time, and further
contrived to have Bump 'overhear' Ceylon singing. He was
bowled over, offered her a spot on his next tour, helped her
negotiate a contract with a major record label, and the rest
was history.

Ceylon had several CDs, all of which had gone platinum,
she had numerous Grammys, American Music Awards and
People's Choice Awards to her credit, as well as a couple of
specials on HBO and VH1. She had a huge crossover audience; everyone loved her because of her warmth, and her
charm and her humor, which amused everyone without offending anyone. She had recently ventured into acting with
several television roles, including a recurring one on a major
sitcom and some small film parts.

"The problem is, they keep trying to cast me as 'sassy,' because I'm not sexy, like Halle Berry or Vanessa Williams. When your fanny is as big as mine is, or *was*, you automatically become 'sassy.' Like a *strong-but-sassy* high school principal. Or a *strong-but-sassy* judge, or single mother or something," she said ruefully. "I just got offered a part in a new sitcom last week."

Martin said that sounded promising. "What's the part?"

Ceylon smiled wickedly. "It's a real departure for me—a mayor in a small town who is not only *strong* but . . . *sassy*," she said merrily.

Martin laughed with her, relishing the genuine enjoyment on her face as she told him anecdotes about her career. And how her grandparents were persuaded that she could have a successful career after they were convinced that Bump Williams would look out for their baby.

"It helped tremendously that they were big fans of his. And it also helped that I would be singing and not working the comedy circuit. A singer, like Lena Horne or somebody, that was okay. A comic, like Moms Mabley? Never! Not in a thousand years would they have let that happen!" Ceylon said fondly.

The best thing to her was the fact that her grandparents lived long enough to celebrate her success with her. Her grandfather passed away six years ago and her grandmother the day after. Ceylon remarked sadly that there was no way her granny was going to live without her husband. "I always knew they would go together. I'm just blessed to have had them for so long and to have been able to take them on a few trips and let them know that I was a success. That was a big blessing," she sighed.

They sat in companionable silence for a while, and then Ceylon cleared the few dishes and put them in the dishwasher. It really didn't surprise her when Martin zeroed in for the kill.

"So what happened Ceylon? How did everything go so wrong for you?"

* * *

Ceylon took her time about looking at Martin. He leaned against the kitchen counter, his long, sexy legs crossed as he waited for her to respond. Ceylon looked down at her toes for a moment before looking up into his patient face.

"I knew you were going to go there, Martin. If you have to know, let's go sit down and be comfortable. This is going to take a minute or two," she said as she took his hand and led him into the great room.

Martin put some soft music on the CD player and settled himself next to Ceylon. Before dinner, Ceylon had changed from her peach pants into a long, pale green cotton jersey dress with long sleeves that she had pushed up to reveal her pretty arms. She toyed with a silver bangle bracelet and appeared to be collecting her thoughts before speaking.

Martin thought again about how very appealing she was, especially in her current vulnerable state. She looked so sweet that he wanted to bite her, just to see for himself how delicious she would be to taste. He restrained himself with great effort, a bit ashamed for having such an elemental reaction to her femininity. The last thing she needed was him all over her, but God help him, that's where he wanted to be. *Who the hell says she isn't sexy?* He had to force himself to listen to her story.

It was short and predictable, really. For years, Ceylon had doled out money to her siblings for one reason or another, usually under the guise of helping one of her nieces and nephews. As her star rose in the entertainment world, so did her value to her venal relatives. After so many years of trying to gain acceptance by her immediate family, Ceylon had the dubious pleasure of being accepted and, to her mind, loved by them. That they loved her money even more was not a possibility that she explored too closely.

After her grandparents' deaths, Ceylon was lonely and vulnerable and fair game for her oldest brother Duane, who wormed his way into her confidence. With his sleazy brand of sincere charm and his MBA, Duane convinced her that he was the best person to manage her business affairs. He even fooled her personal manager Sheldon Brillstein, a seasoned veteran in Hollywood. And for the first year, everything was fine. She made fantastic money and Duane saw to it that her investments prospered. She got so comfortable with Duane handling her finances that she never looked over his shoulder, trusting that her big brother would take care of her. Little did she know that taking care of himself was his first priority.

Duane was taking his first vacation in about two years when Ceylon wrote a big check to the Make-A-Wish Foundation, one of her pet charities. To her enormous chagrin, the check bounced, causing her to call the bank and find out what was going on. She found that her personal accounts and business accounts had been cleared out, leaving her with a zero balance. Then the IRS appeared on her doorstep, demanding payment of past taxes and brandishing several years worth of unanswered summons and demands for payment that Duane had ignored. She lost all of her real estate and personal property except for her stage clothes and her daily wardrobe and effects; the stage clothes were deemed necessary in order for her to continue working to pay back the rest of the money she owed. Everything else, the IRS confiscated.

So Ceylon had to go to work to pay back every penny, and work she did. Rather than file bankruptcy, she dug her heels in and worked like she had never worked before, with every cent save a court sanctioned living allowance going to the IRS and other creditors. She suffered the tabloid feeding frenzy, the cruel jokes on talk shows at her expense, and the rampant gossip with her head held high. She had done nothing wrong, other than trusting a family member, and she was making restitution; she was not going to walk around like a pariah. But her life was truly hell, the kind of hell that creeps up late at night and stays until the early hours; the kind of hell that makes you feel like the biggest idiot in the free world.

Ceylon's talent and the relationships she had built with influential people were the reason she was able to work so much despite her problems. Tommy John, the rock idol, for instance, had written a duet for them to sing on his newest CD and had asked her to perform on several tour dates. He understood better than most what she was going through— his brother-in-law had stolen several million dollars from . him some years before.

Bump Williams was certainly in her corner and she would never want for a place to sing, to tour, or to live, for that matters. He thought of her as his goddaughter, the same way he did Bennie. So, she had, even in the middle of her agony, reason to rejoice, because she had so many good, true friends in the business, people that she considered family. Even though she knew she had friends, she had not turned to them in her need.

"Ceylon, I can't believe you've taken so much on yourself," Martin said slowly. "I'm not trying to criticize what you did but, honey, you have to know there was a better way for you to handle this! You're killing yourself when number one, there are people who would give you any amount of money you needed, and number two, you're paying for something you didn't do! That brother of yours is the one who should be paying, not you. His ass should in jail somewhere, baby. Why didn't you try to find him and bring him to justice?"

He didn't mean to yell, but the thought of everything she had been dealing with was killing him. He reached out for her and stroked her silky brown curls while he waited for her to answer.

"Martin, I don't know how to answer that. On the one hand, he was wrong; he's a thief and liar. But he is my brother, after all. I was in such deep shock after I found out what he did that I just did things blindly, stupidly, I'll admit. I just wanted to get everything straightened out as quickly as possible. And I was so ashamed; I couldn't stand for anyone to know that my own flesh and blood had done this to me. And then my mother begged me not to go after him," she admitted.

At Martin's incredulous look, Ceylon lowered her head. "I know, I know, she's the last person in the world I should want to do anything for. But like it or not, she's the only mother I have. And she wasn't much of a mother, but she gave me something nobody else ever gave me. She gave me a birthday," she murmured. Then she gave a choking little laugh. "She didn't give it willingly, but I'm here. And I have her to thank for it. So I, I . . ." her voice trailed off into a soft sob.

Martin couldn't take it any more; he reached over and pulled her into his arms. "You needed them to love you for so long and when you were at your most defenseless, they took advantage of that fact. Damn, Ceylon, that was just wrong, just wrong, and they shouldn't get away with it. Nobody should have to go through all the crap you've been through, especially not you. You're too sweet for your own good, too trusting and much too forgiving," he said gruffly as he stroked her soft form.

Ceylon wanted to feel like an utter fool, but she couldn't. She was too comforted by what Martin was saying and doing. She tried to pull away from his embrace but he was too strong for her. With a sigh, she settled into his arms and let his warmth sink into her. Finally, she pulled away while she was still in her right mind.

"Martin, honey, thank you for listening to me. Thank you for making me talk. There were a lot of things I needed to get off my chest, I guess. But the worst is over. I'll be finished paying everything off by the end of next year and I can start fresh. It was a mess, but I lived through it," she said philosophically.

Martin looked at her sweet, tear-streaked face for a long moment and then lowered his mouth to hers. The tender, gentle kiss would have gone on forever if the insistent ringing of the telephone had not jarred them apart. With sincere regret, Ceylon answered the phone, staring at Martin the whole time. It was Sheldon, checking to see how she was doing.

"Shelley, I'm fine, thank you for asking," she said, watching the enigmatically sexy Martin as he rose to leave the room and give her some privacy. She smiled broadly as she relived their sweet kiss. "I'm better than fine, if you can believe that."

Martin went to his bedroom and picked up his cell phone. He quickly punched in a long distance number and waited impatiently for the party to answer.

"Titus, this is Martin Deveraux. I'm fine, how about you? Listen, I have a case for you. I need you to find someone for me. Make this a priority, okay?"

When he got off the telephone, Martin felt much better about the situation. Whether she liked it or not, Ceylon needed someone to look out for her. And he was going to be that person, regardless of the consequences.

Chapter Six

Ceylon actually thought she would be able to sleep that night. She was more relaxed than she had been for months, and she felt like weight had been lifted off her very soul, which it had. Talking to Martin helped her release some of the pain and frustration she had been carrying around since the deception. She eagerly made her preparations for bed after talking with Sheldon, and couldn't wait to slip into the cool, crisp linens that awaited her.

All of the beds at the St. Simon's house were oversized to accommodate the hulking masses of the Deveraux men. Ceylon slipped into a long, peach colored gown of cotton batiste with a *broderie Anglaise* bodice and settled down for a long night's rest, a much-deserved night's rest after the emotional purge she had been through. And she had the added bonus of the memory of tonight's kiss to float her into dreamland.

She sighed happily as she closed her eyes against the light of the bathroom. She could never sleep in a darkened room; her fear of the dark was absolutely real. But tonight she did not have to worry about things going bump in the night. Her lips curled into a smile as she remembered how gently Martin had held her, and how soft and passionate his lips felt against hers. But even the warmth that drenched her body at the thought of the closeness they shared was not enough to lull her to sleep.

After an hour or two of tossing and turning, Ceylon gave into the inevitable and wandered into the great room with several of her favorite romance novels. If she couldn't sleep, she would stay awake with a few old friends. She settled herself in a big comfortable armchair, and drifted off to Ethiopia and a big, handsome investigator's arms courtesy of Janice Sims.

The next morning she was dressed and ready for her next project, the sun porches. She wasn't in her usual rush to begin, however, and lingered over her coffee chatting with Satchel, which is where Martin found her. Her eyes lit up with the warmth they almost always had when she looked at him and she smiled pleasantly.

"Good morning, Martin. There's more coffee in the pot."

Martin was not known as a morning person, but there was something so cute about Ceylon's fresh scrubbed beauty that he automatically smiled back. He almost bent over and kissed her, but caught himself just in time. She just looked so pretty in an old denim shirt and jeans with one sandaled foot tucked under her that he was completely disarmed.

"Good morning, Ceylon. Did you have breakfast already?" he inquired. Once again he did not smell the remnants of a meal, but after last night's feast he was hoping for more of the same.

"Yes, I did. I had some lovely cantaloupe and a piece of toast. Would you like some? The cantaloupe is in the refrigerator," she replied.

Martin tried not to look too disappointed, but that was not his idea of breakfast. He opened the refrigerator door and stared mournfully at the contents. *Cantaloupe. Yuck.* He probed and poked around and sighed heavily as he finally closed the door in resignation.

Ceylon enjoyed her view of his rear end and was rather sorry when he stood up and turned around. Today he wore khaki shorts and a plain navy short-sleeved T-shirt. With his hair still unconfined and damp from the shower, he looked fabulous. Sexy, fresh, and desirable, or he would have if he hadn't looked so glum.

"Martin, there are eggs and bacon and cheese and all kinds of things in there. You could make something else if you wanted," she said sweetly.

His expression, if anything, looked more morose.

"What's the matter, Martin, can't you cook?" Ceylon asked teasingly.

He sighed deeply and admitted, "I can burn toast."

"Ohhh, I see. So, if you're going to get any kind of breakfast around here, I need to prepare it for you, is that it? I don't know, Martin, that's a lot of work. What do you think Satchel, is he worth it?"

Satchel cocked his head to one side and looked from Ceylon to Martin for a long moment. He gave a short bark and laid his paw on Ceylon's lap with a winning grin.

"Well, if you're going to gang up on me, I guess I'd better get busy!" Ceylon laughed. She stood up and laid her hand across her breast. "Y'all are just going to work me like my name is Kizzy. I see how this goes. Okay, give me about twenty minutes and I'll see if I can't scrape something up for you, you poor helpless man."

Martin's smile broke across his face like sunshine and this time he did kiss her, a loud smacking one on her cheek. A light, sweet fragrance floated up around him and he was hard pressed to let her go, but he did.

"Thanks, Ceylon, you're the best. It looks like rain, so I'm going to get going on that shower before it starts."

He left the room whistling as Ceylon turned to the refrigerator to decide what to fix. She did not realize that she was singing for the first time since she had come to the island. Her voice trailed out to Martin as he stood in his work area and he closed his eyes to enjoy it. He hadn't heard anybody sing "God Bless the Child" like that since the last time he listened to his Billie Holiday records. He pulled his cell phone out of his pocket and punched in Bennie's number.

"Well, Martin, what's the latest?" she asked cheerfully. "I talked to Ceylon for a few minutes yesterday and she sounds pretty good. So what's going on? Has she scrubbed the lawn or put Satchel in the washing machine or something?"

Martin ignored her attempt at humor and got right to the point. "Bennie, Ceylon doesn't sleep. I thought I heard her the first night I was here, but you know I sleep like the dead, so I didn't really pay it any attention. But last night I got up to let Satchel out and she was in the living room with the television on, pretending like she was reading a book. Wide awake at 4 o'clock in the morning," he said worriedly.

Bennie's next words did not reassure him. "Ceylon hardly ever sleeps," she agreed. "She's a world-class insomniac. Even when things are going well for her she has problems sleeping. And when things are unsettled, sleep just disappears from her life. She's tried everything—warm milk, chamomile tea, white noise machines, breathing exercises, but nothing seems to work. She's been like that as long as I've known her."

"Well, I don't advocate sleeping pills, but how about some melatonin or something? It's supposed to help," Martin said.

"Child, please! Ceylon doesn't take pills of any kind. Not aspirin, Midol, nothing. She has an absolute horror of any kind of pill because a friend of hers died from an overdose. If she has to have an antibiotic the doctor has to give her a shot, because my girl is not going to take a pill," Bennie informed him.

This was not good news to Martin. Sleep was a critical part of life and if you didn't get quality sleep your body reacted in all kinds of ways. Besides, he knew of at least one occasion where Ceylon had slept. He and Bennie chatted for a few more minutes and by that time, the kind of smells he had been yearning for assailed his nostrils.

"Sis, I've got to go. I smell breakfast and if it's half as good as last night's dinner, I'm about to die and go to heaven," he said with a big smile.

"See? I told you Ceylon could cook! Go eat. I know how you Deveraux boys are when it comes to food," she said fondly and bade him good-bye.

Martin entered the kitchen just as Ceylon was pouring a cup of deliciously fragrant coffee at his place setting. In a very short time she had made him steak and eggs with grits and toast. There was also a dish of mixed fruit and a small glass of tomato juice. Everything was arranged on a nice linen placemat and there were fresh flowers in a small round vase. It looked like a magazine illustration and tasted even better. The steak was crisply browned on the outside and juicy and tender on the inside, the eggs over easy—his favorite—were done perfectly and the toast was golden and buttery.

"I didn't ask, but how's your cholesterol?" Ceylon said with a worried pucker on her forehead.

"One-twenty at my last check up. Ceylon, this is beautiful. Thank you from the bottom of my heart," he said sincerely.

Ceylon joined him for another cup of coffee that she had laced with a hint of cinnamon. There was something intimate and romantic about sharing idle talk with a beautiful man over a meal she had made just for him. *I could be heading for deep trouble here if I don't watch myself.* But for once she ignored the little voice in her head, she just enjoyed the moment.

Ceylon didn't attack the sun porches after all. After breakfast, with Martin gallantly cleaning the kitchen as thanks for the delicious meal, Ceylon assisted him in finishing the shower installation. It was located in a secluded end of the main part of the house, and would be finished with a bricked floor and a privacy wall made of fencing, which Martin would put up the next day. Ceylon mainly handed him things and they talked about a variety of subjects while they worked. She was caught off guard when Martin asked what her immediate plans were for the future.

"Well, that's kind of why Sheldon called last night. My record label wants another CD and I'm being considered for a part on Broadway. I'd be replacing the second lead in a musical that is getting some very, very good reviews, so that's exciting," she said, but the excitement did not come through in her voice.

"What's the matter, don't you want to do it?" he asked immediately.

"Oh, no, Broadway is wonderful, the play is wonderful, and I'd only be in New York for about three months. If it's held over, I could be there longer, but I would say I'd be up there for about three and a half months, the way it's looking now." She still did not sound over the top with elation, though.

At Martin's probing question, she looked pensive for a moment and then confessed, "I hate living like a vagabond. I have some friends in New York and I can probably stay with them, or sublet a place, or the show will rent me an apartment or a suite. Sheldon will see to that, believe me! But I get tired of living out of suitcases and hotel rooms. I want a place of my own. I'm pretty much a homebody."

Martin felt a pang as her simple words revealed how much she had lost. When Bennie was in the hospital in California, Ceylon insisted that he and Clay and Renee treat her home as theirs. She made them check out of the hotel they were staying in and brought them to her gracious home in Brentwood. It wasn't a flashy Hollywood mansion, just a warm, exquisitely tasteful home that displayed the charm and beauty of the woman who owned it. It was such a traumatic time in their lives that Martin had all but forgotten his stay at Ceylon's but it suddenly came back to him with eerie clarity.

Her taste was elegant and simple and the comfort that oozed from every room was a balm for the soul. And she had nothing left of it now, thanks to her thieving brother. His jaw tightened in resolve. She was going to get back everything she had lost; he would see to it himself. In the meantime, though, there were a few other things that needed to be addressed and he was not about to shirk those things, either. He almost didn't hear her softly spoken question.

"So, Martin, when are you going back to Atlanta?" she asked wistfully. It sounded more like a plea than a question, but it was too late to take it back. If she didn't put the brakes on fast, she would be falling even harder for Martin Mercier Deveraux and that was not an option, not with her life so unsettled. But she would be lying to herself if she did not acknowledge that she would miss him dreadfully when he left.

"Well, I should have the shower enclosure up by noon tomorrow and then I'll be out of your hair," he said thoughtlessly.

Ceylon blinked as she watched him stowing away the tools he had used that day. Using lunch as an excuse, she quickly went into the kitchen to try and swallow the stupid lump in her throat.

Martin watched her leave, feeling as oddly upset as she appeared to be. Satchel did not make things better when he looked at Ceylon's retreating figure and whined. He looked at his master with reproach in his eyes. Martin gave him a reassuring pat on the head. "Don't worry Satch. I got this, okay?"

Ceylon was in much better spirits that evening. Over lunch Martin told her he wanted to take her out for dinner. It was partially to repay her kindness in cooking for him, he said, but also because she was the best dining companion he'd had in a long, long time.

Her face grew warm with pleasure from his sweet remark and she looked adorably young and flustered. "Is that a nice way of saying I talk a lot, Martin? Because I do, I know I do," she confessed.

Martin took her hand and stroked her soft skin with his thumb. "You do not talk a lot. You are, however, a very delightful and entertaining conversationalist, as well as a wonderful cook," he added as he looked at the remains of the chicken salad. Ceylon's was by far the best he had ever tasted, fragrant with fresh basil and toasted pecans. With sliced tomatoes and cucumbers in a raspberry vinaigrette and fresh hot biscuits, the light meal was surprisingly filling for what was usually considered a 'ladies tea' dish.

Listening to his deep voice while his big hand cradled hers, the compliment was doubly nice. He leaned in closer and touched her cheek gently with his lips, his mustache sending little trembles of delight down her spine.

"Now can I please have some of that leftover pie?" he begged. "Please?"

Ceylon pulled away from him and burst into laughter. "No! A piece of my delicious pie for a measly little kiss like that? Ha! I need a lot more than that for my wares, Martin. What do you think this is, the Sara Lee Outlet Store? Sam's Club? The day-old bread place?"

She rose from her chair and was backing out of the room when Martin caught her in one smooth swoop.

"Ceylon, if you want another kiss, you never have to ask," he assured her as he pulled her close. This time, there was no light, playful exchange of soft pecks, or even a tender, healing caress. This was the kind of kiss that melted steel, shattered crystal and set off alarms; the kind of kiss that gave as much as it took.

Martin's lips connected with Ceylon's seconds before their mouths parted to taste the essence of passion that was

never far from the surface with them. He moaned his pleasure as their tongues met, mated, and danced over each other
in a shimmering explosion of bliss. His arms tightened around
her until she could barely breath, but she didn't care. Her
fingers slid into his silky hair and she just held on, wanting
more and more of the taste of him, the feel of him.

The ringing of his cell phone, which, sadly enough, was
in the pocket of his shorts made them stop. Ceylon jumped
and immediately looked at his pants in wonder. He chuckled
at her expression, although he truly did not find anything
amusing about breaking off that kiss.

"It's just my phone," he apologized.

"Good, I was afraid it was some kind of mood condom or
something," she said breathlessly.

While Martin answered the phone, she took the opportunity to race down the hall, ostensibly to fix her hair but in reality to catch her breath. *Great balls of fire, that man can
kiss. You could rent those lips out for parties*, she fretted as
she paced around the bedroom. She finally went into the
bathroom to behold her face and was alarmed by what she
saw. Her eyes were huge, her cheeks were rosy, her lips
looked lush and recently devoured and her hair was mussed.
And she looked fabulous, better than she had in months. *I
knew that man was dangerous, I just didn't know* how *dangerous. He could be fatal,* she thought. *But what a way to
go!* And the thought made her smile as she touched her still
throbbing lips.

Martin growled a greeting into the cell phone. He was not
happy about breaking off that kiss, but it was just as well. It
certainly wasn't going to end on its own, and he wasn't
strong enough to stop. *That was just too damned sweet, too
good* he brooded as he listened to the voice on the other end
of the phone.

"Yeah, I did say as soon as possible," he conceded. "So
are you telling me you found something already?"

His brow furrowed, he continued the conversation intently, although a part of him wished fervently that the phone had remained silent.

Their first public meal together was wonderful. Martin took Ceylon to a small, beautiful restaurant that specialized in seafood, grilled or baked only. Ceylon was amazed by all the choices and finally asked Martin to order for her. He had eaten at the restaurant many times and was bound to select whatever was best on the menu. And his choices were absolutely superb. Beginning with a sweet red pepper and crabmeat bisque, they then dined on shrimp scampi and angel hair pasta in a light cream sauce that had a subtle, sweet taste of garlic. Ceylon was pleased with her dinner and even more pleased with her companion.

Martin was more charming than she ever remembered him being; not that he was ever rude or obnoxious. He had always been so distant, though, that to see him happily conversational and relaxed was rather unusual. His easy words and the occasional flirtatious remark made her flash her adorable dimples in smile after smile. Martin commented on how beguiling that smile was to him.

"Ceylon, I know you must have heard it a million times, but you have an absolutely beautiful smile. When you smile, it's like you're opening up your entire being to the lucky person on the receiving end. You are one gorgeous woman, you know that?" Martin had no idea what his quietly spoken words did to Ceylon's insides.

All she could manage was a soft "Ohhh" in response. Then her face lit up again in a special way that Martin was beginning to recognize.

"Martin, I believe that's the nicest compliment I have ever received," she murmured. And surprising them both, she leaned over and kissed him quickly and sweetly.

Luckily, the server returned with their dessert before she could get weird about what she had just done. Despite her protests, Martin ordered dessert; a chocolate mousse cake that he assured her was delicious. He went so far as to order an extra big piece, which the server was more than happy to provide. Martin insisted on giving Ceylon a taste, a perfect little bite-sized morsel covered in whipped cream. He held the forkful next to her lips and she obediently opened, like a little girl.

Martin smiled at the look of absolute delight on her face and they shared the rest of the cake along with sidelong looks of utter contentment. Ceylon looked beautiful in a simple, elegant Marina Renaldi dress the color of cream that set off her skin and made her hazel eyes sparkle. Martin wore a linen shirt and pleated slacks of tobacco brown that enhanced his tanned skin. Altogether, they were a stupendous looking couple.

The small, scruffy man across the room seemed to think so; his eyes never left the gorgeous pair. They were so wrapped up in each other that they never noticed him. The man continued his observation and nodded to another man who was seated closer to the couple. At this discreet signal, the second man took out what appeared to be a cell phone and pressed several buttons on it. The ever-alert maitre d' calmly asked the gentleman to refrain from using it in the dining room and with a grudging smile the man acquiesced and put the instrument away. The three pictures he had just taken should be sufficient . . . for now.

The evening had begun fairly early and was ending early due to the thunderstorm that was threatening to start any minute. In fact, Martin and Ceylon got back to the house just as the first drops of the rain that had grayed the skies all day became reality. The house was built with storms in mind; the eaves around the house were especially deep so that the windows could be left open without fear of water damage. But they took no chances and closed a few just in case. After talking for a while, they bade each other good night and went in the direction of their respective bedrooms.

Ceylon really did think she would be able to sleep that night. A good meal with a wonderful companion on top of a long day and the smell and sound of rain should have sent her to sleep in minutes. She took a soothing bubble bath that she did not need in hopes of increasing her chances for a good night's sleep. She slipped into her favorite ivory silk nightgown and relaxed into bed, sure that slumber would come to meet her. An hour later, she was back in the great room, moodily looking over movies, trying to find one to distract her from the long night ahead.

She plumped down on the sofa and tucked her feet up, pulling a soft, handmade afghan across her upper body. She envied Martin, who was down the hall sleeping like a baby. At least Satchel was there to keep her company. He was curled up by the sofa apparently waiting for the movie to begin. Ceylon obliged him by pressing the play button on the remote. Tonight's selection was *The Little Foxes,* an old black and white version of Lillian Hellman's play. As usual, Ceylon did more daydreaming than watching. She was reliving every moment of the day with Martin. And he would be leaving St. Simon's the next day. She sighed deeply and looked out the window just as a brilliant flash of lightning lit the night.

"Can't sleep?" Martin's deep voice cut across her reverie.

She jumped, then looked at Martin in the doorway, looking better than any man had a right to in a heavy brown silk robe. He repeated his question as though she hadn't heard him. Crossing the room to the sofa where she was curled up, he asked why she was up so late. "Scared of the storm? It will probably blow over soon," he said comfortingly.

She assured him that she was not afraid of a little bad weather. "I love rain. I love great big noisy thunderstorms, soft spring rain, icy cold rain, any kind of rain. I should probably move to Seattle," she said offhandedly. Trying not to stare at his inviting length outlined by his bathrobe, she asked him why he was up. His answer was unnerving and exhilarating all at once.

"I couldn't sleep. I was worried you might be afraid of the storm," he said lazily.

"Well, I'm not, not a bit," she said.

"I can see that."

"So you can go back to bed."

"No, I can't," he drawled, coming to stand in front of her. He held out his hand and like an automaton, she placed her smaller one into it.

"Come with me, Ceylon," he said in a low, tender voice.

She stood up slowly and looked at him with her soft hazel eyes. And she went.

Chapter Seven

Without a bit of trepidation, Ceylon went with Martin into her bedroom. She looked around the feminine peach and ivory décor with wonder, as though it was the first time she had seen the room. And in truth, it did look a bit different. There were candles lit on the dresser and bedside table, and the rumpled bedclothes had been put to rights and were turned back invitingly. She finally turned to Martin with a look that was part surprise and part bewilderment.

He led her over to the bed and instructed her to get in. "You *are* going to sleep tonight," he said quietly. He removed her ivory silk robe and watched her as she slid under the covers. He carefully folded the delicate garment and laid it across the peach boudoir chair by the vanity table. And then his intentions became plain as he stretched out next to her on top of the covers.

"Go to sleep, Ceylon," he said in that same quiet, sexy voice. "I'm just going to lie here with you until you nod off. We both know that you can sleep if you're relaxed, and sometimes it helps to have someone lying down with you," he said easily.

And sometimes it drives you right out of your mind, too!

Ceylon rose up on her elbows and was about to protest when Martin snaked a long, muscular arm around her waist and pulled her next to him.

"Don't talk. Don't think. Just sleep," he murmured encouragingly.

Ceylon's mouth closed tightly and she lay there as brittle and stiff as a sheet of ice. She looked around at the dimly lit room, inhaled the fragrance of the scented candles, and felt the warmth of Martin's big body beside her. And before she could formulate another coherent thought, her eyes closed and she melted against his heat, beginning the first real sleep she'd had in months.

The next morning found Martin pounding down the hard packed beach like the hounds of hell were on his heels. It was only Satchel, enjoying the brisk run with his master, but it could have been Cerberus himself for all the turmoil that was roused in Martin at the moment. When he woke up after a surprisingly blissful slumber, his first thought was to get as far away from the house as humanly possible. What had seemed like an innocent gesture had backfired mightily.

Martin, remembering how Ceylon slept easily and readily in Atlanta after Renee's shock, thought that he could help her get some rest. In Atlanta, after Clay and Bennie had arrived home and Renee was resting, Martin had taken Ceylon back to her hotel. He insisted on seeing her to her room, and furthermore insisted that she get ready for bed so that he could make sure she was all right. She acquiesced, emerging from the bathroom in a completely concealing robe and they sat down on the sofa in her suite. In what seemed to be minutes, she was sound asleep on his shoulder and he had carried her to the bed and tucked her in.

Obviously, a little warmth and reassurance would make her nod off, so he contrived his plan of lying down with her for a few minutes. She would go to sleep and then he could go back to his room, he figured. Seldom had he been so completely wrong about anything in his life. She went to sleep, all right, but her fragrant warmth had made *him* sleep better than he could ever remember. He slept so well that his original plan of going back to his own room fell by the way-side. And to make matters infinitely more complicated, he awoke to find the two of them tangled in each other's arms as if this was where they belonged.

He had not only gotten under the covers with her, but his robe had come undone and the slippery silk of Ceylon's gown had shifted during the night so that much of her still bountiful breasts were exposed. And she was nestled next to him in such a way that her luscious lips were positioned against the most sensitive part of his bare chest and her hand was curved around his hip. Needless to say, the combination of warm, pliant Ceylon pressed next to his nearly nude body in a posture of complete abandon was more than enough to rouse all of his male instincts to the fore. His body was proud to remind him that he was a man in bed with a most desirable woman.

Which is why he slipped out of bed as quietly as possible, grabbed the first pair of shorts he could find, and tore out of the house like a man possessed, carrying his running shoes. The fact that he wanted nothing more than to stay right where he was and draw the sensual scenario to a logical con-clusion was what made him run so hard. He didn't want Ceylon to think he was putting some cheap moves on her, of course, and he also didn't want her to think that he was so hard up that copping a feel in the night was his only re-course. *I just wanted her to get some sleep, dammit.* But he had to admit the truth to himself and that was the fact that Ceylon beguiled him and tempted him like no other woman ever had. *That is one dangerous, beautiful woman back there. And that is why I am finishing that stupid shower en-closure and getting the hell out of Dodge today.*

Ceylon was vulnerable, hurting over her brother's deception, exhausted. She deserved more out of life than a momentary liaison with a reclusive, battle-scarred loner. What could Martin possibly offer her? He slowed his run down to a steady jog and ruefully passed his hand over the scar on his face. Slowing down even more, to almost a walk, he looked down at his chest. It, too, bore the remains of his accident; it was scarred in the same manner as his arm. There were also lighter patches on his thigh from where the skin grafts had been taken. Nothing to be proud of and nothing to expose to a beauty like Ceylon. And yet, that was exactly where Ceylon was this morning, resting against those very scars, sleeping like an angel.

Martin finally came to a dead halt and stared out at the early morning over the quiet shore. Only the sounds of the gulls broke the silence as he replayed the events of the night and morning. Whistling once for the wandering Satchel, he turned back towards the house.

Ceylon's reaction to a night of uninterrupted, peaceful slumber was quite different from Martin's. When her eyes finally opened, she felt as fresh and dainty as a budding rose. She savored the heaviness of her eyelids and the total lassitude that enveloped her body. She hadn't felt this absolutely wonderful in years. *So that's what a good night's sleep will do for you, hmmm?* She rose with great reluctance from the bed and floated into the bathroom. When she saw her reflection in the mirror, her reaction was a huge smile. Even with her sleep-tousled hair and drowsy eyes, she looked fabulous!

Her skin had the moist softness of a baby's, her eyes were rested, sexy and happy and her complexion was nothing short of amazing. *All it took was a night in the arms of . . .* Ceylon's eyes got huge as she realized what she was thinking—she had spent the night with Martin Deveraux in every sense of the word. *Well,* almost *every sense,* she amended as she touched her breasts tentatively. Sliding her hands down to her abdomen she narrowed her eyes, assessing the situation. Nope, they did nothing but sleep last night. It had been a couple of years since her last intimate encounter, but she vaguely remembered what a night of love felt like.

While she brushed her teeth and showered, she thought about the night with Martin. *He's obviously still a gentleman—darn it*. Their shared slumber had been innocent and sweet and caring, she acknowledged. Although she further acknowledged that she wouldn't have minded something of a more provocative nature happening between them. From the moment she had laid eyes on him at Clay and Bennie's wedding reception she had been smitten mightily. She had tried, over the years to relegate him to the permanent file marked "Hands Off" but she just couldn't keep him there. She'd always had a passion for Martin that she simply couldn't extinguish.

Everything about Martin appealed to her; his appearance, his demeanor, his deep, sexy voice, his kindness, and his gentleness. There was nothing about him that Ceylon did not adore. She had always suspected that he was a sweet, loving man despite his gruff, antisocial exterior. The past few days reinforced that suspicion. She still got tears in her eyes when she recalled the conversation in which he described his accident and how his bitch of an ex-wife left him cold.

No one deserved to be treated like that, least of all someone like Martin. She always assumed that he was indifferent to her because of his distance and reticence. But now she had reason to believe differently. She had positive proof that indifference was not on the menu anymore. Smiling at her reflection, she traced the spot on her forehead where Martin had kissed her before flying out of bed that morning. Mr. Martin Mercier Deveraux was many things, but indifferent was not one of them, not anymore.

Ceylon sighed happily and cupped her breasts appraisingly before turning on the shower. For the first time in ages, she sang in the streams of warm water, an old-school number called "Ready or Not."

Oh, honey, yes! The Delfonics knew what they were talking about when it came to old-fashioned lovin'. If Martin could have read her thoughts at that moment, he would have either fled immediately or gotten down on his knees to praise the Lord.

By the time Martin skulked back to the house, Ceylon had prepared a big pan of homemade cinnamon rolls from her grandmother's recipe. She was still in a wonderful mood and was singing along with a Marvin Gaye greatest hits CD. That's how Martin found her, setting the table, singing the hell out of "Your Precious Love" and looking like the very essence of spring, even in a pink T-shirt and baggy jeans. Moreover, there was an incredible fragrance in the kitchen; it smelled like cinnamon, vanilla and pure heaven.

Martin castigated himself up and down the beach, so much so that he was not sure how he was supposed to behave. What exactly was the protocol for coming face-to-face with a woman you'd inadvertently groped all night? Ceylon, luckily, had no such second thoughts. She looked him right in the face and then let her mischievous eyes enjoy his shirtless, muscular frame from head to toe.

"Good morning, Martin. And thank you. I haven't slept like that since I was a child," she said sweetly. And before he could react, she gave him a big hug and kiss, right on his hated left cheek. Without stepping away from him, she asked if he had enjoyed his run. He mumbled an affirmative and she smiled hugely in return.

"I guess you did. Your physical exertion seems to have outstripped your routine of personal hygiene," she said calmly.

Martin looked down at her with a mixture of amusement

and pique. "Did you just say what I think you said?" he asked gruffly.

"Yes, baby, I did. You stink. You smell like a barrel of granddaddies, is what my granny would have said. You need a shower, quick," she said frankly, backing away from him.

Martin took a step towards her, which made her back up more. "I heard that women like a musty man. It's supposed to be quite sexy in some cultures," he growled menacingly.

Ceylon backed around the table, giggling. "Well, we don't live in that culture, now do we? We live in the highly deodorized, scented, synthetic culture! And I love me a good smellin' man. You're sexy enough when you're bathed, you don't need animal musk to help," she ended in a shriek as Martin caught her up in his arms.

To her delight he proceeded to rub his unshaven face all over hers and use her freshly showered and scented body as a towel. Ceylon squirmed and shouted with laughter, which made him all the more determined.

"There!" he said with satisfaction. "Now I'm not the only person who needs a shower around here," he added as he ambled off to get clean.

And he was not kidding, Ceylon found. She sniffed her T-shirt and her arms, both of which smelled just like Martin, distinctly musky and wild, like someone who had just engaged in heavy physical exertion. She sighed and gave a delicate shudder as she remembered how enticing his big, sweaty body had felt on hers. As she went into her bedroom to quickly shower and change she smiled. *I'm NEVER washing that shirt again.*

After they were both showered and attired in clean casual clothes, the morning began again. Martin made an absolute pig of himself over the cinnamon rolls, to Ceylon's amazement.

"Martin, it's just biscuit dough rolled up with melted butter, sugar, cinnamon, and dried cherries. Anything a raisin can do, a dried cherry can do better, is my motto. My granny taught me how to make them when I was a mere child," she said, watching him devour his third.

"They taste like you," he mumbled around a dangerously big mouthful. "Rich, buttery and unexpected. Perfect," he added, licking a bit of the mellow, sweet vanilla frosting off his upper lip.

"Flattery will get you anywhere with me," Ceylon said flirtatiously. "Do you need a hand with that enclosure?"

Martin assured her that he did not. "It will take about four hours of concentrated effort if I am not distracted by any pretty brown women with big cat eyes. Of course, I'm bound to be starving by the time I get through, so . . ."

He flashed her a look that was just innocent enough to be convincing and she sighed deeply. "All right, I can take a hint. I can probably find you something for lunch. I'm sure there's some peanut butter or sardines around here."

Martin stuck out a long leg and snaked it around her chair, drawing her closer to him. Giving her a series of wet kisses on the cheek, he murmured, "Aw, baby, you can do better than that. You're gonna give me dead fish from a can after I slave outdoors in the sun?"

Ceylon's throaty laugh rang out as Martin's moustache tickled her neck. "Just don't worry about lunch. You'd better get to work because it looks like it's coming up a cloud."

Martin drew back and looked at her. "Where did you get that Southernism from? What does a city girl like you know about such things?"

"My grandparents were from Alabama, honey. I have many more of those very phrases at the very tip of my tongue."

As it was indeed dark and overcast, Martin did as Ceylon suggested and got to work on the last part of the shower project. Ceylon tidied the kitchen and the bedroom in no time flat, but felt no urge to continue her marathon cleansing of the house. Instead, she decided to call Bennie, who was delighted to hear from her.

"Well, Ceylon, I have to say you sound like your old self again. I think that St. Simon's is doing the trick for you," she said happily.

And she meant every word of it. Bennie and Ceylon had shared brief daily conversations since the start of her vacation, but Ceylon was really sounding like she was back in fighting form. Her response to Bennie bore out that theory totally.

"Oh, Bennie, I haven't felt this good in years! I feel rested, I feel strong, and I definitely feel like working again. And it's not just the house or the island, as you well know. Thank you for not being nosy, but you know very well that your brother-in-law has more than a little to do with my new attitude. Bennie, he's . . . it's . . . we've . . . ummm, ummm, ummm! Do you hear me? *Ummm!*" Ceylon sighed happily.

Bennie knew the sounds of impending passion when she heard them. She discreetly covered the mouthpiece of the phone and whispered "YES!" before answering Ceylon. "So, you two are getting along well?"

"Better than well," Ceylon was happy to inform her, and proceeded to share details about their time together. "But he's going to have that stupid shower finished today and he's going back to Atlanta," she said sadly. "Which is going to break my poor heart right in two. Do you think he'll keep in touch with me this time, or is it going to be one of our typical encounters where I don't see him again until the next time I happen to be freeloading at your house?" she fretted.

Bennie scolded her immediately. "If you ever use that word to me again I'll snatch you baldheaded! You're like a sister to me and my whole family adores you! We love it when you come to visit, especially the boys! Remind me that I owe you a pop upside the head when I see you again," she threatened. "Furthermore, I don't think Martin is going to just waltz back to Atlanta without a definite plan for seeing you again. You always thought he wasn't interested in you, but I have eyes, Ceylon, and I used to watch him looking at you whenever you were around. Martin's always been interested in you, but he would've never done anything about it."

Ceylon sat up straight on the sofa where she was slumped. This was news to her! "What do you mean he wouldn't have done anything about it? What do you mean he used to look at me? What do you mean, *period?*" she sputtered.

Bennie laughed softly at her dear friend. Ceylon had it bad for Martin, but Bennie had known that for some time. "Honey, in all the time I have been married to Clay, I have never seen Martin with a woman. After what that wench of an ex-wife did to him, he just went into a deep freeze and stayed there. He took off to Key West and lived down there for years, away from his family and friends. And from what I can gather, he and Malcolm were best friends as well as being identical twins. They hardly spend any time together now, and I think it's because of the accident and the fact that he was so badly scarred," she said.

Ceylon felt tears coming to her eyes over Bennie's pronouncement. "Are you telling me that he is so self-conscious about his face and his body that he wouldn't have tried to approach *me*, the original 'two tons o' fun' gal? I am *not* all that. Especially not now when I don't have eye water to cry with! I'm broke as a he-haint and I still got dumps like a truck so what's the big deal?" Ceylon regretted her flippancy immediately as Bennie tore into her once again.

"Ceylon, do me a favor and slap yourself right across the mouth 'cause I can't get to you this minute. If I was there, *ooh!* I would give you such a smack! I don't know what to do with either one of you! You and Martin can be two of the most trying people in the world, I swear. If I didn't love you two so much I'd turn you both in to the loony bin and collect a reward!"

She and Ceylon both burst out laughing then as they recalled the rumor that was popular in Michigan many years ago; that if you turned someone into the state institution at Traverse City, you would not only get a reward, but a bushel of Traverse City's famous cherries, too.

"Okay, okay, I'll behave myself. But if I slip, and you just *have* to ship me off, freeze some of those cherries for me." Ceylon chuckled as they said good-bye.

All too soon, the happy, restful day was drawing to a close. Martin had indeed finished his work and the outdoor shower was a thing of beauty. Ceylon heaped lavish praise on his handiwork while she cursed its completion under her breath. The thought of Martin leaving was just too depressing. She refused to let any of her very private feelings about his departure show, however, and remained outwardly cheerful as she served him the lunch she had promised. And it was not the peanut butter and sardines she had threatened him with earlier.

Martin was more than pleased with the corn chowder she made; it was velvety and rich with potato, bits of red pepper, celery, and full of crab and crayfish besides. With a nice crisp green salad and some freshly baked chive bread, it was a treat for the eye as well as the palate. Martin praised her cooking to the skies, as usual.

"Damn, Ceylon. I know my mother can cook. And Selena and Bennie are also great cooks. Even my brothers throw down in the kitchen. But you've got them all beat. I think you're some kind of witch, I really do," he said, only half joking.

Ceylon laughed and disagreed. "It's a mighty poor witch that would let her wayward sibling walk off with everything she owned. If I was any kind of self-respecting witch, I'd be tracking him down and getting my life back together. Or putting a spell on him or something."

A bit surprised at having revealed so much, she stood up

abruptly and began clearing the table. Martin looked at her closely as she busied herself. Her very posture touched him; it was plain that her situation was far from settled and she was still at odds with herself. He stood up and walked over to where she was rinsing dishes in the sink in preparation for the dishwasher. He wrapped his arms around her and held her for a long moment before speaking.

"Ceylon, I've been meaning to talk to you about that . . ."

Ceylon cut off his words as she turned around in his arms. "Oh, Martin, I don't want to talk about my troubles now! You've got to get ready to leave and I'd rather your last hours here be pleasant ones," she said softly. Her eyes were full of the anguish she was trying to keep at bay and it touched Martin's very soul.

"Leave? Have you looked out the window? It's getting ready to storm again. I can wait until tomorrow to get back to Atlanta. In the meantime, why don't you let me clean up and you can take it easy for a change."

Ceylon was so happy to hear that he wasn't going that she beamed like a five-year-old at a birthday party. She readily agreed to Martin's proposal and made herself scarce. *He's staying, he's staying!* she chanted happily to herself. It was just another night, but she really didn't care. She enjoyed his company so much that any extra hour she got was golden.

They spent the rest of the day talking and listening to music. Ceylon fixed a light dinner of grilled chicken and rata-touille with saffron rice. The pleasantness eased into the early evening with the sound of steady rain accompanying their conversation. They sat on the sofa after dinner watching movies and occasionally touching one another like teenagers on a first date. Nether one of them wanted to bring up the idea of going to bed, but it hung in the air like a cloud of dense fog.

Finally, Ceylon couldn't take it anymore. "Martin, I think I'm going to take a bubble bath and go to bed," she said succinctly. *There, let him do what he wants*. Suiting action to words, she quickly kissed Martin and made record time getting to her bedroom. She heaved a deep sigh of regret as she prepared a nice hot bubbly tub. *Well, I can't force myself on the man. We're both adults; we both know what the deal is,* she thought grumpily as she sank into the scented bubbles. Or maybe she didn't really know. She stuck one long, brown leg out of the fragrant warmth of the tub and let the foam run down as she admitted that she would give a lot to know just what was on Martin's mind at that very moment.

Martin's total being at that instant was focused on the woman down the hall. Picturing Ceylon naked in a tub full of bubbles was sheer, unadulterated torture. The thought of what her satiny skin would look like clad in moisture and aromatic foam had the same relaxing effect as free fall parachuting. His respiration increased, his skin went hot and cold in turns, and his libido staked a feverish claim on his consciousness that drove him straight into a cold shower.

It didn't do a single thing to cool off his molten core. Cold showers never worked to chase away true ardor. Mild horniness, maybe. But when you were being driven mad by the object of your heart's true desire, cold showers served as an aperitif; they only made your appetite keener. Martin pulled on an old pair of drawstring pants and put his eye patch back on over his wet hair before lying down on his bed to stare at the ceiling.

Ceylon. He was more convinced than ever that there was a tiny bit of sorcery lurking about her somewhere. This morning, for example, should have been uncomfortable, awkward. There should have been polite half silences and strained conversation. Instead, Ceylon enveloped him in her arms and in her fragrant aura and they spent a sexy, happy morning together full of laughter, which led right into a warm, comfortable evening. It should have ended with them sharing something else, he thought moodily. *Okay, get your mind off of that and concentrate on something else. Do not let yourself go crazy over this.*

Martin had rid himself of happy endings, fairy tales, and all the other trappings of what is fondly known as modern romance eight years before. He knew firsthand how illusory those things were and how painful it was when the illusions shattered. And they would shatter, of that he had no doubt.

Martin was suddenly struck with how maudlin he was being. He sat up abruptly and laughed at his own angst, the sudden movement making his still damp hair swing forward. Satchel, who was flopped near the bed, looked at him quizzically.

"Satchel, this is proof positive that the woman is a siren. I'm here for a few days and I turn into a whining adolescent," he said in a mock stern voice. "Let this be a lesson to you, boy. Women are trouble. They'll make you lose your mind if you're not careful. Got me talking to myself like a horny teenager . . . I'm a grown man, dammit!" *A lonely, tired man with a huge desire for a woman I have no business wanting.*

Satchel raised his head with a mild expression as if to concur with Martin's assessment. Martin laughed softly and assured his pet that he hadn't quite gone off the deep end yet.

"But first thing in the morning, we are heading out of here. We're getting out of harm's way before permanent damage is done. Okay, boy?"

Whether or not Satchel would agree with his master would never be known. At that very moment, the sickening buzz heralding a power failure was heard from outside and the house was thrown into dark, eerie silence. Martin was immediately on his feet and on his way to Ceylon.

Chapter Eight

Ceylon's first reaction at being in the dark was the same as always—she panicked. She knew that she wasn't in any danger, but the disorientation of being in complete blackness overtook her with its usual swiftness. She began vainly trying to figure out where she was and how to get some light going. In the middle of the bedroom, there was a candle on the dresser if she could just find it. She thrust her arms out and waved them in the useless way that people do when they are desperately trying to find something to hold onto. In seconds, she found something. Martin's arms were around her and holding her tight.

"Oh, Martin," she breathed softly.

"Are you okay, baby? I know you don't like the dark. This happens every so often when there's a bad storm. Come on over to the bed and I'll light a candle," he added as he led her over to the big four poster bed.

In no time she was sitting on the edge of the big bed with Martin beside her. He found the matches on the nightstand with no effort at all and lit the candle, giving a welcome amber glow to the room. Martin looked down at her face, flushed with relief.

"You must think I'm the biggest sissy in the world," she said selfconsciously.

Martin could not trust himself to speak at that moment. 'Sissy' was hardly the word he would have used to describe the soft armful of woman cuddled next to him. He cleared his throat and suggested gruffly that she get some sleep.

"The lights will be back on soon, but in the meantime, you may as well get comfortable and go to sleep."

He tried not to stare at her beautiful skin glowing in the candlelight, tried not to acknowledge the short silk nightshirt she was wearing, and tried mightily not to think about the fact that there was nothing under it except her warm fragrant self. He adjusted the covers around her neck like he would a small child. After making sure she was comfortable, he instructed Satchel to go to the great room and the obedient dog left immediately.

Ceylon watched Martin through half-closed eyes, hoping that he was not planning to leave her. Her fondest wish was granted when he at last lay down beside her. She flashed him a sexy, yet innocent smile and turned to face him.

"Good night, Martin," she sighed peacefully. She kissed him softly and snuggled into his shoulder for slumber.

Martin ground his teeth and willed his body to behave in a decorous manner. It was going to be a long, long night.

"Good night, Ceylon."

The scented darkness of the room surrounded him. Cool rain-scented breezes both refreshed and caressed his body; at the same time an unmistakable heat slowly coursed through him. Soft hands touched him all over, stroking his chest, his hard muscled abdomen, sliding down his hard thighs, bringing him closer and closer to a dangerous point of erotic longing. His own hands joined the sensual massage that was taking place; he returned the stroking motions caress for caress. Her skin was like satin, her breasts were full and firm and delicious to the touch. He felt as though he were drowning in her passion—mere touching wasn't enough, not nearly enough . . .

Martin came awake slowly. The dream was too profound, too arousing to let go. It was then that he realized it was no dream. He and Ceylon were wrapped up in each other and very little else. Their mutual desire had taken over when their conscious minds were at rest and they had turned to each other in sleep. Ceylon's nightshirt had come undone and her breasts pressed against his chest, her hands pulling him closer and letting him know in no uncertain terms that she wanted him.

Her long lashes lifted and her perfect lips curved in a smile of complete bliss. She rose gracefully to a sitting position. Slowly, as though she was still dreaming, she removed the satin nightshirt, allowing it to float to the floor in the soft amber light of the candle. Martin pulled her back into his impatient arms and their mouths came together in the silent language of lovers.

Martin loved her mouth with his own until the sweet, moist heat was not enough. He trailed his lips down her neck, down her supple chest until he found the sensitive, alert nipples waiting for him. Taking one into his mouth, he applied an even more passionate kiss that made Ceylon moan as she trembled from the force of her response.

His long, silky hair was draped over her exposed breast and it was all she could do to remain conscious. Just the sensation of his mouth on her hot skin was sending her into a place that she had never, ever been before, a place where there was nothing but Martin. The feel of his big, hot body sliding over hers as he began to plumb the depths of her was making her dizzy with joy and entirely too close to a total release.

She breathed a sigh of relief and frustration as he finally turned his attention away from her ultra-sensitized breasts. He stopped only long enough to help her remove his loose fitting cotton pants, the only barrier between their eager bodies. When he was completely naked he stopped caressing Ceylon long enough to retrieve protection from the beside table that he put there after their first night in the same bed; when he was ready, they slid into each other with the ferocity of passion too long held at bay.

Martin wasn't ready for the shock of sensation that overtook him as he experienced the moist welcome of Ceylon's heated body. The pleasure became so piercingly keen that it was almost like pain; the motion of their bodies as they established a pulsing rhythm took his breath again and again as he lost himself in the power of the most profound loving he ever had. Nothing in their kisses, nothing in his memory could have readied him for the reality of Ceylon's arms wrapped around him, her softness, and her surrender.

He couldn't stand the pressure that was building, the release that was beckoning, the power of the connection that was forcing him to relinquish all his pain, all his frustration and longing. With every thrust he drew closer to a completion that threatened to drown him in *Ceylon*, that would unite him with *Ceylon*, that would turn him into *Ceylon*, that was *Ceylon*, that was beautiful, that was *Ceylon*, that was everything, that was eternity, that was Ceylon, *Ceylon*, *Ceylon*, *Ceylon*, *Ceylon* . . . in one final thrust he both lost and found himself completely in Ceylon . . . they were one.

When Ceylon awoke, many hours later, there was no question about what had transpired in the night. She did not have to rack her brain or make a surreptitious survey of her erogenous zones to determine whether anything of a passionate nature had taken place between her and Martin. Every part of her body was still tingling, vibrating with the passion that Martin had awakened in her all night long. She wanted to blush or feel just a bit of shame as she thought about the things they had shared, but she was far too honest.

She couldn't possibly pretend that she had not reveled in every single erotic moment of the long, passion-filled night. She was so blissful at the recollection that she had no desire whatsoever to open her eyes.

She'd have been perfectly content to lay there naked and throbbing all day, but for the fact that Martin was not beside her and there was an elusive fresh fragrance tickling her sensitive nose. She forced her lids open and sighed with delight. Her bare body was covered with a peach striped sheet and an array of wildflowers still bearing the morning dew. There were flowers all over her body, all over the pillows, and some in her hair. Ceylon sat up with a huge smile on her face, adoring the romantic gesture by her unseen lover.

Gently, so as not to disturb his handiwork, Ceylon slid out of bed and stretched like a happy cat in the bright sunlight. She should have been terribly sore but she felt like she had experienced a lovely long Pilates workout, thanks to Martin's skillful loving.

The words of the classic Cole Porter tune, "How Long Has This Been Going On," expressed just how Ceylon was feeling on the bright and beautiful morning. She sang eloquently as she showered with some of her precious Tresor shower gel that she saved for very special occasions. Her money was tight, but this was a celebration as far as she was concerned. She used lavish amounts of the lotion and sprayed herself liberally with the matching eau de parfum before putting on a favorite Josie Natori robe in silk charmeuse with a vibrant pattern of flowers. And not a stitch underneath; if she had her way she wouldn't have it on too long anyway. After finger-combing her brown curls and putting on some luscious lip gloss, she went in search of Martin, figuring he was out running on the beach.

To her complete surprise, he was in the kitchen, arranging a tray with the most appetizing looking food she had seen outside the pages of a magazine. He was shirtless and wearing the kind of jeans that made even sane women lose their grip—old, washed until they were almost white, chamois soft to the touch, and fitting his body like denim paint. She could barely tear her eyes away from him to comment on his activities.

"Sweetheart, what are you doing? I thought you couldn't cook," she said in amazement.

"I said I could burn toast, which I suppose I could if I wasn't careful. I never actually said I couldn't cook," he hedged. "This was supposed to be a surprise. I was going to bring it to you in bed. And my preferred greeting is this," he added as he cupped her face in his big hands and kissed her gently but thoroughly, so thoroughly that she felt dizzy when he stopped.

"Good morning, baby," he said in the deep voice that never failed to thrill Ceylon.

"Good morning, darling. And you *are* my darling for fixing me this lovely breakfast. What is it?" she asked. "And where is Satchel?" she added after looking around the room for the ever-present Akita.

"Satchel is running on the beach, he'll be back in a little while. And why don't you sit down and I'll show you what you're getting for breakfast."

Martin, once he was persuaded that eating on the deck was just as romantic as eating in bed, was happy to show off his considerable kitchen skills to Ceylon. He made her an amazing repast of authentic *pain perdu*, the true French version of French toast, but he stuffed the thick slices with a luscious mixture of cream cheese flavored with peach brandy and finely chopped pecans. The fragrant slices were covered with fresh peaches in a brandy-laced syrup. To make matters worse, he had broiled country ham and scrambled eggs with cream and chives.

Ceylon's eyes got huge as she looked at the beautifully prepared and presented meal. It smelled heavenly, right down to the creamy cappuccino with a hint of cinnamon.

"Martin, honey, I can't possibly eat all of this!" she protested.

"Well, just eat what you want, baby. You could stand to gain a few pounds, you know. As much as I love every sweet inch of you, I have to confess I liked it when there was a little bit more Ceylon to hold onto."

Ceylon took a bite of the *pain perdu* and moaned with happiness. "Oh my Lord. Martin, you should have given me some cold cereal or something. You may never get rid of me now," she said cheerfully.

Martin watched her daintily sip coffee before he answered her.

"Ceylon, what in the hell makes you think I want to get rid of you? I want you to come back to Atlanta with me," he said quietly.

Ceylon stopped completely, her forkful of eggs forgotten as she stared at Martin.

"I'm sorry, I don't think I heard you correctly," she murmured.

Martin smiled a secretive, sexy smile at her as he enjoyed her look of innocent confusion. He guided the fork to her mouth and waited while she opened her mouth like a hungry child. As she swallowed the perfectly prepared eggs, he spoke.

"I want you to come home to Atlanta with me. I want to get to know you better, Ceylon, and I want you to know me. I want to spend time with you. I want to be with you. I want to share more than this breakfast with you. You're here to rest and relax and you can do that with me in Atlanta, can't you?" he asked, trying not to let her see how important this was to him.

He wasn't very successful at hiding the desire in his heart, though. Every time he looked at her, her morning-flushed face, her incredible smile, and the sheer beauty of her, his longing for her was plain. He knew, long before their night of passionate lovemaking had ended, long before dawn, that he could no more leave her on St. Simon's than he could leave one of his arms or legs. He needed to be with her as much as he needed air to breathe. He was making a concerted effort to phrase his suggestion casually, but he knew he was failing miserably. Ceylon knew that he wanted her; what he didn't know was how she would respond.

It took her almost a minute to compose herself. It was quite evident that Martin was completely serious and equally evident that her answer was of the utmost importance to him in more ways than the obvious. Her fabulous dimples flashed as she smiled her sweetest smile at the man who had come to mean so much to her in the past few days.

Before Ceylon could reply, a sound like the roar of a jungle beast cut through the morning's peace. Satchel came pounding towards the deck barking and snarling and making it quite plain that he meant business. Martin didn't have time to do anything but leap up from the table when Satchel's target took off at a run; it was the two men who had been following Martin and Ceylon around the island. One man stumbled and fell; the other managed to get away. In the confusion caused by the savagely barking Satchel and the murderously angry Martin, his presence wasn't noticed.

Ceylon clutched the front of her robe with one hand and covered her mouth with the other hand. At once she realized how ridiculous that must look and crossed both arms across her chest. Martin held Satchel by his collar to keep him from tearing the man's throat out and he had the slightly built man by the scruff of his neck.

"Ceylon, call 911," he said in a deceptively calm voice.

She immediately went into the house to do just that, but not before muttering a truly unladylike word under her breath. *Now what?*

Chapter Nine

The brilliantly warm Atlanta sun streamed through the windows of the last place Ceylon had expected to find herself—the well-appointed kitchen in the home of Lillian Mercier Deveraux. The charm of the soothing peaches and cream color scheme of the spacious room was lost on Ceylon at the moment. She stared out into the gardens from the windows of the breakfast room trying to figure out how things could have gone so awry so quickly. She had been there almost a week, ever since the paparazzi ambush at the St. Simon's house. Martin had taken her to Atlanta and dropped her off at his mother's house in less time than it took to tell about it. Actually, since her marriage a year before, it was the house of Ceylon's mentor, Bump Williams, too.

Bump and Lillian renewed their friendship when Bennie, Bump's goddaughter, started dating Clay. They had been each other's first love years before in their small hometown in Louisiana, and it took very little time for those feelings to rekindle. In very little time a passionate courtship ensued which culminated in a very romantic wedding. Bump sold his Los Angeles home and moved to Atlanta, where he bought Lillian a fabulous sprawling home in which to begin their new life. But as warm and welcoming as her hosts were, Ceylon was not feeling too happy with developments. Even though she didn't say this to Lillian, who was at the moment trying to get Ceylon to eat, her hostess sensed it.

"Honey, I know things are unsettled right now, but starving yourself isn't going to make things better. Would you like some tea?" she asked.

Ceylon smiled at Lillian, who spoke in a deceptively soft tone of voice. The older woman was slender, brown-skinned, and bore a rather startling resemblance to Nancy Wilson, right down to the stunning streak of white in the front of her shiny black hair. Lillian was the gentlest person in the world until some ill befell someone she cared about; once that happened, a mother lion had nothing on her for protectiveness. If she decided Ceylon needed rest and good food, that was what she was going to get, whether she wanted it or not.

"No thank you, Lillian, but could I have some hot water?" Ceylon answered. Lillian didn't show any reaction. She just poured Ceylon a cup from the tea kettle that was singing on the range and joined her at the table, looking pointedly at the delicious mixed fruit and fragrant blueberry muffins on Ceylon's plate. Ceylon immediately picked up a fork and began eating.

Lillian repeated her earlier statement. "I know that things are out of hand right now, but in a couple of weeks you'll be in New York doing that play. Then you and Bump will be recording the soundtrack for *Idlewild* and you'll be too busy to worry about tabloids or anything else. You'll see," she said comfortingly.

"Lillian, you're right, of course you're right, but there's a few other things that need to be . . . seen to," Ceylon murmured, suddenly staring at a piece of canary melon as though she'd never seen fruit before. She suddenly realized that she was talking to the mother of the man she loved, the man who'd been splattered across the cover of every tabloid in North America with the galling headline of "Beauty and the

Beast." Those horrid photos still made her cringe; not for her sake, but Martin's. Martin barely spoke to her as he bum-rushed her off the island to his parent's home and left her without a word. He had disappeared off the face of the earth, it seemed; she'd not heard a word from him in the past few days. Thanks to that mess on St. Simon's he probably never wanted to see her again, and who could blame him? She was still surprised that Lillian had been so welcoming, consider-ing the circumstances that had forced her into the woman's home. She said this to Lillian, unable to keep the embarrass-ment out of her voice.

Lillian reached across the table and grasped Ceylon's hand. "Look, honey, I told you when you got here that you don't owe anyone any explanations or apologies. And you never have to apologize to me for loving my son! You're the best thing that's happened to Martin in years, Ceylon."

At Ceylon's look of surprise, Lillian laughed out loud. "Girl, I've known for a long time how you feel about Martin. I knew the first time I saw the two of you in the same room; it's all over your face every time you look at him. And quiet as it's kept, I have a pretty good idea of how he feels about you, although he might not admit it. Deveraux men are known for their mule-headedness," she said as she paused to pour more tea for herself and more hot water for Ceylon.

"I'm sure that Martin isn't too happy about having those pictures splattered across those disgusting little papers. He's been such a private person since . . . well, since the accident. It wasn't your fault that those weasels invaded your privacy; it wasn't like this was something you asked for, for heaven's sake!" Lillian set her cup down abruptly and made a noise of disgust.

"I don't know how those people can look themselves in the mirror, considering the havoc they wreak in people's lives. Just terrible! I know how humiliating this must feel to you, Ceylon, but please realize that the people who care about you are on your side all the way. And the people who care about you include Martin, even though he may be a little distant right now. Just don't give up on him. And don't leave him alone too long; he thinks too much as it is. In the past, when that horrible woman abandoned him, yes, he had a lot of pain to work through. But now he doesn't need to be over in that big mausoleum of a house brooding. He really doesn't. If I were you, I'd drop by for a little visit to let him know *he's* on *your* mind, too. Now that would give him something to think about," Lillian added with a sassy smile.

Ceylon sat back in her chair with a look of utter shock. Lillian laughed again.

Bump walked into the room in time to hear the last words, as well as his wife's wicked chuckle. "Okay, that just sounds evil. What are you women up to at this hour of this morning?"

Lillian's eyes brightened the way they always did when her beloved husband entered the room. Bump Williams was still as good-looking as he'd been in their youth. He was tall, about 6'4" and still lean, thanks to Lillian's constant vigilance in matters of diet. His salt and pepper hair was still thick, his dark brown skin unlined, and his face was usually full of merriment, as it was now. He repeated his question after kissing Lillian.

"What are you two up to? By the way, your daughter cheats, dear. Don't ever play golf with her, she's a poor sport," he said indignantly.

Lillian laughed out loud as Bump joined them at the table and helped himself to a blueberry muffin. "Oh please, the two of you have no business playing together! Neither one of you can stand to lose and neither one of you plays fair. Where is Angelique, anyway? Didn't she come home with you?"

"No, dear, she didn't. She said she had some errands to run and that she would definitely be here for the cookout," Bump reported dutifully.

The word "cookout" made Lillian remember a few things

that needed to be seen to and she excused herself, leaving Bump and Ceylon alone in the breakfast room. He gave her his complete attention, checking her over carefully.

"Well, darlin' girl, how are you doing? Are you ready to take on Broadway? Because if you don't feel up to it, other arrangements can be made, you know."

Ceylon's eyes got huge and she immediately affirmed that she was ready. "Oh, no, Bump, I need to get back to work! Sitting around feeling sorry for myself isn't going to get any bills paid, and it's not going to make people forget about the latest fiasco in what passes for my life these days. When something like this happens the worst thing you can do is stay home and have a pity party. The only way to make people forget about a stupid incident is to get out there and shine," she said emphatically.

Bump's pride in his protégé was visible as he reached over and squeezed her hand. "You're absolutely right, Ceylon. Let your talent speak for itself. Broadway won't know what hit it when you take over. Even though it's just for a month, it'll give you some great exposure. And when you wrap up there, you can come back home and we'll start on the soundtrack," he added. He stopped when he noticed the look on Ceylon's face. "Something's bothering you, Ceylon, what is it?"

"That word, 'home'," Ceylon admitted. "I don't have one, Bump, and I'm tired of it. You know, everything happens for a reason, and even though I'd still like to have a few moments alone with that low-life little tabloid monkey, having those pictures taken did serve a purpose. It made me mad as hell!"

She blushed and covered her mouth, as she had no intention of disrespecting Bump by swearing in front of him. Bump made a gesture that indicated he understood that she was merely expressing her anger.

"Bump, I have no idea what took over my brain after Duane stole all my money, but I want it back. I want all my money, I want all my stuff, I want my house, and I want my old life. I'm tired of killing myself to repay money that was stolen from me by my own flesh and blood. And most of all, I want that thieving, miserable, skunky brother of mine found and put *under* the jail, you hear me? I've had enough of this mess; I want it over and done with. I want my life back! My *mother*," she pronounced with disdain, "had a lot of nerve to ask me not to press charges against him. And I was a true fool to agree with her, I have *no* idea what made me think that was a plan!"

Ceylon's eyes were bright with anger and her cheeks were flushed from emotion. She'd held it all in for so long that letting it out stirred up powerful feelings she didn't know were there; resentment, anger, frustration, shame, and determination. Bump was slightly taken aback, not by what she was saying, but the way she was saying it.

"You know, my little sister has a temper just like yours. Elizabeth could be the sweetest little thing in the world until you did her wrong. It would take her a while to get really mad, but when she did, look out! You have that very same look in your eye. The one that says 'I'm crazy, don't mess with me,' the look that black men have learned to dread from black women," he said.

Ceylon started laughing. "I do not have that look," she denied.

"Oh yeah, you do, with the corner of your eye twitching and everything. It's right there, I can see it!" Bump teased her. "But it's okay. It needs to be there because it's about time you got mad enough to make him pay back what he owes you. That look is *supposed* to be there. I ain't mad at you, not a bit."

Bump stood up and pulled her up with him, giving her a tight hug. "Well, baby girl, I'm glad you finally got your right mind back. It's one thing to be sweet and considerate and it's another thing to let people run roughshod over you. I'm proud of you, Ceylon."

Then he added something that caused the fire in Ceylon's eyes to flash again. "And it should all be over soon, anyway. That detective Martin hired is supposedly making some good progress."

Ceylon pulled away from Bump and narrowed her eyes. "*Detective?* What detective?"

Bump shook his head and groaned. "See? There goes that look again."

Lillian was completely correct on one count. Martin was holed up in his huge Midtown home and he was also starting to gather the cloak of a recluse about him. As much as he wanted to act as though nothing was wrong, he still felt the aftermath of the tabloid disaster. Martin tried to pretend that everything was status quo, but he couldn't even convince Satchel of that lie. Every since he walked in on Ceylon on St. Simon's Island, his life had changed. Permanent, irrevocable changes had been wrought against his better judgment, even against his considerable will. The one thing he wanted to avoid at all costs was a romantic entanglement and he managed to get himself involved with someone whose every move was deemed public domain. Before the accident, he might have been able to tolerate it, might have enjoyed basking in the limelight with a talented, beautiful star like Ceylon, but not now.

He'd been going to work every day, trying to act as though nothing out of the ordinary had occurred when nothing could be further from the truth. He imagined that he heard conversations stop every time he turned a corner in the massive suburban headquarters of The Deveraux Group; no doubt his exploits were on the lips of every employee. Oddly enough, he was more concerned about Ceylon than himself.

He'd had enough time on his hands to convince himself that the pictures of the two of them sharing an intimate brunch were enough to make her look like an utter fool. Like she was so desperate that the best she could do for male companionship was a broken-down scarred hermit like him. His jaw tightened in fury as his angry thoughts escalated to the point of savagery. Then there was the matter of Ceylon's silence. The fact that he hadn't heard a single word from Ceylon since bringing her to Atlanta was enough to convince him that she shared this opinion.

He pounded away on the treadmill in the home gym he'd set up in an unused bedroom. The air conditioning was on at its highest to offset the heat Martin was generating through his exertion. It was as if he thought he could outrun his demons if he kept moving, so he did just that. Running until his heart rate was up, he was covered in sweat and could better control his rage. *Nobody said life is fair*, he reminded himself. If life were fair, he'd be exercising his body with Ceylon's instead of punishing the treadmill. If life were fair, Ceylon would have all her worldly possessions back, her career would continue to soar, and she'd be with a man who would cherish her as much as he could. He laughed at the irony. Ceylon needed a man who could adore her, protect her, and go out in public with her without attracting unwanted attention. *Well, hell, two out of three ain't bad.*

He didn't realize he'd spoken aloud until Satchel gave a short, disgusted bark.

Martin threw up his hands and slowed to a walk to conclude his workout. "You're absolutely right, Satchel. I've been at this 'poor-me' festival long enough. Just because Ceylon hasn't called me all week is no reason to wallow in it. I'm going to take a shower and do something about it. Is that okay with you?"

Satchel barked again, clearly signifying the canine equivalent of "It's about time."

Less than thirty minutes later, Martin pulled on his favorite faded Hawaiian print shirt, its bright colors muted by much laundering. He was also attired in the faded-out jeans that Ceylon found so sexy on St. Simon's. A sudden movement from Satchel made Martin pause in his dressing to question him.

"What's up, boy?"

Satchel left his spot in the sunny corner of Martin's bedroom and dashed down the hall, then pounded down the stairs to stand expectantly by the front door with his tail wagging happily. Martin followed Satchel at a more leisurely pace. He raised an eyebrow when the doorbell sounded a sharp note.

"You're not getting psychic on me, are you Satch? You're not going to be wanting your own cable show are you?"

Martin's lame joke died in his throat as he opened the front door to see Ceylon, cool, fragrant and gorgeous, standing directly in front of him.

Without waiting for him to speak, Ceylon pushed a large bouquet of wildflowers into his chest and sashayed past him to pet Satchel who was wriggling and barking his joy at seeing her.

"You've got a lot of explaining to do, Buster," was all she said.

Martin barely had time to acknowledge the fact that Ceylon had come to him before she started in on him. Straightening up from her canine caresses, Ceylon removed her big sunglasses and gave Martin the full effect of her big, long lashed eyes in which the fires of passion glowed deeply.

"I suppose you wonder what I'm doing here," she asked haughtily as she looked around the spacious foyer in which they stood. "After breakfast I took your mother's very good advice, as well as the keys to her car, and here I am. Lillian gives very good directions. At any rate, there are a few things you need to know about me," she said carefully, using an elegant finger to tick off her points.

"First of all, Mr. Man, I do not appreciate you dropping me off at your mama's house without so much as a kiss-my-foot and then not calling me even once! If you think you're getting rid of me that easily, you've got another think coming. Second of all, I've had an epiphany, and when I have them, I like for the object of my affections to be somewhere in the near vicinity so I can share these insights. Lord knows they don't happen that often. And third, I'm pretty much sick of being treated like a ditz. Between Bump and Sheldon, my future is being planned for me, something I don't really care for but just like about everything else these days I don't seem to have a choice in the matter. Everyone seems to be keeping things from me and deciding what's best for me and I've had all I can take of *that*, thank you very much. And to top it all off, I find out that you've been doing it, too, which is why I'm here. *What* detective? When did you hire a detective and why didn't you tell me? Didn't you think I had a right . . ."

The indignant torrent of words was stilled as Martin brought his mouth down on Ceylon's, silencing her quite effectively. But not for long; as soon as their lips parted she pushed him away, but not as if she really meant it.

"Oh no, you don't! You know I can't think when you do that, and I need to keep my wits about me so I can tell you off," she murmured.

Martin ignored her words and leaned down again for another soft, sweet kiss. Ceylon jumped away from him and swatted him with her purse; luckily, a small clutch bag.

"Stop it! I'm serious, Martin Mercier Deveraux. I'm a very angry woman. You don't want to fool around with me right now," she warned.

Martin looked at Ceylon and thought that the timeworn cliché was correct; she was certainly beautiful when she was angry. She was casually attired in a gauzy tunic and wide legged pants in a soft, creamy vanilla color, which brought out the richness of her skin. Her sexy feet were in flat bone sandals with a thin thong strap and she wasn't wearing any jewelry except a big mother of pearl cuff bracelet and matching earrings that were big flat discs. Her glorious hair was in charmingly curly disarray and her eyes were bright with indignation. He wanted nothing more than to take her upstairs and show her exactly how much he'd missed her, but decided correctly that this would not be a prudent move.

"You're absolutely right, Ceylon. I apologize," he said simply.

Ceylon's mouth had been open to launch another barrage at him, and she closed it quickly, while looking at him to ascertain how much of what he was saying was sincere.

Martin took one of Ceylon's hands in his and kissed it. "You have every right to be upset. I didn't handle this too well, Ceylon. I owe you an explanation if you'll allow me to give it you."

Ceylon made an insouciant gesture that meant "Yeah, whatever," but her attempt at being aloof faded rather quickly. "Okay. You can explain, but only if you show me around your house," she conceded.

Martin kissed the back of her hand and immediately gestured to the interior of the house. "Your wish is my command."

The outside of the house was very like the Martin she had been acquainted with before St. Simon's. It was a cool gray stucco, Italianate in design with tall multi-paned windows. The trim was chic matte black, with matching old-fashioned canvas awnings. There wasn't much lawn in the front, but there were austere pots of geraniums on either side of the front steps that led up to the front door. It was a somber, imposing home that looked perfectly in place with the rest of the neighborhood.

The large foyer had a terrazzo floor and led into a formal living room lined with windows. If she had thought about what Martin's home would look like, she would not have imagined it to be so elegantly furnished. It looked like the drawing room of an Italian manor, with furnishings that were obviously antique and selected with great care. Some of the rooms were barely furnished, like the dining room, or what Ceylon imagined was the dining room. There was a huge table in the center with a Carrera marble base and a thick beveled glass top, but no chairs.

The living room more than made up for its bareness, though. It was in the front of the house and was dominated by two big leather sofas that faced each other across an elegant fireplace. Ceylon sat on the burnished cushions and let out a soft 'ooh' as she sank into the comfortable depths. Everywhere she looked there was something beautiful, exquisite and unexpected. Tooled leather footstools, silk duppioni pillows, and an elegant leopard patterned cashmere throw gave the room life and harmony without clutter.

Floor-to-ceiling bookcases on either side of the fireplace were filled with books as well as various *objets d'art*. She noticed several hand-tooled leather boxes, huge perfect seashells, and what looked like several ostrich eggs in a low tulipwood bowl. A glass case held many specimens of semiprecious stones and one wall displayed a collection of antique stringed instruments, some of which she could not identify. The walls were rag painted and glazed by hand to give them a subtle patina that welcomed and embraced the visitor. Ceylon asked Martin if he had done it all by himself.

He enjoyed the look of surprise on Ceylon's face as she looked around the lower level of the house. The few people he ever had in his home were stunned, having been conditioned to expect track lighting and chrome from bachelors. But Martin liked comfort and had an innate sense of style. He freely admitted, though, to having some help with certain things.

"Actually, Bennie helped a lot with selecting colors and fabrics and things. And believe it or not, Angelique was a great help, too," he added. "Angel is very artistic, although she doesn't really believe it. But my favorite part of the

house was my own idea. Come with me." He smiled and
held out his hand.

Ceylon went willingly and oohed and aahed over the
kitchen. It was a cook's delight, with a big Sub-Zero refrigerator and a massive stainless steel range that could have
serviced a restaurant. She was still rhapsodizing over the
enormous work island that seated six and the glass brick
wall that separated it from the dining room when Martin told
her that although he loved this room, that was not what he
had to show her. He looked in vain for a vase and settled for
a big crystal ice bucket in which to place the bouquet of
flowers.

He then took her into the barren dining room and walked
over to the louvered folding doors that formed one wall of
the room. "I had this added when I bought the house," he
told her as he opened them wide.

Ceylon was totally speechless. The dining room opened
out to an atrium that covered the back of the house and ex-
tended all the way up to the roof. It was made entirely of
glass, of course, and filled with all manner of tropical plants,
from orchids to palm trees, that nearly reached the top. She
was unaware that she was holding her breath as she entered
the amazing green paradise that was the true center of the
house. A slight rustling noise and a scurrying made her come
back to herself.

"Martin, what was that?"

"Quail. I let them run loose in here to control the insect
population. I like things to be as organic as possible," he answered.

And sure enough, Ceylon got a glimpse of a few plump
gray-brown birds peeking at her curiously. Before she could
comment, though, her attention was drawn to a big cage that
contained two beautiful parrots. Or cockatoos; Ceylon wasn't
too sure. They were astoundingly gorgeous, though, and she
went over to the cage for a closer look.

"What pretty birds," she cooed.

To Martin's surprise, the two birds hustled right down to Ceylon's level for a good look. They clung to the side of the cage and made cooing sounds right back to her.

"Damn. I've never seen Bette and Tallulah take to anybody," he said. "They're pretty evil for the most part."

He had originally bought the birds for a lark and to amuse Bennie's nephews and niece who all adored Martin and thought he was a pirate. The boys thought his eye patch was the coolest thing going and admired him greatly for his scar, which they imagined had been earned in battle on the high seas. It was Bennie's niece Lillian who had asked him about his bird, insisting that all pirates had to have a parrot. The fact that Martin's mother shared the same name as the child made her feel especially close to all members of the Deveraux family. Despite the fact that they lived in Detroit and didn't visit Atlanta that often, Martin was so gratified at their acceptance of him that he bought the two big birds on a whim. He lived to regret the decision more than once as the birds were cantankerous, raucous, and refused to speak. And they would undoubtedly outlive him; the lifespan of a parrot is legendary.

They seemed charmed by Ceylon, something that Martin took as a good omen. He had not had a single clear, coherent thought since he had first kissed Ceylon on St. Simon's Island, but as far as he was concerned it was all good. She was here in his home and she seemed content. He didn't know how long she would stay, nor did he care at that moment. It was enough that she was here now.

He finally dragged her away from the atrium long enough to show her the rest of the house. There was quite a scene as the birds screeched like maniacs when she left their sight and didn't stop until she came back where they could see her. After she assured them that she wasn't leaving, they seemed slightly mollified, but Martin took no chances and closed the doors behind them. He took Ceylon upstairs and showed her the unfurnished guest bedrooms, his study, and the master bedroom.

Entering the room where Martin slept did strange things to Ceylon. She couldn't take her eyes off the bed, a gigantic four-poster that looked as big as an aircraft carrier. She was so entranced with the bed, she could barely take in the cool, yet sexy ambiance brought about by the Venetian-finished walls painted in an antique parchment color that looked tea-stained. The room was also accented by the crisp ivory linens and the weathered shutters that served as window coverings. Two antique brass fans graced the high ceiling and there was a big antique armoire against the wall across from the bed that hid Martin's expensive stereo equipment. The room was unusually long and encompassed a sitting area as well. Martin informed her that he had knocked out a wall to join what had been a smaller room to this one.

The resulting room was light and airy, with tall windows on either side of the bed, two windows in the sitting area, and French doors that took up the center of the wall to the left of the bed. Before Ceylon could inspect the view, Martin threw open the French doors to reveal a balcony that over-looked the atrium. The lush, tropical smell of rich soil and heavy greenery assailed Ceylon's senses and she sighed deeply. She could just imagine sharing an intimate breakfast with Martin on that balcony, or reclining on the chaise and listening to music. And she refused to allow herself to con-template what could happen in that bed.

"Martin, your home is absolutely lovely. And this bed-room . . . mmmm!" she said, as she walked about the space admiring the gleaming hardwood floors, drawn once again to that magnificent bed. "Martin, this is huge! I'm a tall woman, but I don't think I could get in that thing," she exclaimed. Her words turned into a small shriek as Martin lifted her ef-fortlessly and plopped her into the middle of it.

"See? Not a problem, Ceylon," he said in that deep sexy

voice that drove Ceylon mad with desire. Not today, though. She wasn't through with him, not yet.

"Very cute," she said mildly, trying not to notice the fact that his shirt was unbuttoned, that his shower-damp hair was unbound and hanging over his shoulders, and that he was able to make her tremble without even touching her. "But I'm not finished with you, Buster. I want to know why you dumped me off at your mama's house and never looked back, and why you took it upon yourself to hire a detective to find my brother without so much as mentioning it to me! How do you think that makes me feel?"

Before Martin could muster a reply, he was treated to the sight of Ceylon daintily removing her enticing little sandals from those pretty feet as she made herself comfortable against the big bank of pillows at the head of the bed. He opened his mouth to speak again but Ceylon rattled on, apparently still on a roll.

"I've been doing quite a bit of thinking, Martin and somewhere along the line, my life got completely out of my control. My granny didn't raise me to be anybody's doormat. yet that's exactly what I've become, laying flat on the floor like I have WELCOME on my back. I have *no* idea what twisted notions from childhood let me allow my mother, of *all* people, to convince me to just let that slick-behind Duane walk off with my money, but I've come to my senses. I've given enough to my family and I don't owe them a thing. Never did. I don't owe *anybody* anything, as a matter of fact. Even the people who have helped me through the years, like Bennie and Bump and Renee and you, I don't owe them anything except to be myself and do the best I can. Because when people care about you, that's all they want for you, the best. And . . . and . . . hey, stay where you are, Buster, we're not done with this," she warned as Martin made a move from leaning against the armoire.

Martin didn't pay her words any attention as he stepped away from the armoire and started towards the bed, taking off his shirt as he did so. Maybe it was the fact that she mentioned his name as one of those who had been on her side, or the fact that she looked so very sexy in the middle of his bed, but whatever it was it was making his control slip fast. Ceylon scooted further to the side of the massive bed as Martin continued to approach.

She tried to look apprehensive, but could only look aroused as he reached his target and sat down on the side of the bed, reaching for her as he did so.

She tried to push him away succeeding only in angling into a more comfortable position in his arms. "Martin, this isn't getting us anywhere," she whispered.

"On the contrary, I think this is getting us right where we need to be," Martin said. "I do owe you an explanation, and an apology. You're absolutely correct, Ceylon, but I don't see why that," he paused to kiss her softly, "is mutually exclusive from this."

Ceylon sighed deeply and submitted to Martin's embrace. When his lips and tongue stopped pleasuring hers, her only response was to remove the large earrings and hand them to Martin, along with the big mother of pearl cuff.

He was so beautiful to her eyes; his long, glossy hair unbound and cascading past his shoulders, his long eyelashes, his aquiline nose, his golden skin, his everything. He looked so good glazed by the mid-morning sun that Ceylon wanted to take a bite out of him. She smiled seductively at the thought. Unfortunately, Martin chose that moment to make a most eloquent apology.

"Ceylon, I wanted to get you someplace where the press couldn't bother you anymore and I knew Mom and Bump would make sure of that. I didn't call you, baby, because I thought you didn't want to hear from me. I was the cause of some pretty major embarrassment for you and if you had wanted to wash your hands of me, I would have certainly understood," he admitted.

Ceylon was just getting really comfortable in Martin's

arms when he made this pronouncement. Her mouth opened, ready to issue an eloquent rebuttal, and he silenced her the best way he knew how, with another long, blistering kiss, letting his tongue play along her lips and tantalize the tip of her sensitized tongue until she moaned in frustration. He relented then, and let the kiss take over, drowning her in all the passion he was feeling. She returned his kisses with equal fervor and began stroking his big arms, moving her soft curves against him in a way that caused him to pull away.

"Ceylon, baby, slow down, I'm not finished talking," he moaned.

"Oh, yes you are, darling," she purred and showed him that further conversation was indeed superfluous.

Chapter Ten

Martin allowed Ceylon's lips to silence all conscious thought, but he took over everything else. He rose to remove the faded jeans, tossing them carelessly to the floor, and as an afterthought, his bikini briefs. While Ceylon unbuttoned her gauzy top, Martin reached into the top drawer of his nightstand and withdrew a box of condoms. Without a word exchanged, he helped Ceylon remove her top, then slid the loosely fitting drawstring pants down her lush legs. He even went so far as to lay them carefully on the upholstered bench at the side of the bed. Ceylon lay on her side, looking seductive and somehow innocent at the same time. In two long strides, Martin was back in the bed and reaching for Ceylon, pulling her into his arms to kiss her thoroughly. Her soft, willing lips responded to his so seductively that the slow, languorous lovemaking he planned was replaced by the desire for something much more immediate, more primal.

Staring into eyes that reflected the passion in his, he slid his hands behind her back to release the clasp on her delicate lingerie and pulled the flimsy barrier away from her rounded breasts so he could kiss them as thoroughly as he had her mouth. Ceylon almost wept with pleasure as he kissed and licked his way around her right breast. When his hot, questing tongue swirled around her taut, erect nipple and pulled it into his waiting mouth, she screamed his name in passion. His only answer was to repeat his action on her left breast while she quivered helplessly.

Martin finally relented long enough to bring his head up to kiss away her tears of frustration. "Don't do that baby; why are you crying?"

Ceylon tried to answer but the words came out as a soft cry of passion as Martin began removing the last barrier to her femininity with a lover's skill. The panties joined the long-gone brasserie and Martin was free to explore every inch of her body with avid hands. He started by stroking her inner folds with his fingers until he felt a gush of moisture that signaled her readiness. He increased the sweet torture by finding her clitoris and stroking it in a circular motion until Ceylon thought she was going to come apart at the seams.

"Let it go, Ceylon; come to me, baby, let it go," Martin encouraged her until she abandoned herself to the urgent sensations surrounding her. But the torture wasn't over as Martin then kissed his way down the same path his hand had taken, loving her as thoroughly with his mouth as he had his hands. Only after she screamed out in ecstasy a second and third time did Martin allow Ceylon to begin to return the favors as their lovemaking continued.

If she had been able to think clearly, Ceylon might have been amazed at the ease of the passion flowing between her and Martin. Rational thought simply was not possible, though, in midst of the erotic bliss they shared. It was somehow better than the first time. This time was not the result of subconscious yearning; it was deliberate, sweet, hot, and consuming. In the bright sunlight of the day, they immersed themselves in the cleansing fires of love. When they were finally able to come up for air, Ceylon rested on Martin's broad, naked chest, purring with contentment.

After a final, deep sigh of bliss, she put one long leg over Martin and raised herself up so that she straddled him. He levered himself up on the pile of pillows at the head of the bed and lay back like a sultan, gazing at her bronzed bounty. It was evident from his sexy smile that he was pleased with what he beheld. He put his hands on her shoulders and stroked her soft, firm arms while committing her body to memory.

"Ceylon, you have the sexiest skin in the world. And some gorgeous breasts," he added. "You're a little bit too thin, still, but you're the most beautiful woman I've ever had the pleasure of knowing." He pulled her forward and kissed her softly before she could say a word.

When she was able to speak, she did so frankly, without ignoring the compliment he was paying her. "Martin," she murmured. "Thank you for saying that, but I am hardly skinny. And I was a pretty big package before, if you will recall. If you had ever seen me naked, you would have changed your tune," she said selfconsciously.

"I did see you naked," Martin said calmly. "Well, almost naked. And I was quite pleased with what I saw, baby, so talk what you know."

Ceylon's mouth fell open with shock and Martin was happy to educate her. "Once when you were staying with Clay and Bennie, I came over to the house. I went out on the patio and you were in the pool. I didn't know you were out there at first, not until you surfaced. You had on this gold bathing suit and it was just about the color of your skin. From where I was standing, you looked completely naked, like some kind of goddess rising out of the water. The sun was going down and everything had this red glow and you looked absolutely fantastic. Beautiful, unearthly, surreal, amazing . . ." his voice trailed away as he recalled how profoundly stunned he had been when he saw Ceylon emerge from the water as the sun turned her into molten, shimmering gold.

"Oh my. What did you do then, Martin? I remember that swimsuit, I even remember swimming, but I don't remember seeing you that night," Ceylon said in a bemused voice.

Martin chuckled. "That's because I got the hell out of there. When I was able to remember how to walk, I turned around and went straight home to an ice-cold shower, which did not do a bit of good, as I recall." That reminded him of something else that he was happy to share with Ceylon.

"I've taken more than my share of cold showers on your behalf, woman. I'm not taking any more. From now on, when you bat those big cat eyes at me, or come around me smelling good enough to eat, or put those soft little hands on me, I am not going to be responsible for the consequences," he threatened.

Ceylon was still in shock over his recollection of the evening swim, so much so that she was not paying him a bit of attention. She finished playing with his hair and stroked his big, broad shoulders, punctuating her strokes with soft kisses. "I love the way you feel," she said dreamily. "All that hard muscle and smooth skin. You know, the first time I saw you, I literally couldn't breathe."

Martin felt his face grow hot with embarrassment. "Yeah, I'm sure this mug scared the life out of you," he said ruefully.

Ceylon leaned over and bit his lower lip very gently. At his exaggerated "ouch," she smiled smugly.

"That's what you get! Martin, I looked across the room and there was this tall, strong, beautiful man who made my heart stop! I thought you were the most desirable man I had ever seen, and I still do. I told Renee that if you were married I would have opened a vein right in the ballroom and I would have, too."

She put one hand on either side of his face and looked at him with all the adoration she was feeling. "Martin, everything about you is beautiful to me. I love your height, your gorgeous hair, your long eyelashes, your nose, your hands, your build, your grace, your manners," she enumerated, kissing him after each attribute.

"You are sexy, gentle, sweet, kind, built like a god, and so smart it scares me. The fact that you wear an eye patch and have a scar does not make you less appealing to me. You are my total package, my dream man, my every fantasy come true."

Fearing she had gone too far, Ceylon resorted to a bit of humor to lighten the mood. "Let's face it, baby, you are alla that and a box of Godiva chocolates. Raspberry truffles at that. And I have a huge appetite for chocolate right . . . about . . . *now*," she whispered as she moved her hips to accommodate his massive hardness.

"Anything you want, Ceylon, anytime you want it," he groaned as they once again answered passion's call.

After making love for what seemed like hours, Martin had explained about Titus Argonne, the investigator he'd contacted while they were still on St. Simon's Island.

"Look, Ceylon, I wouldn't have told him to get your brother arrested or anything unless you said so. At least I *think* I wouldn't. Who knows. He's a punk and needs to be dealt with, but it's your call. All I told Titus to do was try to run the guy to earth and figure out where your money got to, and that's all he's doing right now. If you want him to go all the way with it, no problem. I've known Titus for years; he's very thorough and very discreet and he gets results. I was just so angry about what happened to you that I had to do something. Am I forgiven?"

As they were naked in the shower when he asked these questions, Ceylon had no choice but to let him off the hook, although she had to add a codicil. "The thing is, Martin, we have to trust each other, which means we have to confide in each other and talk to each other. We can't just go off half-cocked and do things that will affect the other without talking it out. Don't you agree?"

Martin was so entranced by the feel of Ceylon's soft, lush body slick with bath gel that he would have admitted being the other gunman on the grassy knoll. "Yes, baby, whatever you say," he murmured absentmindedly.

Ceylon smiled at the bemused tone of Martin's voice. "I don't think you're listening to me, sweetheart. What do I have to do to get your full attention?" she asked as she rubbed her soapy body against his.

"Oh baby, just keep doing that and you'll have my full everything," Martin groaned.

That night, Lillian and Bump hosted an outdoor party for Ceylon to celebrate her going to Broadway to replace the star of the revival of *Bubbling Brown Sugar*, who was out on sick leave for a month. Family and a few close friends were in attendance, but it still resembled a huge bash like the ones in *InStyle* magazine; the family was now so large that even a casual brunch after church resembled a party. There were few restaurants that welcomed the sight of the Deveraux clan; there were just so *many* of them.

Bennie and Clay were the first to arrive with their three boys. Anyone looking at the two of them would have assumed wrongly that they were newlyweds from the sweet affection that flowed between them. Even after years of marriage, it was obvious that they couldn't get enough of each other. They looked much the same as they had as bride and groom, except that Clay's hair was shorter and Bennie's hips were a bit fuller, courtesy of her three sons; weight that she didn't begrudge and that Clay was crazy about. He loved the fact that Bennie's figure was lusher.

Vera Clark Jackson, a longtime Deveraux group employee, was next to arrive, this time with her husband, the legendary

John "Tank" Jackson, middle linebacker for the Atlanta Falcons. Due to his hectic travel schedule with the team, as well as personal appearances all over the globe, Vera and Tank didn't have the luxury of the kind of togetherness that other couples shared. Vera was a stunning brown-skinned beauty with a witty style all her own. She captured the timeless elegance of a Dorothy Dandridge with her short, perfectly coiffed short hair, thick slanting eyebrows, and understated charm, but she had the liveliness of a hip-hop diva and an unbeatable clothes sense. This only made sense since she had been editor-in-chief of *Image* magazine for some years. *Image* was The Deveraux Group's high fashion publication. It had been around for years when Vera took the helm but she was the one who'd put it one the map, so to speak. Vera, like Bennie and Ceylon, was also from Michigan, but she was from Saginaw. The two Detroiters still considered her a homegirl, though.

"Okay Miss Ceylon, let me get a peek at you!" Vera exclaimed in her down-home way. "I'm loving that look, girl! You need to let me put you on the cover of *Image*."

Ceylon blushed and shook her head, although she, too, was fond of her outfit. It was a copper-colored silk sweater with a huge cowl neckline worn off the shoulder. The sweater came past her hips to mid-thigh over a pair of matching silk georgette palazzo pants. The fullness of the pants offset the slim fit of the sweater and the color did fabulous things to her beautiful skin.

The backyard had been turned into a pretty yet casual setting for a summer party, with colorful lanterns and flower shaped candles floating on the pool. There was a big white tent set up by the caterer for the enormous buffet, and a DJ was set up and already playing lively Latin jazz. Vera left Tank in the backyard and went inside to push her point with Ceylon.

Giving Bennie a big hug, as usual, and a bigger one to Lillian, she enlisted their aid.

"Listen, I want to put Ceylon on the cover of the Christmas issue," Vera said animatedly. "She's beautiful, funny, smart, talented, and much admired. And she's a perfect candidate for a big spread. What do you think?"

As expected, everyone was in favor of the idea except Ceylon. "I don't think so," she demurred. "I think I've had quite enough publicity for one year." She tried to laugh, but it was a poor imitation of her usual throaty chuckle.

Vera looked stricken. "Oh Ceylon, I didn't think about that! You know that this wouldn't be anything like that mess. This would be elegant, tasteful and express the real you," she said hurriedly.

"Express the real who?" inquired the voice of the youngest Deveraux, Angelique. She sauntered into the kitchen with the air of a stick of dynamite begging for a match, which was her usual attitude. Angelique was never known to bite her tongue, and was in fact known for biting the heads off others with little or no provocation. Her hot temper was as well known as her beauty and those who were overly taken with the latter often got a taste of the former.

Angelique surveyed the women standing around the big work island and patiently repeated her question, this time getting an answer from Vera, one of the few people with whom Angelique got along. She also admired Ceylon greatly, which was a rarity for Angelique.

"I was asking Ceylon to do the cover story for the Christmas issue of *Image*. I thought it would be really gorgeous and show her off to her public, but she disagrees, and I can't blame her," Vera said ruefully.

Angelique looked Ceylon up and down before speaking. "Well, I agree with Vera," she said slowly. "That would be off the hook. A nice way to end the year and a good lead in to next year when the movie comes out," she said casually.

Everyone tried not to look shocked at the sight of Angelique being thoughtful and insightful, and also tried not to look at each other.

Angelique fixed the awkwardness by changing the subject. "I was sent in here to tell you that your husband is looking for you," she said to Vera, who raised an eyebrow and muttered to herself before leaving the group to return to the backyard.

"Your husband is threatening to take over the grill," she said to Lillian, who immediately took off for the outdoors. Angel then turned to Bennie. "Have you seen what the boys are doing?" which caused Bennie to beat a very hasty retreat, leaving Angelique and Ceylon alone. Bennie's sons were known to be quite lively and the mischief they could get into defied all understanding.

Before Ceylon could get anxious, however, Angelique got right to the point. "The boys aren't doing anything, for a change. I just wanted to get you alone. I know all about you and Martin," she said bluntly. "My brother has had a lot of pain in his life, caused by a real trifling woman. And if you think . . ." her words were cut off by a deep, blessedly familiar voice.

"If she thinks what, Angel?" Martin had silently entered the room from the opposite side. He looked so incredibly sexy in a band-collared, short-sleeved ivory linen shirt, double pleated silk and linen blend slacks, and huaraches that Ceylon forgot anyone else was in the room. She immediately went to Martin and wrapped her arms around him.

"It's about time you got here, handsome," she purred. Martin hugged her closely and gave her a quick, hot kiss before fixing his gaze on his sister again.

"What were you about to say, Angel?" His voice held no real menace but anyone could hear the unspoken warning.

Angelique wasn't put off, however. Airily she replied, "Who knows what I was going to say? I say lots of things."

She looked back over her shoulder as she headed for the back door and out into the festivity.

"Don't let Angel get next to you," Martin counseled. "She can be a handful, but there's no real harm in her."

Ceylon surprised Martin by agreeing. "She's just be protective of her big brother, which is quite sweet. We'll work it out. She and I have always gotten along."

After one more brief kiss, which held the promise of many more, they went out into the fragrant summer evening to join the party.

The party took on additional life after the arrival of Marcus, Martin's youngest brother. Like all his brothers, he was tall and handsome, but he was arguably the most animated of the group. Gregarious and charming, he was the only unmarried brother and to hear him tell it, he would remain that way permanently. Marcus had too much fun dating, although he was dateless that night, strictly by choice. Marcus made it a rule to never date the same woman for more than ninety days, and he never brought one around his family, lest she start thinking her tenure was permanent.

He sat between Vera and Ceylon as Vera explained her earlier *faux pas*. He agreed that Ceylon would make a lovely subject for a holiday cover story, although that was hardly a surprise. Vera and Marcus worked together quite often and always made a smashing success of their projects. They were as close as brother and sister and their thinking was eerily similar in matters of business.

Marcus reached over and took Ceylon's hand. "Ceylon, you know Vera, and you know she'll make this something special, something to celebrate your talent and showcase you as the woman you really are: talented, compassionate, giving, and beautiful. It's about time we reminded the public of the very special person you are," he said persuasively.

They were joined by Sheldon Brillstein, Ceylon's personal manager, who came up just in time to hear the last remarks. "Brilliant idea. This is just what you need, Ceylon. At least think about doing it," he said mildly.

Ceylon sighed. She looked at Sheldon, called Shelley by his friends, and knew it was a *fait accompli*. Once Sheldon decided something was good for a friend or a client, he was relentless. He was tall, handsome, and utterly convincing when the best interests of a client were involved. He still harbored guilt over what had been done to Ceylon. He felt that he should have been able to detect Duane's felonious intentions and protected Ceylon better. Sheldon wasn't going to rest until he felt her career was right where it should be. He was in Atlanta not only to celebrate with the rest of her friends, but also to personally escort her to New York to her apartment suite in the Plaza, where she'd be staying while she took over the lead in the revival of *Bubbling Brown Sugar*.

"You know, Ceylon, New York would be the perfect backdrop to showcase you," he said mildly. "Stepping into the starring role on Broadway, emerging from the ashes, just like the city did after September eleventh. That's a real hook, don't you think?" He asked the question of the table in general, but Ceylon knew it was directed at her.

"And, of course I don't know anything about these things," he lied, "but it seems that your participation would make this a particularly successful issue for *Image*, increase the circulation, sell a lot of copies, whatever. I don't know CeCe, it just seems like it would be a good thing all around," he sighed.

Ceylon looked at Sheldon with loving exasperation. "You only call me CeCe when you're really trying to get something, Shelley. Okay, I'm going to spare everyone your next move, which is that whole yenta thing you do so well."

This remark elicited a laugh from Vera and Marcus. "Oh y'all don't know the lengths this man will go to. Shelley's own grandmother has nothing on Sheldon when it comes to nagging! Okay Vera, I'd be honored to be featured in *Image*. Just make sure those photographers make me look good!" she said merrily.

Ceylon went in search of Martin, to share the news with him. She had just spotted him in conversation with Clay when Malcolm, his identical twin brother, entered with his wife Selena and their three pretty daughters. Ceylon reached his side just as he was exchanging greetings with Malcolm and his family. As always, a little discomfort crept into the air when Martin and Malcolm met. It was the awkwardness both men had felt since the accident. He would forever have his twin as a reminder of how he should look. And for Malcolm, looking at Martin was like looking into a broken mirror. He could never rid himself of a vague feeling of guilt in Martin's presence.

Tonight, though, things were different. Ceylon walked over to Martin and slipped her arms around his waist, looking up at him adoringly and with no self consciousness whatsoever. Raising on tiptoe to kiss his cheek, she happily informed him of Vera and Marcus's plans for the Christmas issue. She turned to Malcolm and Selena and said "I'm going to be a cover girl, can you imagine that? Tyra Banks better watch her back," she laughed.

For some reason, the bubble of pain that normally encased the brothers seemed to have burst, just because Ceylon made things appear so normal. The two couples spent a good bit of time together that evening and enjoyed each other's company thoroughly, so much so that Selena suggested they come over to their house for brunch the next day. Without realizing what she was doing, Ceylon immediately was accepted as part of a couple.

"Selena, how nice! We'd love to come, wouldn't we Martin? What time do you want us and should we bring anything?"

Martin and Malcolm looked at each other and for the first

time in a long time, shared a joke. Only Malcolm heard him say "Is this where I say 'Yes, dear?' "

Malcolm snorted. "Trust me, that's about all you'll get to say. Just nod and smile like I do."

The utter normalcy of the remark capped off the contentment Martin felt at the moment, and that's exactly what he did, nodded and smiled.

Chapter Eleven

Martin was taking Satchel for his third walk of the day. They usually jogged in the mornings and took another walk in the afternoon, but this was a bonus. Satchel couldn't have cared less about the reason for the extra stroll; he was just glad to be out, as usual. His master, however, needed the time to think. For the first time in years, Martin wasn't sure what his next move should be. Ever since Ceylon came into his life, things kept getting more wonderful, more exciting, and much more complicated. Ceylon roused feelings in him that he hadn't expected, and her mere presence in his life put him into situations for which he hadn't prepared. There was his relationship with Malcolm, for example.

The day after the party, they went to Malcolm and Selena's house for brunch and it was a huge success. Growing up, Malcolm and Martin had the special closeness that's so often a part of being identical twins. They knew each other so well that they would finish each other's sentences; they antici- pated each other's thoughts and were truly each other's half. The accident had changed all that. In his worst moments Martin sometimes entertained the morbid idea that it was like having a twin die; after all, they shared nothing but a birthday now.

It wasn't anyone's fault, but no one seemed to be able to bridge the gap that loomed between the brothers. The fact that Martin took off for Florida after his recovery hadn't helped; his absence from the family seemed to make his injury and loss even more painful. And since he had returned to Atlanta, the twins hadn't been able to regain their former closeness. It seemed that things were irrevocably broken between the two men. The brunch, though, was the beginning of a wonderful healing.

Ceylon was her usual effervescent self, chatting with Selena and Malcolm, playing with their three daughters, admiring the house, and helping Selena in the kitchen. Selena was a very busy OB-GYN who didn't have a lot of time to cook. Malcolm actually did most of the cooking, and they had a wonderful housekeeper who came in three times a week. Selena's specialty was elaborate breakfasts, which she saved for the weekends, and she'd outdone herself this time. They dined on softly scrambled eggs, salmon patties, grits, baked tomatoes, grilled mushrooms, fruit salad, and fragrant banana nut muffins. Hot coffee, grapefruit juice, and iced tea were available to quench the thirst, and the conversation was light and easy. Everything was progressing nicely until Ceylon had looked at Malcolm and asked what Martin was like growing up. Everyone froze, except Ceylon, who didn't notice anything amiss and elaborated on her question.

"Tell me some of the things you guys did when you were little. Who was the quiet one and who was the wild one?" she asked, looking from one brother to the other.

Selena immediately jumped up and fetched a photo album, returning to the dining room with it in record time. She dropped the book into Ceylon's lap and invited her to take a look.

Martin smiled, remembering how Ceylon had oohed and cooed over every single picture of him and Malcolm as babies and small children. Her reaction on seeing them as college students had been priceless.

"My goodness, the women must have driven your poor mother nuts! They were probably all over you boys! Selena, didn't you start dating Malcolm in college?"

"Yes, I did. I fell in love with him when he and Marty had the band," she had answered. She'd flipped through a few pages of the album and pointed triumphantly to a picture of the young men in blazers with padded shoulders, tight jeans, even tighter T-shirts, and long curly hair. They each had a small, oddly shaped electric guitar, and everything about their postures suggested 'rock star.'

Ceylon had, of course, wanted details of their musical exploits, which Malcolm was happy to supply. She'd known that his brother Marcus had a great singing voice, but the fact that he and Martin were musicians was news to her.

"Well, it's like this. Marty and I had always had some kind of little group, all through middle school and high school because it was fun, we made a little money, and we met a lot of girls. Lots and lots. Ouch," he said in mock pain as Selena popped in him the back of the head.

"It was a long time ago, baby, don't hate on me now," Malcolm said laughing. "Anyway, we thought we were *bad*, thought we could actually make a living at this, didn't we?"

Martin agreed fervently. "Oh hell, yeah. We were gonna be the next Brothers Johnson, the new Isley Brothers, the black Hall and Oates or *something*. We were gonna quit college to launch our recording careers. We just knew some big producer was waiting for us with a multimillion dollar contract!"

Ceylon was entranced by the story and wanted to know what had derailed their train to the American Music Awards.

The men looked at each other and said in unison, "Clay."

Martin took up the story. "Pop had passed away and Clay was in charge of the company and trying to take care of

Mom and Marcus and Angel and we thought we were grown and could have some business. We went and told him our big idea and he didn't say a word . . . then. A few weeks later he says 'Let's go to Louisiana and see the family,' so we said cool and we drove over to visit our relatives. Mom and Pop are both from there, as you know.

"So we're hanging out with the kinfolks, chillin', whatever, and Clay says let's go to the country for a minute and we drive out into the middle of the dang bayou to some little bitty town that's like a wide space in the road. There's basically nothing there but a little general store, a few shotgun houses, and a little ol' filling station. Yeah, that's right, a *filling station* 'cause you couldn't call it really call it a gas station, it wasn't even brand name gas in the pumps. It was called something like Bubba's Home Gas; I think you could strip paint with it and use it for lighter fluid, too. So we pull up to this palace and Clay says 'let's get out of the car.'"

At this point Malcolm took over the story, just like when they were boys. "So we're standing there dressed like Crockett and Tubbs and thinking we're finer than wine and Marty looks up at the sign on the place and starts poking me in the arm. This great big brand-new sign reads 'Marty & Mal's Fill 'em Up. Cold Beer, Live Bait and Gas.' We look over at Clay and he gives us this big sneaky grin and puts his arms around our shoulders.

"He looks at us, then at the sign and says he wants us to be a big success in our new career, but he also wants us to have a back up plan. And this is our back up plan."

Martin finished the story. "So of course we *jumped* in the car, went back to Atlanta as fast as possible, enrolled for the next semester, and stayed our butts in school until Mal got his MBA and I got my law degree. And neither of us ever got anything less than an 'A' in any class, either."

Ceylon commented that it was a great accomplishment. The brothers looked at each other and laughed. Martin answered for them both. "It's amazing what you can accomplish when you know there's a bait shop with your name on it if you mess up. It wasn't diligence; it was *fear* that kept us on track."

The rest of the day was spent in laughter and reminiscing, as well as making plans for more outings. The only person who didn't seem to know that a huge hurdle had been overcome was Ceylon, which was ironic since it was she who was the catalyst. Martin had to acknowledge that he wouldn't have gone to Malcolm's house voluntarily; it took Ceylon's warmth and affection to make such a gesture seem normal. She'd even been the impetus behind his new relationship with his nieces.

Ever since the accident, he'd had almost no relationship with his brother's children, basically because he didn't want to scare them. Before the accident, he'd been their dearly loved Uncle Marty, playing with them, spoiling them rotten, and showering them with affection. When he'd had the accident, they had been quite young, Amariee the oldest at six, Jilleyin had been four and Jasmine only two. He'd never forgotten how they came to see him in the hospital and started crying. The heavy gauze bandage around his head and the raw, exposed burns had scared them senseless, and he couldn't blame them. Rather than risk repulsing them for the rest of his life, he chose to avoid them. He still sent birthday and Christmas presents, but they were dispatched through the mail when he was in Florida and through his mother after he returned to Atlanta.

He never admitted it to anyone, but he felt the loss of his role of beloved uncle quite keenly, especially after Bennie's children were born. They were used to seeing him the way he was. They only knew him as their cool uncle with the cool dog. But like his relationship with Malcolm, he didn't know how to salvage it. Until the day Ceylon took it upon herself to invite Malcolm and Selena over for an early dinner and insisted that they bring the girls.

Martin's reverie was broken as Satchel perked up as they

neared the part of the park where they always ran together. "Okay, I'm letting you off your leash. Don't go crazy," Martin admonished him. Satchel gave his customary bark of assent and trotted ahead, stopping to smell everything in sight as his master continued to stroll and think.

The girls were enchanted with their uncle's house, especially the atrium, which is where they spent a good bit of time while the adults chatted and had drinks before dinner. They had grilled shrimp as an appetizer, followed by boiled crabs, corn on the cob and little red potatoes, also cooked on the grill. The girls were thrilled with this repast, as it was served in the backyard on tables thickly covered with newspaper and each guest had a mallet with which to crack the crab shells. It was a noisy, happy family meal and everyone was helping everyone else eat, cracking shells and excavating the meat. Jasmine in particular had trouble besting her crab and Martin helped her, smashing the shell and fishing out the succulent meat for her until the other girls cried foul and demanded he help them, too.

Martin laughed out loud at the memory, then shivered slightly as the wind played along his neck. He still wasn't quite used to having short hair, although it had been his idea and also a result of that evening.

After everyone had eaten their fill, Martin and Malcolm had gallantly cleaned up the backyard and the kitchen, which had given them a chance to talk, something they couldn't seem to get enough of since the ice had been broken at the brunch. Selena and Ceylon were in the living room chatting about fashion and hairstyles and Amariee, now practically grown up at fourteen, wanted styling advice from Ceylon, who, after all, had been a top stylist in her former life. This had all spelled boredom for the two younger girls, who were left to their own devices. They'd apparently grown tired of watching their mother and sister have their hair played with and come and found their father and uncle.

Martin remembered them standing on either side of him

and staring for a long moment. Finally Jasmine, always the boldest, made her request. "Uncle Marty, can we comb your hair? Aunt Ceylon is combing Amariee's hair and we want to comb something, too. And we don't have any dolls over here," she added wistfully. Jilleyin hadn't said a word, but looked longingly at Martin's thick, abundant ponytail. Bemused, Martin agreed without realizing what it would mean. Malcolm, who'd been watching the Braves' game on the big screen TV, tried with varying degrees of success to control his laughter as Martin found himself sitting on a low footstool while his nieces took down his ponytail and groomed his hair to their heart's content. When it was finally time for everyone to leave, Ceylon and Martin were standing in the doorway to bid them good-bye. Selena asked the younger girls how they'd spent the rest of the evening.

"I didn't see you girls for a while, what were you and your daddy up to?" she'd inquired.

Jasmine was happy to inform her what they'd done. "We combed Uncle Marty's hair, Mommy! We combed it and combed it!"

Martin smiled gamely and grimly and as soon as the door closed behind them he'd turned to Ceylon. Picking up a handful of his now tangled hair, he'd said very few words. "Cut it off. Now."

And Ceylon, bless her heart, hadn't tried to argue with him. She merely went upstairs to her makeup bag where there was always a pair of hair scissors; like many hairdressers, she never left home without them. As she'd told him, there always might be a hair emergency somewhere. They'd gone into the atrium and to the soothing sounds of a Ramsey Lewis CD entitled *Maiden Voyage (and more)*, Ceylon skillfully and lovingly removed almost nine years of hair from his head. The change the haircut made was amazing. Now he looked younger, more dashing, and even sexier; at least that's what Ceylon told him. And from the reactions he was getting in public, she might have been right.

Martin finally shook off his deep thoughts and whistled for Satchel, who immediately came running. It was time for his nightly call to Ceylon and he wanted to be laying down in his big bed when he heard her voice. He hated the fact that she was in New York, but she was busy, productive, and happy, and that's all that mattered to him. The fact that he was lonely as hell without her was something he'd have to deal with.

Martin would have been gratified to know that Ceylon was at least as miserable as he, if not more. The work was wonderful, the suite was fabulous, and the fact that she was getting back on track as a performer was great, but the way she missed Martin was horrible. She had to work very hard to avoid a total funk; that's how badly she wanted to be with Martin. She sat in the sitting room of her Plaza suite staring at Vera Jackson, who was back in New York to conduct the interviews that would lead to the cover story for the Christmas issue of *Image*. It was the one day of the week that she didn't perform and she and Vera had spent the day shopping, chatting, and getting massages, manicures, and pedicures, all courtesy of *Image* magazine. Vera explained everything to her when she arrived in New York two days before.

"Honey, Marcus is on me every month because I don't use up my expense account, so this is one time we're going to use the money. We're going to get some new outfits for you for the photo shoots *and* you get to keep them, too. That'll make Marcus happy for a change."

While not exhausted from the day's activities, Ceylon was still in her own little world, for sure. The sophisticated furnishings were wasted on her. Even though Vera sat directly across from her on the sleek settee that graced the room, she could have been invisible. Ceylon was completely immersed in thought.

"Earth to Ceylon, earth to Ceylon," Vera called, waving a

slender hand in her direction. "Where'd you go?" she added playfully as Ceylon snapped out of her trance and realized that she'd been ignoring Vera. "This wouldn't have anything to do with a certain tall, handsome fellow from Atlanta, would it?"

Ceylon sighed dramatically and slouched in a very unlady-like manner on the loveseat she occupied. "I'm so sorry, I didn't mean to space out on you like that. And you're absolutely right, it has almost everything to do with Martin," she admitted. "I'm crazy about him, and I want to be with him. But there's so much that's not settled in my life. I can't inflict myself on him in this state."

She held up a hand to forestall the reply that she knew was about to come from Vera. "No, it's true. Vera, all my wages are still attached by the government and will be until the end of this fiscal year. Except for a small stipend for what they laughingly call living expenses, I don't have an income. When I check out of this suite to go back to Atlanta to record the soundtrack for *Idlewild*, I won't have anyplace to live. I'll be staying with Bump and Lillian, I suppose, or Bennie and Clay. I'm used to being an independent woman, to having my own. I can't stomach the idea of living off of someone else, especially in a love relationship. My grandparents thought it was appropriate for the man to take care of the woman, but I can't handle that. Every woman needs to have her own identity, her own income, and the ability to take care of herself. Until I have this mess straightened out, I can't even imagine what this relationship is all about." She sighed unhappily. Having spoken her piece, though, she had to add something.

"Despite all that drama, I have to tell you I just plain miss my man! Vera, I'm so crazy about Martin I can't see straight! I think about him day and night, you hear me? Mmmm, he's so . . . umm . . . he drives me nuts, girl!" She and Vera both started laughing as Ceylon fanned herself to demonstrate the effect Martin had on her.

"I hear you girl. Those Deveraux men are potent! In all the time I've known her, I've never seen Selena without a smile on her face and you know how Bennie and Clay are together. You'd swear they'd just met last week instead of being married for almost five years. The Deveraux men got it goin' on when it comes to making a woman feel special. I envy you, honey," Vera said and she was only half teasing.

"And I know what you mean about missing your man; John is gone so much that when he's home it scares me. One time I was so tired I couldn't see straight and I'd gone to bed extra early. I woke up in the middle of the night and there was this big naked man in the bed with me and I was about to knock him smooth out with that bowling pin I keep under the bed—and then I realized it was my own husband!"

They both laughed and Vera sighed. "I'm not going to kid you, it's hard on a marriage when one person has to travel a lot. Let me ask you, Ceylon. What are you going to do when everything is back in place, when everything in your life is in order again? Because it will be, very soon. I claimed it for you; you're going to get back everything you lost and you'll have even more than you dreamed of, you can rest assured. But what are you going to do with Martin while you're off in California and going on tour and whatnot? It ain't easy to be married like under those circumstances. I'm a witness to that!" Vera held up a hand in testimony.

Ceylon sat up completely while Vera made these remarks and her face had undergone a variety of expressions. Now she looked bemused.

"Well, Miss Prophet-Psychic-Friend Vera, where should I begin? Thank you for believing that everything will come back to me. I need that kind of positive energy. But dear heart, Martin and I aren't anywhere near to discussing marriage. And quiet as it's kept, I have no intention of moving back to California. I've discovered that I like being around people who care about me, people who I love. Atlanta isn't exactly a hick town, either. There's plenty of recording studios down there. For that matter, Bump has a recording studio in his house!

"There's plenty of work in the south for entertainers. Plenty. Who knows, I might open a supper club or go into artist management or God willing, I might just keep making movies! *Idlewild* was a lot of fun and I know in my heart it's going to be a huge success. Bennie and Clay are talking about expanding into TV production, so who knows? All I know is that I don't have to be in California or New York to continue to have a career in music. And if all else fails, I'll go back to frying hair. I kept up my license, you know," she said with a wicked smile.

Vera smiled, too, and then noticed the time. "Ceylon, it's getting late. I know it's about time for your nightly chat with your Boo, and mine should be calling as well." Her eyes suddenly sparkled wickedly. "He's coming up here this weekend for a long romantic weekend, so while you're relaxing tomorrow, I'm going to be racking up the La Perla lingerie. I want this weekend to be extremely special," she said sweetly.

"Ooh, girl, John 'the Tank' Jackson won't know what hit him! Go get some beauty sleep. Who knows, I might feel like shopping, too," Ceylon answered.

The two women hugged each other and Ceylon watched out the door of the suite until Vera disappeared into the elevator to go to her own floor. With a happy sigh, she hastened to draw a deep bubble bath so that she could be bathed, creamed, and perfumed when Martin called. It was ridiculous, but she treated their nightly calls like dates; it was the only way they could date right now, even though he had come to New York for her opening night. That was a truly special memory, one that she relished. As she sank into the gloriously scented bubbles, she thought about that night.

Martin had arrived at the Plaza and come directly to her suite. When she threw open the door and saw him standing there with a Tiffany blue shopping bag, she melted on the spot. He was tanned, and the deeper coloring made him look even more exotic to her hungry eye. They stared at each other for a long moment and moving as one they were in each other's arms. Ceylon vaguely heard the door shut as Martin kicked it closed, all while they were kissing madly.

It felt so good, so right to be in Martin's arms that she was ready to blow off the opening and told him so. He laughed at her gently while reminding her that there were a few other people in attendance who might take issue at her non-appearance. By then they were sitting on the settee in the sitting room; or rather, Martin was sitting on it and Ceylon was sitting in his lap and they were making up for lost time. Ceylon stroked Martin's beloved face and told him again that she was surprised at how much she liked his hair short.

"I thought you were handsome when it was long, but I have to say that you're even better looking with it this length," she murmured as she stroked his high cheekbones and caressed his ears and neck before kissing him again.

Ceylon trembled and sat up from her reclining position in the giant bathtub. The water had cooled considerably and the bubbles had dissipated while she remembered that passionate weekend with Martin. She released the tub's stopper and adjusted the shower to quickly rinse off the soap. Wrapping herself in one of the large, fluffy towels on the heated rack by the tub, she stepped out onto the thick bathmat and prepared to start drying herself off. She stopped when she caught sight of her reflection in the mirror. She fingered the amazing necklace she was wearing; she still wasn't used to its beauty. Ceylon smiled as she remembered how Martin had presented it to her.

Martin had come bearing gifts but Ceylon had been too excited to see him to even remember the bag until he presented it to her with a flourish. She'd been so pleased that she immediately tore into the contents without all the usual 'oh you shouldn't have' nonsense. The bag contained a big box of Belgian chocolates and a sterling silver frame with a picture of Satchel. Martin explained that Satchel had commissioned this gift; he didn't want her to forget him while she was away. There was also a smaller box with a three-carat brilliant cut diamond pendant suspended from a beautiful platinum chain. Ceylon's eyes had grown huge and Martin had fastened it around her neck while saying that it was a perfect stone for a perfect woman. And then things had heated up to the point that Ceylon would have been late arriving at the theater if Martin's cooler head hadn't prevailed.

Ceylon finished drying and applied body cream from her neck to her toes, as well as toner and moisturizer to her face. She started to put on some her of favorite lingerie, then decided to slip naked into the king-sized bed, feeling slightly wanton as she did so. She turned the television on and lowered the volume, then settled back against the pillows and glanced at the bedside clock. The phone would be ringing any minute and she'd hear her Martin's deep voice. Fingering the necklace again, her thoughts went back to opening night.

The flowers in the dressing room were breathtaking; it seemed that everyone she'd ever known had sent some kind of tribute. The show's producer, the cast of the show, Bump and Lillian, Bennie and Clay, *Image* magazine, The Deveraux Group, the list went on and on. And there seemed to be as many people as there were flowers; Sheldon, of course, Vera Jackson with a photographer, the mayor of New York, several old friends and, looking like he'd just stepped off a *GQ* cover, was Martin in a fabulous black suit with a long jacket worn with his favorite style of band collared shirt. He seemed to know that she was tired and a bit overwhelmed because after kissing her gently, he slipped his arm around her waist and kept it there, which was a good thing. When Bump and Lillian walked into the hot, overcrowded dressing room, Ceylon began to cry from happiness. If Martin hadn't been holding her up, she might have also fainted from excitement. She had no idea they were coming to New York but felt like a million bucks when Bump looked at her like she was crazy and asked how she thought he was going to miss her Broadway debut.

Happy tears moistened her eyes when the phone rang, bringing her back to reality. "Hello, baby," she purred into the mouthpiece.

"Hmmm. Do you always answer the phone that way? I could have been room service for all you know," Martin teased her.

"No, baby, I know your ring. I always know when you're on the line," she said in her sexiest voice.

"Do you know what I want when I'm on the line?" he drawled in the voice that never failed to elicit a physical response from her.

"Mmm-hmm, I do, because I want the same thing from you," she answered.

"What are you wearing?" he asked softly.

Ceylon had been waiting for this and was more than happy to answer him. "My exquisite diamond necklace, Tresor body cream, and a big smile," she crooned.

"Stop. Hold it right there before I forget what I have to tell you," Martin said abruptly. "You're going to get me breathing hard and talking crazy and you need to know this," he said in a totally different tone of voice.

"Ceylon, Titus found Duane."

Chapter Twelve

The next morning Vera's morning stretches were disturbed by the sound of someone tapping persistently on the door of her suite. She rolled into a sitting position, then stood and donned a bathrobe, which had been tossed on the chair. Turning off the Pilates tape in the VCR, she opened the door to find Ceylon standing there with a stunned expression on her face. Before Vera could utter a sound, Ceylon started talking.

"Forgive me for barging in on you, but I needed to tell someone about this. I've already ordered us breakfast and lots of coffee, it's on the way," she added as she walked past Vera and took a seat in a comfortable looking wing chair near the picture window.

It was obvious that she was in some distress, from the sound of her voice to the very fact that she'd come to Vera's suite without even calling first. Vera didn't ask any questions, she just nodded.

"Let me put some clothes on and I'll be right back," she said. "Me doing Pilates in the nude is *not* something you want to witness," she added with a laugh.

In minutes she was back in the living room, attired very

similarly to Ceylon in comfortable lightweight cotton jersey
pants and a matching tank top. Her feet were bare and even
with her skin devoid of all makeup and her hair mussed, she
was still strikingly gorgeous. Her face was full of concern
for her friend as she took a seat on the sofa. Ceylon huddled
in the wing chair, repeatedly stroking the bridge of her nose
with her forefinger, something she did when she was upset.

"Ceylon, come sit over here. You look terrible! Tell me
what's happened. Did you and Martin have a fight?"

Ceylon made a face and rose from the chair to slouch
over to the sofa and flop down on the end opposite Vera.

"No, no, Martin and I didn't have a fight. It's just that he
gave me some unexpected news. You know that detective he
hired, the one I told you and Bennie and Selena all about the
night of the party? Anyway, he's managed to track Duane
down. It seems that he's found himself a nice little hideaway
on some island where they have all these offshore banking
establishments that don't ask a lot of questions about where
the money comes from. Ol' Duane is having quite a time
with my money, it seems. It also seems that he may be up to
some of his old tricks. Only this time he's playing with some
people who are way, way out of his league and he could be
headed for big trouble," Ceylon said tensely.

Vera could see how upset Ceylon was, but her concern
was for her friend, and not for her low-down brother. She immediately said "So? That's his lookout. All we care about is
getting your money back from him, right? That guy Martin
hired, is he bringing him in? Did he call the cops on him or
something? Did he have to beat him up?" she asked with sincere hope in her voice.

Ceylon had to laugh a little. Vera sounded so blood-
thirsty! "No, no, no! Titus, I think that's the detective's name,
Titus Argyle or something strange like that. Anyway, he just
found Duane. He knows where he is and what he's been up
to, and he thinks he's pretty sure where Duane stashed the
bulk of my money. He checked in with Martin to find out

how I wanted it handled, if I just wanted to get my money back or if I wanted him to have Duane arrested."

Vera's eyes widened. "No wonder you look so tired, girl. I'll bet you didn't sleep a wink last night! You shouldn't have stayed down there fretting all night. You could have called me, you know."

Both women jumped as a sharp rap on the door let them know that room service had arrived. Vera let the server in, showed him where to place the table, and tipped him generously. She then busied herself preparing a plate for Ceylon and one for herself. Ceylon had ordered fresh fruit, English muffins, and two pots of coffee, as well as a couple of bottles of mineral water and a bucket of ice; Vera drank more water than anyone Ceylon had ever met. While she was fixing the plates, Vera continued to utter comforting words to Ceylon.

"Well, as long as you get your money back, that's the important thing. I know it was hard for you to let Duane walk away, but I don't know if I could have let somebody haul my kin off to jail, no matter what they'd done to me. I'm about as soft-hearted as you are when it comes to family," Vera admitted. "Believe me, no one is going to think any less of you for not prosecuting Duane."

She handed Ceylon a plate with one hand, and a cup of hot coffee balanced on a saucer with the other. Ceylon carefully set the coffee on the end table next to the sofa before answering Vera.

"That's just it, Vera. I told Martin to have Duane's butt dragged off that island and shipped back here FedEx if that's what it takes. I'm going all the way with this one."

Vera luckily had a mouthful of iced water and not hot coffee when Ceylon made this announcement; the contents of her mouth dribbled down both sides as she gaped in shock.

"You didn't! Did you really? Well, shoot, girl, good for you! He needs to pay for what he did and pay big. So is this why you're all tied up in knots? Are you second-guessing yourself? Do you think you did the wrong thing or something? Because you didn't, you know, you absolutely did not. The man is a felon, a crook, a liar, and a thief, and he needs to do time," Vera said confidently as she tried vainly to sop up the water from her bosom. "I'll be right back; this isn't working."

She returned in minutes clad in a well-worn FAMU football jersey, which had obviously been a part of her wardrobe for years. Ceylon hadn't moved from her corner of the sofa and was at the moment staring at the blank television screen as if it held the secrets of the universe.

She finally looked at Vera and admitted that it wasn't a crisis of conscience that was causing her angst. "I'll tell you what it is: it's the fact that I'm *not* having any regrets that's making my stomach knot up. I don't feel any guilt over what I told Martin to have that Titus do. I don't feel any compassion for Duane and no remorse over having my blood kin locked up like a common thug. If anything, I feel triumphant and self-righteous and you *know* how much I dislike smug, self-righteous people! I feel like some kind of prosecutor or something, like I'm suddenly in charge of deciding people's fates," she declared, although no one could have looked less like a stern avenger than she did at the moment. She looked pale and uneasy and in need of a big hug, which is what Vera gave her after first taking the untouched plate of fruit from her hands.

"It's going to be okay, kiddo, it really is," Vera assured her.

And Ceylon wanted with all her heart for her words to be true.

The bright sunlight in the Caymans was dazzling enough to make a man lose his vision, which is one reason the man wore very dark sunglasses. The other reason that he wore the glasses is that he didn't want to be noticed, and eyes with odd coloring such as his always attracted attention. He wanted to be inconspicuous and blend in with his surroundings and so far, he'd succeeded. Duane Anthony Carter had no idea that he was being observed.

"Bartender, another Red Stripe for me and whatever the gentleman is drinking," Duane said grandly.

He and his companion were seated at Duane's favorite outdoor bar, enjoying the scenery, which consisted of luscious, barely-clad women. They were also conducting business. At least the companion was trying to be business-like; Duane was doing more preening than anything else. The lilting island music, the beach, and the bevy of beauties that paraded about half-naked all contributed to his excellent mood.

Duane was a good-looking man, with smooth brown skin, a neatly trimmed head of coarse black hair, and a thin moustache. He was an even six feet tall, with an average build that had just the slightest bit of a paunch beginning, the result of his love for the high life and evidence that he despised exercise of any kind. The fact that Duane found his belly adorable was a sign of his narcissism; he referred to it as his "chippie's playground." That he referred to women as "chippies" was a sign of his level of maturity. Despite being in his late thirties, Duane had a remarkable lack of that quality. After the extremely sexy woman he was watching left his view, he turned his full attention to what his companion was saying.

"After my family was forced into exile, much of our fortune was left behind, our bank accounts frozen and inaccessible. The only way we can get the money at this point is to have it transferred into an American bank and converted into American dollars. This seems to be a simple matter, but because I am temporarily without a country, it is impossible for me to gain access to an American bank," he explained in his meticulous, charmingly accented English.

Joseph Nbuku was a very well groomed man of Duane's approximate age and size, although his body bore the evidence of an extremely rigorous regime of physical fitness or an extraordinary gene pool; he was taut, lean, and muscular. His dark skin was smooth and unmarked, his rather small eyes magnified slightly by the small round glasses he wore. His hair was cut down to his scalp and he was attired in plain but expensive casual wear—as opposed to Duane, who had gone island all the way in a loudly patterned shirt and colorful shorts. Nbuku leaned forward to emphasize the urgency of his plight.

"What I need, Mr. Carter, is an agent, an intermediary, . . . how you say . . . *liaison*, someone to act as a conduit of my family's funds."

Duane took another long swallow of the icy cold Red Stripe beer and nodded as though he were listening intently to the man's story. Nbuku took this as agreement and went on with his proposal.

"I need someone with an American bank account to simply accept the transfer of seven million pounds sterling into their account. For this simple service he would be given twenty percent of that amount for their trouble and for aiding the royal family in their time of need. It's just that simple, Mr. Carter," Nbuku said quietly.

Now he had Duane's attention. With the current rate of exchange, seven million pounds amounted to about twice that number of American dollars. Twenty percent of that was a nice chunk of change, no matter how you looked at it. And all he had to do was let this guy deposit some money into his account? It sounded easy enough, almost too easy. Duane's eyes narrowed and he looked at Nbuku for a moment before speaking.

"Mr. Nbuku, this sounds rather interesting. I'm not going to pretend as though this idea has no merit. But I have to ask how you came to pick me as the perfect candidate for this opportunity. You don't know anything about me, so what makes you think I can be of assistance to you in this matter?" Duane asked carefully. He didn't want to insult the man, but at the same time, he wanted to let Nbuku know that he was a man who was careful and logical in his business dealings. To his surprise, Joseph Nbuku seemed to be relieved that Duane had asked the question.

"Mr. Carter, I knew that you were the right person to approach with this. I recognize that this is an unorthodox proposal, but it was a chance I had to take. When I came to the Caymans, I used some of our remaining available funds to begin a campaign to regain our family fortune. In doing so, I made an . . . acquaintance at the bank here, the same bank that you use. I explained in confidence what was needed and my . . . acquaintance was able to point me in the direction of three men who had the kind of acumen to be able to handle this situation. I am not ashamed to tell you, Mr. Carter, that I observed all three candidates before deciding upon you as the perfect man. The other two men, they were careless and sloppy in their conduct, frequently intoxicated and frankly, lacking the kind of character necessary for this undertaking," Nbuku explained. The sincerity in his voice was unmistakable.

"You see, Mr. Carter, I am making myself quite vulnerable in this enterprise. I will be putting the fortune of the royal family into your hands, so to speak. I will be entrusting you to carry out your end of our bargain because if you so chose, the money would be in your accounts and I would have no recourse to claim it from you; it would be your word against mine and the authorities would not be able to aid me. This is why it was imperative that the candidate be someone who could be trusted completely and I feel that I have found that person in you."

Duane was of course flattered by the man's opinion of him, and convinced by his admission of using underhanded means to get his name. A man who was capable of bribery was, in Duane's mind, a man he could use. But he had to at least appear to be hesitant; it would probably up the ante for his share. And there were lots of details to work out; even Duane knew that there were limits on how much money that could be deposited into a bank account without lots of questions being asked. American banks were much more interested in regulations than their Cayman counterparts. There was much strategizing to be done, but first Duane had to make Nbuku sweat a little.

"Mr. Nbuku, this is a very interesting proposition you've given me, but I need time to think about it. Perhaps we can talk later. I need some time to crunch a few numbers, try to get the big picture, you know what I mean," he said with a shrug of his narrow shoulders.

Nbuku seemed relieved that Duane was asking for additional time; in fact, he seemed delighted at Duane's words. "Mr. Carter, thank you so much! The fact that you wish to give this further consideration pleases me to no end; it shows me that you are indeed a serious man who knows what he is about! Let me give you numbers where I can be reached and I will await word from you," he said as he reached into his pocket for a card on which to scribble his information. "You won't regret this, Mr. Carter, I assure you. I thank you in advance and the royal family thanks you also. I shall wait to hear from you." He stood up and made a sharp, short bow to Duane before leaving the bar.

Duane picked up Nbuku's card and read it over before stashing it in his pocket. As he ordered another Red Stripe, he grinned. This was going to be easier than picking his sister's accounts clean. Fourteen million dollars in his account and the joker had admitted that once it was there, Duane had total control over it and there was nothing anyone could do about it. Life was too good sometimes, it really was.

In a shadowy corner of the same bar, the man removed his sunglasses and looked again at his target. Duane Anthony Carter was about to get some very, very bad news.

* * *

Ceylon managed to get through the day without completely sinking into a funk. This was mostly due to the fact Vera kept her busy all day by taking her to a fabulous day spa in Harlem for a facial and massage. By the time she got to the theater she was ready to give a great performance as usual. As a matter of fact, her performance that night was one of her best; she received an additional standing ovation in which she generously included the rest of the cast. She was still exchanging happy remarks with her fellow actors as she left the stage door of the theater, so engrossed in conversation that she didn't notice that someone was watching her until she almost reached the car that picked her up and dropped her off each day.

A shadow fell across her in the dimly lit alleyway and she gasped and turned around. In an instant the adrenaline surge that signaled fear had turned to ecstasy.

"Martin!"

In minutes, it seemed, she and Martin were in her suite at the Plaza. They'd had very little in the way of conversation on the drive over. Ceylon was content to be wrapped in his arms in utter bliss. As soon as they got into her living room she locked the door behind them and turned to behold her lover in all his glory. Martin got better looking each time she saw him. He was dressed casually in a pair of dark summer weight slacks and a cotton sweater with the sleeves pushed up. The only jewelry he was wearing was his Corum watch, and his tanned skin and short hair made the most of his chiseled good looks. Ceylon couldn't take her eyes off him, or her hands for that matter, as she was reaching for him as soon as the door closed.

They embraced for long moments, each reveling in the comfort and heat generated by their embrace.

"I'm so glad you're here, Martin. Why did you come up without letting me know?" she said at last.

Martin tightened his arms around her again and kissed the top of her hair, smiling as her familiar fragrance assailed his nostrils.

"It's called a surprise, baby. I love to see that look on your face when you're happy or excited. And because," he slowly released her enough to tip her chin up so she was looking up into his face, "I had a feeling you wouldn't be able to sleep last night. Was I right?"

Ceylon sighed and stepped reluctantly out of his embrace. She took his hand and led him over to the sofa, where she pushed him down so she could sit in his lap. "Yes, well, I'd be lying if I said I slept," she admitted. "Martin, what you told me about Duane, and what I told you, it's huge, isn't it? There's no turning back, is there?"

Martin looked into Ceylon's troubled eyes for a long moment. "No, baby; there's no turning back. Titus has located Duane and on the strength of what you told me, he's started a plan in motion that will restore the money he's taken from you and bring him back to this country to face charges. Please don't tell me that you've changed your mind about this," he entreated. "Baby, please tell me that you're sure that this is the right thing to do."

The sigh that issued from Ceylon seemed to come from the very soles of her feet. "I'm not having second thoughts, Martin, and that's what's making me have second thoughts," she mumbled without meeting his gaze. Martin patiently turned her face to his while she tried to explain her jumbled thoughts. "I'm so angry at Duane that I can't wait to have him punished for what he did to me. I want every single penny that he hasn't already spent back in my bank accounts where it belongs; nobody *gave* me that money, I *earned* every cent of it and I deserve to have it returned to me—with interest, after what he put me through!" Her eyes flashed with anger that quickly died out. "But for some reason I'm really uncomfortable thinking of myself as somebody's judge and jury. Who am I to decide who needs to be punished. Isn't that what God is for, after all? Wouldn't it be enough for me to get my money back and let the chips fall where they may after that? I know I sound like Boo-Boo the fool here, but I have to be honest with myself about this issue. This is a real big deal here."

She lowered her head again, hesitant to meet Martin's penetrating gaze. He didn't speak for a moment, and when he did, his words were soft and comforting.

"Ahh, Ceylon, you're just too sweet for your own good. You're always trying to do the right thing and make everybody happy, trying to be fair and honorable in a world where everybody's out for themselves. I think . . . no, I *know* that's one of the reasons that I love you so much," he said quietly.

Ceylon's heart seemed to stop for a second, then resume its beating with a vengeance.

"You love me?" she breathed, not daring to believe her ears.

Martin laughed a deep and hearty booming sound. "Don't sound so surprised! Of course I love you, Ceylon! Why would I have jammed my long legs into business class on a hot ass crowded plane in the middle of summer to come up here to be with you? I love you more than anything, woman, and you know it. Just like I know that you love me, too. I may be crazy, but I ain't stupid," he growled as he started kissing her neck like he meant business, which he did.

Ceylon giggled like a schoolgirl and tried in vain to make him stop. "Wait, Martin! Ooh, stop, baby! Let's get you relaxed and comfortable and . . . ooh!"

She finally had to leap off his lap to get him to stop his cheerful seduction. She took off for the bedroom with Martin in hot pursuit. She escaped into the bathroom where she stopped. "Look at that fabulous bathtub, Martin. We're going to get in it and bathe each other from head to toe and then we're going to order some champagne and then . . . well, if you have any strength left in your body, then we'll see," she said with a wicked glint in her eye.

Martin admired the huge tub and the gold fixtures, which included two handheld showers while he removed his clothes. "Oh, yeah, baby, than sounds like a plan for sure. And don't worry about the strength of my body; where you're concerned, I've got plenty," he said as he enjoyed the sight of Ceylon removing the casual clothes she'd worn to the theater. He loved watching her curves come into view, the sight of her luscious full body tantalized him to no end.

In minutes they were enjoying the sensation of a torrent of warm water flowing over their bodies from the handheld showers. Ceylon investigated the various settings on one of the showerheads while Martin investigated her body. Martin loved looking at Ceylon's luscious figure, especially after the first time they made love and he'd discovered that her delicious behind had two beautiful dimples right above the curve. She was rounded and lush like a sculpted nymph and he did not think he could ever get enough of looking at her, although he was not lying when he said he liked her just as well when she was heavier. He tried to explain it to her as they soaped each other's bodies.

"Look, I'm a big ol' country boy one generation away from the bayou. I like what I like and I like butter, " he stated firmly.

That comment made Ceylon's brow pucker. "Honey, what have dairy products got to do with anything?"

Martin laughed. "No, baby, not that kind of butter. *Butter*, that soft, tasty, squeezable stuff that very lucky men find on very special women." He pulled her close to him to demonstrate what he meant. "That sweet baby softness that feels warm and tastes juicy and delicious. Butter, baby. That's what you're made of," he growled and helped himself to a mouthful.

Ceylon sighed happily and allowed herself to be seduced

by the honest lust in his voice and the sensuality with which he devoured her. There was definitely something to be said for a man with a healthy appetite, and Martin's showed no signs of flagging. They had engaged the catch to stopper the tub so by the time they had soaped each other thoroughly, it was full enough for a long, sensual bubble bath. They sank into the fragrant bubbles and sighed with repletion. It was made in such a way that the fixtures were in the middle wall, so that each of them could lie back against the smooth porcelain surface of the deep sides without hitting a spigot. Martin's long legs cradled Ceylon's until she mischievously slid her feet down his thighs to his most sensitive spot.

He immediately groaned with pleasure as she zeroed in on his penis, which immediately responded to her touch.

"Oh damn, Ceylon, that's . . . umm . . ." his voice died away as she continued to stroke his now growing erection with her toes.

Ceylon smiled smugly as she enjoyed the sight of Martin's obvious pleasure. That is, until Martin grabbed her feet and started massaging them. The look in Ceylon's eyes was priceless as his sensual touch began to awaken sensations she'd never experienced before.

"Surprise, baby," Martin said softly. "I'll bet you didn't realize that your feet could generate that kind of feeling," he teased her. "Didn't you know that your feet are erogenous zones?"

And she hadn't, not in a million years. Martin rested one foot in his lap and concentrated his efforts on the other one, stroking and massaging it until Ceylon sighed with passion. "You have such sexy feet, baby. I've been wanting to do this since the first time I saw these pretty feet," he murmured. He lowered his head slightly and ran his tongue across the bottom of her foot and ending by taking her big toe into his mouth and sucking on it gently at first, then increasing the pressure as Ceylon's eyes closed and she began to tremble from the sensual assault. Martin wouldn't relent, though; he continued in this fashion until both her feet had been thoroughly treated to his sexy ministrations.

Ceylon was helpless against the sensations that filled her body. Waves of pleasure spiraled up her body until she writhed in ecstasy and moaned his name aloud over and over, begging him to stop and then begging him to keep going. When it was finally over, she shuddered in completion and rose to a fully sitting position, her enjoyment evident in her flushed face and her fully erect nipples.

"Mmm, Martin . . . don't you move, baby, I've got something special for you, too," she purred as she slid closer to him, close enough to grasp him in both hands under the still warm water. It was Martin's turn to sigh in ecstasy as she proceeded to massage his now massive erection with her gentle, loving hands. She explored every inch of his tumescent member and was about to lower her head to further pleasure him when he choked out her name.

"Ceylon! Umm . . . let's get out of here, baby, before you drown."

Before she could protest, he stood up and hastily pulled her up with him, then rinsed them both. He wrapped Ceylon in a towel and put one around his waist before swinging her up in his arms and carrying her into the bedroom, where he placed her gently in the middle of the big bed. He immediately took off his towel and turned to face her. "Now then, my love, where were we?"

Ceylon hesitated only a moment before resuming her activities from the tub. She sat up and removed the towel, proudly showing her bronzed bounty to the man she adored. She reached over and stroked his face, leaning in for a kiss as she did so. "I do love you Martin, I do," she said softly. "And I think we were right about here," she added as she began to finish what she'd started in the bath.

There were no more words, only the sounds that two people make when they are consummating their love in the most intimate way possible.

Chapter Thirteen

Duane thought over the proposition laid before him by Joseph Nbuku, trying to figure out the best way to take advantage of the situation. No matter what Nbuku said, it wasn't going to be easy to direct that much cash into a single account in an American bank. Hell, even into a dozen accounts in a dozen banks, it wouldn't be easy, but it could be done, of this Duane was sure. There had to be a way for him to cash in on this. He was so busy musing over his good fortune he didn't notice the tall man who'd come over to his table. Not until the man spoke did Duane look up.

"Mr. Duane Carter? I'm Thomas Allen. I'd like to have a word with you, if I could." Without waiting for an answer, the stranger pulled out a chair and sat down. Even from a seated position it was easy to see that the man was tall, at least six feet four inches. He had an unusual look to him, a broad, almost Slavic face that looked out of place with his olive complexion. He had high cheekbones, short, coarse, dark blond hair and eyes that were slightly Asian, an odd shade of bluish gray. He should have looked uncomfortably alien in the lively, friendly bar, but for some reason he looked as though he belonged there. He wore navy blue shorts and a plain white T-shirt that showed off his muscular frame. A pair of expensively nondescript sunglasses perched on top of his head as if he'd just shoved them up there, which he had.

Duane simply stared at the man. It didn't look like it would do any good to tell him to shove off, and he was curious besides. The last stranger to approach him was going to make him rich; he wanted to hear what this man had to say.

"Mr. Carter, I saw you talking with Joseph Nbuku earlier. I'm sure that whatever Nbuku had to say involved money, large sums of it. You should be aware that Joseph Nbuku is a con artist. He's bilked hundreds of American citizens out of hundreds of thousands of dollars and he has a very large price on his head, placed there by the American government," he said quietly. "I represent that government. I'm an agent for the United States Treasury Department and I have a proposition for you, a much better one than Nbuku offered."

Duane immediately shook off the effects of the beer and sat up straight. "Look, Mr. . . . what did you say your name is?"

"Thomas Allen."

"Okay, Mr. Thomas Allen. You claim to be a Treasury agent and that Joseph Nbuku is a con artist. Just what kind of proof do you have?" Duane said roughly.

The man looked Duane steadily in the eyes before producing a wallet with a badge and identification card. "If you'd like to place a call to Washington, feel free to use my cell phone," he said mildly, shoving it across the table with the wallet. "As far as proof, I can tell you pretty much what Mr. Nbuku told you; that he was a member of the royal family, that he needed to get their money out of the country, that he needed help from an American citizen with an American bank account and that this benevolent person would be given a percentage of the money as a means of showing the appreciation of the royal family. Am I right so far?"

Duane didn't have to answer. His slack jaw and blank expression said it all.

"I have in my hotel suite a pile of evidence against Mr. Nbuku—that's just one of his aliases, by the way—and I'll be happy to show it to you any time you'd like to see it. By the way, did he mention which country he was fleeing? Was it Gambia or Ghana or Zaire? Because he changes countries the way you change shirts. Sometimes he's an ambassador, sometimes a prime minister, sometimes a prince; it just depends on his mark. Whatever story will work the best, that's the one he tells," the man said offhandedly.

He waited a few moments for the enormity of what he said to sink in for Duane. He hadn't bothered to ask the man a single question, hadn't asked him for an iota of proof, just went for it like a trout after a hand-tied fly.

The man leaned forward to impress his next words on Duane. "Mr. Carter, I've been looking for someone like you, someone who can help the government in its effort to stop this kind of scam. It's known as the Nigerian scam, the African scam; it goes by many names, all of them a slur on the continent because it makes it seems as though the African people are con artists when nothing could be further from the truth. There are just a handful of unscrupulous people conducting these kinds of scams but they've been spectacularly successful as there are people, not as astute as yourself, who get taken. Be that as it may, you're in a unique position to render your government a service and collect a reward. Not as sizeable as the percentage Nbuku offered you, but unlike that offer, this one is legitimate."

In less than a second, Duane asked the question the man knew was inevitable. "How much?"

When Ceylon initially told Martin that she would be in New York three weeks longer than planned, he was upset. Her original engagement was for four weeks, now it would be seven weeks altogether that she'd be away from Atlanta. It was great for her and the family; Bennie and Clay and then Malcolm and Selena would now have a chance to go visit and see the show. They would take turns on successive weekends so that each couple could babysit the other's children; they were too considerate of Bump and Lillian to ask them to handle all six children at once. And they were too conscientious as parents to allow just anyone to stay with their children; besides, their housekeepers needed the time off. A Deveraux household was not an easy one to manage. So the extra weekends were a boon for them, but a punishment for Martin, at least until he came to a decision that would change his life forever.

The weekend he'd spent with Ceylon included brunch at a tony restaurant in Tribeca, a spot where celebrities often appeared. Ceylon had been approached for autographs and she was too generous to refuse. Martin excused himself to wash his hands in the restroom while she chatted quietly with her fans. As he left the men's room he caught a snippet of conversation that caused his blood to run cold.

"So that's Ceylon Simmons, hunh? Damn she's fine! She looks way better in person than I thought," a man's voice grudgingly admitted.

A second voice chimed in, "Yeah but did you see what she was with? I thought she was in *Bubbling Brown Sugar*, not *Phantom of the Opera*! That is one scary man!"

The next sound Martin heard was the cackling laughter of the duo. He refused to turn around and look at them, for fear of what his reaction would be. He made his way back to the table and hoped that his face didn't reveal what he felt at the moment. Luckily, the radiance of Ceylon's welcoming smile made him forget what he'd heard. He'd had almost nine years to get used to people's reactions to his face; he couldn't let things like that bother him. They finished their meal in peace and enjoyed the rest of their time together until Martin returned to Atlanta.

But the incident bothered him more than he liked to admit; not for his sake, but for Ceylon's. He knew that she was the woman he wanted to spend the rest of his life with, and he was damned if she'd have to go through the rest of her life shackled to an ogre. Ceylon thought he was beautiful, but Ceylon, bless her heart, saw beauty in everyone. The fact that she loved him to distraction blinded her to his obvious imperfections. The one thing he knew was that he loved Ceylon with all his heart, loved her enough to do something he'd never considered before, but would do for her sake, for their sake. Which is why he picked up the phone as soon as he got back to Atlanta.

He dialed a number in Detroit and was soon speaking to Bennie's best friend and sister-in-law, Renee. After engaging in small talk and inquiring after her four little girls, he asked to speak to Andrew, her husband who just happened to specialize in reconstructive surgery. He explained to Andrew what he wanted and Andrew was more than happy to give him not only the information he sought, but some names and numbers, too.

"Well, Martin, it's not as difficult as you might imagine. Even though the accident was so long ago, there's no reason you couldn't have a prosthetic eye put in if you wanted to. If the eye socket wasn't too badly damaged and the muscles are intact, the eye will even move like your other eye; the muscles will control it. Even if the socket was badly damaged, a good oculist can design a cup that will fit right into the socket to cradle the prosthesis and it'll fit right in. And believe it or not, this is an outpatient procedure. You don't have to undergo surgery or anything like that; you go to an oculist for the procedure. I know a couple of ophthalmologists in your area who can hook you up."

Martin thanked him for the information and asked another question. "What about the scar, Andrew? Is there anything that can be done to remove it?"

Andrew assured him that there was. "I know the scar

looks bad to you, Martin, but you have to realize that it's faded over the years and it's not as prominent to the eye as you think. The fact is that it won't be completely gone, but the newer laser techniques can diminish it to the point where it's less noticeable, even to you. Normally the laser technique isn't recommended for African Americans, but your skin is so fair that it should be alright. The one thing you must do is go to a board certified plastic surgeon, not one of those plastic surgery mills. I know a brother in Atlanta who's an absolute genius. If you like, I can call in a favor and he can get you in sooner than if you made your own appointment," Andrew offered.

Martin accepted the offer with gratitude. "Listen, Andrew, can you kinda keep this under your hat? I, umm, haven't talked this over with anyone and umm, well, you know how that is," he said gruffly.

Andrew did indeed know. He knew from having flown to New York with Renee to see Ceylon perform that Ceylon and Martin were a couple. And he knew first hand that what Martin was planning could have some dire consequences.

"Okay, Martin, whatever you say. But take some brotherly advice if you will; talk to Ceylon. Don't spring this on her because she'll hate it if you do. I've learned from painful experience that the only surprises women like are in the form of something delightful like flowers and jewelry, not something drastic like this. Talk to her, man. You won't regret it," he advised.

After concluding the phone call, Martin did something he rarely did, which was to go to the mirror and remove his patch, staring at his reflection. He gently touched the spot where his left eye should be, then ran his fingers down the familiar jagged scarring. He examined the furrows that the patch made in his skin; they were dangerously close to being permanent. Just what he needed, more scars. He looked for long minutes and finally returned the patch to its resting place. Without another thought on the matter, he went to the telephone and dialed a familiar number.

Malcolm and Martin entered the sports bar together, drawing attention because of their height and good looks. After getting draft beers from the bar, they availed themselves of an empty pool table. Despite his injury, Martin could shoot a mean game of pool, something he demonstrated aptly by beating Malcolm three games in a row.

"Showoff," Malcolm muttered. "So, tell me, something, little brother, when are you making an honest woman of Ceylon? I know you love her, so when's the wedding?" The twins had been born five minutes apart and there was always a question of who was the older, since Lillian claimed she couldn't remember.

Martin didn't answer Malcolm immediately, he was too busy making another spectacular shot which sent three balls racing to their pockets.

"Soon. I'm waiting for the ring to come in, I've already ordered it. I'm not crazy enough to let a woman like Ceylon go, she's the best thing that's ever happened to me. In fact, that's kind of why I wanted to hang out tonight. I wanted to run something past you."

"Sure, like what?"

"Like I've decided to have the surgery. I've decided to get a prosthetic eye and do something about this scar," Martin said quietly.

Malcolm stared at his twin for a long moment before speaking. "Okay. If that's what you want to do, Marty. But why now, why after all this time? Has Ceylon said something to you about your appearance?"

Martin immediately denied the question, shaking his head at the censure in his brother's voice. "Oh man, no. Ceylon doesn't know anything about this! She happens to find me dashing, thank you very much. But I want to do this for her, if that makes any sense. I took a good long look in the mirror and there's really no reason for me to be walking around like this. I can look better; I can look pretty much the way I used to look, as a matter of fact. So I'm going to do it. Partly to look better for her, but mostly for myself, for my own ego," he said frankly.

"Look, I wasn't trying to imply anything about Ceylon, I know she's crazy about you. But you have to know that people are going to wonder, and ask questions and get all in your business about it. You know how people are," he counseled. "But if that's what you want to do, I'm all for it. When are you having it done and who's doing it and how do they do it? And I'm going with you," he added. "I've got to look out for my little brother."

Martin was so overcome with emotion by his brother's declaration that he didn't offer a rebut. "For the last time, I'm the oldest! There's a little brother in here for sure, but it ain't me, it's you. How many times do I have to tell you, I remember every detail of being born, including coming out first?"

The two men both laughed and kept the argument going as long as possible. It felt good to be friends again.

Ceylon was restless. It had been two weeks since she'd seen Martin, although they talked daily. He surprised her at the end of her second week of her original run and now she had three more weeks to be in New York. The actress whose place she was taking was due to be back in action after three more weeks of therapy for a badly pulled muscle obtained while horseback riding, and despite the fact that Ceylon was enjoying her role thoroughly, she wanted to be back in Atlanta. That was where her heart was, where she was starting to feel like home, despite the fact that she didn't have a physical home to call her own.

That might be changing any time though. Martin's detective, Titus Argonne, was going forward with his plan to wrest Ceylon's money away from Duane, and then he was going to drop the matter. Ceylon couldn't go through with having him arrested after all. That was a big topic of discussion with Martin before he went back to Atlanta and although he didn't agree with her, he understood her reasons and didn't fight her on it. He could see how important it was to Ceylon and instructed Titus to get the money and run, and that was it. Case closed.

So now it was a matter of having too much time on her hands. Once a show was in production, rehearsals ceased, so she didn't have the regular grind of daily practice to keep her occupied. She did voice exercises daily, following the precept that the first twenty years you make it on your talent, the second twenty you make it on technique. Bump taught her this and she followed the rule to the letter. Ceylon had no intention of being one of those singers who started to sound weak and pathetic because they hadn't trained their voices. She worked out in the hotel's gym on occasion, but the show was extremely physical and she got plenty of exercise in five performances weekly plus a matinee.

She wrote letters, she e-mailed, and she surfed the web on the computer in the suite, but there was no disguising the fact that she was bored, lonely for Martin and, about to go out of her gourd. She started going to the theater earlier and earlier, just to have people to chat with. The cast and crew had welcomed her with open arms, thank goodness, and she was getting closer to them as the days went by. Her co-stars, Joe Fuller, Henry Hall, and Nekeia Hankins, had become pals and she looked forward to seeing them everyday. She and Nekeia looked forward to their daily girl-talk.

Ceylon was staring intently at a calendar on the wall beside her mirror when Nekeia came in and flopped on the daybed.

"Look at you, counting the days until you get back to Martin, aren't you?" she teased.

"Yes I am," Ceylon admitted. "And until we get started on the soundtrack for *Idlewild*, I'm really looking forward to doing that," she added, eyes still fixed on the pages that had neat little X's in each box.

"Not as much as you're looking forward to getting back to that man," Nekeia said in an annoying singsong.

Ceylon gave the younger woman her full attention then. "Nekeia, did you know I used to be a hairdresser before Bump Williams discovered me? Do you know I have the power to make your hair leave your head without even touching you? Don't mess with me, woman!"

Nekeia grabbed her head full of wildly spiraling curls and shrieked. "Oh please! Girl, you know I was just playin', don't take my hair! I'm just sayin', if I had a man at home that fine I'd be dying to be with him, just like you are. Girl, the way he looks at you makes *my* toes curl, you hear me? Now, *that*'s a man!" she sighed.

Ceylon was about to toss a pillow at Nekeia's head when she stopped and clutched it to her heart. "He really is, Nekeia. But he has no idea that he's fine. None. And he really is the most beautiful man I've ever seen. It was love at first sight almost five years ago. There was something about him that made my insides quiver and God help me, every time I see him they do it again. I don't want him to change one single thing for me, I just love him the way he is from head to toe," she confessed.

Nekeia looked at the glow on Ceylon's face and sighed. "Now that's true love," she said sagely.

"Well, it's not just the way he looks, of course, although I do love that," Ceylon hastened to add. "It's everything about him. He's kind, considerate, protective, sometimes a little *too* protective. He's had a lot to deal with and he did it almost heroically. I admire him tremendously because of the way he handles himself. He's not perfect, far from it, but he's perfect for me. Every day in every way I feel like we're getting closer and closer. Now *that's* true love. I wouldn't change a thing about it."

Andrew's recommendation helped Martin get an appointment with Dr. David Whitney, Atlanta's preeminent plastic surgeon. It usually took months of waiting to get in to see him, but due to his friendship with Andrew, he was able to work Martin in, albeit after regular office hours. Martin didn't mind the lateness of the hour. He was just grateful that the doctor was able to work him in, which he told him after entering the examining room.

Everything about David Whitney was bigger than life; he was tall, broad, loud, and friendly, and had some of the biggest hands Martin had ever seen. Martin was wondering how the man managed to create such miracles with those big hands when the doctor noticed him looking at them.

"Checking out the bear paws, huh? Yeah, well, you're not alone. Everybody wonders how I do it and I can only tell you that I have a gift for it. When I was in medical school people used to make fun of my hands and said I should be anything but a surgeon because my hands were so big. Then when I did my surgical rotations they said I should be anything but a plastic surgeon because I couldn't do the delicate work. My hands were too clumsy, see?" His eyes twinkled as he told the story.

"But for some reason, everything they said I couldn't do I excelled at. I never paid any attention to anybody's assessment of my skill; I was used to that. Everybody took one look at me and just knew I was a big scholarship jock, a football player. When they found out I was a pre-med major with a music minor, they just laughed. But I'm doing what I wanted to do and I guess if I were keeping score, I'd be having the last laugh. Now let's take a look at that scar," he said, angling a light down to better examine Martin's face.

After long moments of scrutiny, David asked Martin some questions about the kind of results he was hoping to get from the surgery, and about the previous treatments he used. He perused Martin's medical records, which had been sent to his office earlier.

"There are several ways to remove a scar. If a scar is very deep, we actually go in with a knife and remove it, remove the underlying tissue and close it up, leaving a hairline mark which will, we hope, disappear after normal healing. If it's extremely deep, we use a combination of excision and sanding—dermabrasion to you. After the first surgery we inject the site with saline to make it hard, and in a second procedure we sand it down. Sometimes if the scar isn't too deep, we just sand it down and improve the appearance of the affected area.

"Of course, we also use lasers these days. A lot can be accomplished with lasers, especially when the scarring isn't too deep. Normally the use of laser and sanding on African Americans is discouraged because of the pigmentation in our skin. You run the risk of removing the top layer of skin where the melanin is and you're left with light patches on the skin. But your skin is fair enough that it won't be a problem. And that scar, while prominent, isn't deep; there's no keloiding there at all. I think you'll be a perfect candidate for laser surgery, which can be done as an outpatient. I think I might keep you overnight just because I can, but that's it. Any questions?"

Martin did have a few questions for the doctor, mostly about the timing of the surgery. "Doctor, I'm also having a prosthetic eye put in. Should I have the eye done first or the scar? Does it matter? And how quickly will my face heal?"

Pleased that Martin was asking such intelligent questions, David was more than happy to answer him. After giving Martin the answers he desired, he explained about scheduling.

"I'll have my scheduling nurse call you tomorrow and

we'll try to get you in when there's a cancellation. Normally you'd have to wait a few months, but any friend of Andrew Cochran is a friend of mine. He's helped a brother out more times than I can count. Nothing I wouldn't do for Andrew. Okay, so you'll hear from my office in a few days. Just be ready to come in on maybe one day's notice, okay?"

"Not a problem. And thanks for everything, Doctor."

The group gathered in the hotel suite were diverse, to say the least. They looked like graduate students conducting a study session, except for the extreme concentration on their faces and the fact that a few of them were older than most students. The three men and one woman were seated on the sofa and chairs that decorated the suite, and one man sprawled on the floor, but all eyes were directed towards the man who was speaking.

"Okay folks, this is the last step in the process, so let's make sure we've got it down pat," Titus Argonne said with a deceptive mildness. Although Titus was an investigator, he was nothing like the larger-than-life characters depicted in movies and novels. He was low-key, professional, and extremely good at what he did. His staff shared the same attributes and he knew he could rely on them completely, but he liked to have all his ducks in a row before making a major move like the one they were about to undertake.

Joseph Nbuku, real name Jason Norris, removed his glasses and pinched the bridge of his nose. "Tomorrow morning Duane Carter and I will board a plane to Miami. We will go to the main branch of the Biscayne Bay Bank where Carter will open a bank account and have the funds from his Cayman account transferred there in a wire transfer that should take about one hour to complete. After the transfer is complete, he will give me his passcode and account number and I will initiate a wire transfer of the funds from the royal family. While this is being done, you, Titus aka Thomas Allen, will

arrive on the scene to arrest me and take me into custody."
Jason recited this with the slightly blasé air of an honor student who's accustomed to getting straight A's.

Titus nodded his head briefly, and then surprised everyone by crumpling a piece of paper and hurling it at Jason. "Don't sound so bored, Buddy. And stick to the script this time. It was supposed to be two million pounds sterling, not seven. Ad-libbing at this point can cost us big!" he reminded the young man.

Everyone laughed, including Jason, who tried to defend his decision. "Oh man, you're not going to let me forget that, are you? I told you, man, Carter is just greedy. The more money I talked about, the more eager he was to get involved. I'm talking about the royal family and he never asked me what royal family. Royal could have been their last name for all he knew! But I won't do it again, I swear."

"That's the nature of con artists. They're greedy and their greed always works for us. Just remember, boys and girl, nobody can get scammed unless they let their greed get the better of them. If they can be convinced they're getting something for nothing, the con has found his mark.

"So after the bogus wire transfer, you two burst in with me and we 'arrest' Jason and haul him out of there. Then we arrange a transfer back to the Caymans for the one and a half million we've convinced Carter he's going to get for aiding his country's government. Only this time the money is going back to its rightful owner, the sister who he stole it from in the first place. The funds will be available for her to retrieve within forty-eight hours and by the time Carter figures out the money isn't there, there won't be anything he can do about it."

Titus looked at his watch. "I'd suggest everybody turn in because we've got a couple of early flights tomorrow. We'll rendezvous at the usual place in Atlanta when this is all over and if it goes as well as I think it will, we'll have something to celebrate. Be careful tomorrow and do pretty. A very nice lady is counting on us."

Chapter Fourteen

As the fateful flight from the Caymans was preparing to leave for Florida, another plane was headed to Georgia. Ceylon was so excited she could barely contain herself. She was on her way back to Atlanta at last. The original lead of *Bubbling Brown Sugar*, Geneva Malik, had fully recovered from her injuries and was itching to get back to work. The cast and crew had a lovely going away party for her and she was finally able to bid adieu to New York and head home to the man she loved and the friends who felt like family. She'd checked all her luggage through to Atlanta, so when she got off the plane she headed for the baggage claim area immediately. This was where Martin would be meeting her. *Martin*. She'd missed him more than she thought possible. When she got her hands on him, she wouldn't be responsible for what happened that night. *And it's going to be a long, long night*, she thought happily.

She began looking upwards, scanning the baggage claim area for her first sighting of Martin, when she glimpsed, to her surprise, Malcolm. She waved uncertainly and walked towards him with a question on her lips.

"Malcolm, what happened to Martin? Why isn't he . . ." the

words died on her lips as she realized that the man in front of her, the man with no patch and two eyes, *was* Martin.

She immediately fell into a dead faint, to be deftly caught by Martin before her body could hit the ground.

"Didn't see that one coming," Martin muttered to no one in particular.

A few hours later, Ceylon was seated at the work island in Martin's kitchen waiting for the teakettle to boil. She was uncharacteristically quiet, not really trusting herself to speak. Once she'd gotten over the initial shock that Martin had put in a prosthetic eye without saying a word to her, she had the secondary shock of seeing a totally different man in front of her. He just didn't look like her Martin any more; the man she beheld was a stranger. There was something about seeing her beloved with two long lashed brown eyes that was distinctly unsettling to her.

The eye didn't look false; on the contrary, it actually moved when the other eye did, which at first made her feel a little strange in the stomach. Surprisingly, though, she got used to the movement of the eye rather quickly. If someone didn't know Martin, they would have no idea that the eye was prosthetic; it looked very natural. And therein lay the problem, at least part of it. Ceylon *did* know Martin intimately, or at least she thought she did. Apparently not, if he could spring something like this on her. They tried making small talk, which failed miserably. Finally, Ceylon asked how the family felt about the new Martin. He shrugged and gave an offhand answer. "They're every bit as thrilled as you are. I'm taking Satchel for a walk." Without another word, he left the house.

To tell the truth, Martin was as uncomfortable with Ceylon as she was with him. He supposed she was upset because he hadn't confided in her. Well, she'd have to get in line for that, since almost everyone else in the family was behaving oddly, with the exception of his twin. Ironically, Malcolm was the only person Martin confided in regarding the impending surgery and the prosthetic eye. And Malcolm understood completely, hadn't tried to dissuade him, hadn't acted overly excited about it, just agreed to accompany him to the oculist. Malcolm was also beside him when he got the initial reactions from the family, which seemed to run the gamut from shock to surprise to more shock. The most touching response had been from his niece, Amariee.

She sat next to him at the breakfast room table at Lillian's house and looked him over carefully. They were alone at the time, and she him asked several intelligent questions about the procedure, questions that might have been discouraged had another adult been present. Her main concern was whether his new eye hurt him or not. He also told her that he was going to have his scar removed in a couple of weeks. To his utter surprise she reached over and touched his scarred cheek.

"You know, Uncle Marty, when we saw you in the hospital we cried because you were hurt so bad, not because you scared us. We loved you, Uncle Marty, and we still do," she said solemnly.

The thought of that scene still put a lump in his throat. The scene with Ceylon, well that was another story altogether. She hadn't yelled at him or berated him, yet; but the way she looked at him, like he was a lab specimen or something, that was something he wouldn't forget in a hurry. He and Satchel continued their walk; he really wasn't ready to face more of Ceylon's obvious revulsion just yet.

In the meantime, Ceylon was in the middle of a conversation with Lillian. The older woman called to see how things were going; she had a pretty good idea that Ceylon would be a bit shocked right about then.

Upon hearing that Martin was out with Satchel, she took the opportunity to gently probe Ceylon's state of mind. "All right, dear, you can tell me. How do you like the change," she wanted to know.

Ceylon sighed deeply. "Well, Lillian, I was stunned at

first. Absolutely stunned, to the point of passing out cold when he came to pick me up at the airport. Really pretty, that was. Poor Martin goes out of his way to avoid scenes and I seem to get him caught up in them every other day or so," she said with a strained laugh. She was quiet for a minute, and then spoke again, this time with assurance.

"I've been sitting here trying to figure out why I'm so uncomfortable with this, Lillian, and it comes down to me being a big spoiled brat because he didn't say anything to me first, like he had to ask my permission or something. This doesn't have anything to do with me; it has to do with Martin and how he feels about himself and I need to be supportive of him and not critical. In a way it's like him getting *his* own back, like I've been whining about getting *my* own back. You know, all this time I've prided myself on not being a diva, but when I'm not getting all the attention, look out, I just get my big butt all up on my shoulders, don't I?" she said with evident shame.

Lillian laughed. "Oh, sweetheart, no one thinks that! It's just that no one knew anything about it except Malcolm and he kept his brother's business to himself. Angelique, well, she just burst into tears and ran out of the room, so who knows what she's feeling, I've never been able to figure out my only daughter," Lillian said with a sigh. "Bennie and Clay were wonderful, of course, but it's been one bizarre reaction after another, believe me. After eight, almost nine years of wearing a patch, he suddenly has an eye and nobody can figure out why he suddenly jumped up and did it. You know Martin. I can't think of anyone who's more private than he is. This is like putting his business all out on front street for the whole world to see and I know it's bothering him, but he's so stoic . . ." Lillian murmured softly.

"Well, sweetheart, as long as he has you on his side everything will be okay. I've told you before how good you are for Martin, I'm so glad you're in his life," she said sincerely.

After she and Lillian ended their call, Ceylon felt her

eyes fill with hot tears of shame. It had finally dawned on her why Martin did something he'd shown no inclination to do since the accident. He'd done it for *her*; he wanted to look his best for her, he wanted to erase any trace of the accident for her. He'd endure any amount of gossip, rude questions and stupid remarks just for her. To say she felt humbled was a gross understatement. Ceylon felt just terrible. She suddenly stirred, rising to empty the cup of now cold water and pouring another cup of hot from the still steaming kettle. She was sipping it when Martin and Satchel came in from their long walk.

Martin observed her sipping the weird beverage and commented that she and Bump were the only two people in the world he'd every seen drink hot water for pleasure. Ceylon smiled wanly and admitted she'd done it since she was a young girl. "Don't know why, actually. It soothes me somehow."

She looked at Martin, who stood with his hands in his pockets looking uncomfortable. She cringed inwardly, knowing she'd done that to him. She thought about how awkward it had to be for him at The Deveraux Group, suddenly walking in without his patch. How many questions and comments and stares he must have gotten and how he'd just taken it, day after day, hoping that when she came back she'd be understanding, his oasis in a desert of discomfort. And what had she done? Clowned, big time, then sulked like a spoiled, selfish diva.

She took a quick, deep breath and resolved to make it up to him for the rest of his life if he let her. She carefully put her cup in the sink, then walked over to Martin and put her arms around his waist.

"Let's go upstairs, my darling. I have so many things to say to you and we need to be as close as humanly possible when I tell you how very much I love you and how very much I regret my behavior of today. Will you come with me?" she entreated.

Martin looked into her eyes, under long lashes starred with tears. He saw so much love in her face that the love he felt for her intensified to a degree that made his heart pound erratically.

"Absolutely, baby," was all he said, but there was a wealth of meaning in the words.

They held hands tightly they climbed the stairs to the upper level of the house, neither one saying a word. They entered the large bedroom and stood looking at each other for a long moment. Finally Ceylon spoke. "Let's get ready for bed, shall we?"

They showered together and did all the little things couple normally do when preparing for slumber, but sleep wasn't what Ceylon had in mind. She had Martin sit naked in the middle of the bed while she retrieved a bottle of lightly scented massage oil purchased from The Body Shop. She climbed into the bed with the aid of the little set of steps he'd thoughtfully provided for her and got behind him in a kneeling position. She applied a small amount of the oil on Martin's broad shoulders, then handed him the bottle. Using her small, capable hands, she proceeded to rub the oil across his shoulder, wincing inwardly as she felt the tension in his taut muscles. Slowly, under her loving care, she began to feel the tension ebb away from his body and she began speaking.

"Martin, I owe you a tremendous apology, my darling. There was no excuse for my behavior, none whatsoever. I had no right to act as though you'd committed some kind of crime against humanity, like you'd done something to deliberately hurt me. It's not about me; it's about you and I should have been more understanding of that fact," she murmured as she stroked his hard, muscular back. She continued to stroke with one hand as she reached for the oil with the other hand. Pushing him slightly to indicate that he should lie down on his stomach, she straddled his body so she could finish the massage.

"My darling, as long as I've known you, you've never

shown me anything but kindness and consideration, and the one time I had a chance to show you some of the same, I demonstrated nothing but selfishness. I'm ashamed of myself, and very, very sorry," she murmured, but the softness of her voice wasn't enough to disguise the catch in her voice. Martin had taken all he could.

He rolled over suddenly and grasped Ceylon's upper arms. "Look, that's the woman I love you're talking about and I ain't having it," he growled. He gave her a playful shake, and then enfolded her in his embrace. "Butter, I appreciate what you're saying, baby, but there's no need to say it. If I had handled this better, you would have been better prepared for it. But honest to God, Ceylon, I couldn't think of a single way to do it that would've been any easier, so to hell with it, I just did it. I promise to try not to spring things on you in the future if you promise to not take it personally when I do. Because I'm bound to screw up at some point. I know me very well," he said dryly.

Ceylon continued to stroke his big body while she cuddled against him, listening to the sound of his deep, soothing voice. "Martin, I love you. You've got to know that whatever else might happen, that's not going to change. Not now, not ever. We're learning about each other and we're bound to make some mistakes along the way. But as long as we try to understand each other and talk things out, we'll be fine, don't you think?" she turned her face toward his as she spoke. "And is 'Butter' your new pet name for me?" she asked with amusement.

Martin held her for a long moment, loving the feeling of her softness against his body. "Yes, baby. As long as we communicate with each other, we'll be fine. For example, I want you to know that I think you have on too many clothes," he said seductively as he tugged at the bath sheet she'd wrapped around her body after their shower. "And hell yeah, you're *my* Butter," he growled.

Ceylon gave him one of her throaty chuckles as she

pointed out that it was a towel, not clothing in the strictest sense of the word. Martin gave her a look that said he didn't care what it was, he just wanted it off, and she was happy to comply, undoing the offending wrap and preparing to toss it aside. Martin stopped her from discarding it by spreading it out on the bed, to Ceylon's puzzlement. It was Ceylon's turn to be directed as Martin asked her to turn over on her stomach. He then applied the same massage oil to Ceylon's back and began to caress and knead every inch of her body until she felt as relaxed and supple as he did, but not so relaxed that the feeling of his hands on her body failed to create an aching neediness that only he could relieve.

When he started giving all his attention to her derriere, the sensual onslaught became too much. His hands cupped and caressed her silken flesh, creating a heat that could only be extinguished in one way, fondling the luscious twin globes until she moaned aloud.

"Martin!"

Martin didn't stop in his adoration of that particular part of her anatomy; he got even more creative as he licked each adorable dimple and kissed both cheeks. Ceylon cried aloud as his lips caressed her. She felt so hot and aroused she thought she might burst, especially when one hand slipped under her undulating body to grasp a sensitized breast, and the other one slid down her buttocks into her most feminine part, the part that craved his touch desperately.

Ceylon bit into the end of the towel to keep from screaming out loud, and Martin finally relented.

Slowly releasing her so that he could don a condom, he quickly returned to her shivering body, hovering over her until she could feel his heat. "Scoot up, Butter, and grab the headboard, we're going to try something different," he whispered in her ear. Ceylon's eyes widened, but she did just that. Grasping the headboard tightly with both hands she found herself kneeling on the firm mattress with Martin holding her around the waist. He entered her from his straddling po-

sition, very slowly at first, with the tempo increasing as
Ceylon adjusted to the new position. At her first cry of passion, Martin plunged more deeply, his hands moving up her
body to caress her aching breasts then slide down to hold her
hips, bringing her even closer to him. Their bodies pumped
in a wild, frenzied rhythm until Ceylon began to shudder
from the force of the orgasm that rocked her. Martin ground
his body against hers until the last wave had consumed them
both, then gently turned her in his arms until she was lying
on her back, sighing with contentment.

He pulled her into his embrace once again; kissing her
with a wildness she'd not experienced with him, but one she
relished, matching his tongue stroke for stroke and grinding
against him as she felt him entering her again. The sex was
hot, passionate, and wild, and it seemed to go on forever.
Martin couldn't stop plundering her body and she wouldn't
let him stop. Finally, complete exhaustion made them fall
into each other's arms, totally sated. The room was a mess,
the pillows and bedclothes were everywhere, the original
Thomas Blackshear painting over the bed was crooked, and
both of them struggled mightily to draw a normal breath.
Neither one of them could speak for a long time; finally
Martin raised his head to mutter, "Baby. Ceylon, that was . . .
good."

Ceylon opened her eyes to behold that wreckage around
them and smiled. "Yes, Martin, it was. Let's do it again . . .
tomorrow," she whispered and immediately fell into the
deepest sleep she'd had in years.

The next morning Ceylon managed to wake before Martin,
who was sleeping the sleep of a very satisfied man. She squinted
around the room in wonder; it looked like the WWE Smack-
down had taken place in there. She dangled her feet over the
side of the bed, looking in vain for the little set of steps
which had gotten kicked against the wall during their loving.

Shrugging, she hopped out of the giant bed and began setting the room to rights. She slipped on a summer weight robe and fluffed the pillows, putting them back in place; Martin was so dead asleep she could lift his head and drop it and he never moved. She retrieved the linens and covered Martin with a sheet; everything else was going into the laundry. To her amusement, Satchel peeked around the doorway as if to ask what the heck had happened in the usually perfectly ordered room.

"Stay out of grown folks' business, Satchel. You want to go out?"

Naturally he did, so Ceylon took a very speedy shower, dressed in jeans and a white T-shirt of Martin's, and took him for a stroll. When they returned, Martin was still dead asleep, so Ceylon decided to make him breakfast in bed. She made a fluffy mushroom and cheese omelet, crispy bacon, and whole grain toast, and cut up a couple of kiwis and added some big yellow Mt. Rainier cherries, which she thoughtfully pitted and sliced in half for easy consumption. She mixed the fruit and added a few drops of lime juice and a drizzle of honey, giving it one last stir. She placed the fruit in a pretty little glass dish, and then arranged everything on a big tray. As she poured coffee into the thermal carafe she found in the pantry, she suddenly realized this was a heavy load to be toting up the steep stairs of Martin's house. Just then, Martin made his appearance in the kitchen, hair damp from the shower, clad exactly like Ceylon right down to the bare feet.

His face lit up when he saw the wonderful breakfast and took in the sight of his lover looking as appetizing as the meal. He immediately kissed her good morning and sat down on one of the tall stools around the work island, pulling her between his legs for a long embrace. "Oh baby, last night was . . . look, I'm gettin' old, we can't be doing that every night," he moaned.

Ceylon laughed merrily and put her arms around his

neck. "If you're an old man, I'm a skinny woman! But last night was . . . umm . . . *umm*," she sighed as she tried to come up with an adequate phrase. "Last night was exceptional, just like the exceptional man I love," she said quietly. They kissed, again, softly and tenderly. She pulled out of his embrace abruptly and informed him he had to eat while the food was hot. "In fact, let me nuke it for a minute," she said worriedly.

Martin assured her it was fine and picked up the tray and carafe. They went into the atrium to eat at a small glass topped table with beautiful, restful jazz pouring from the hidden speakers. After the wonderful meal, Martin asked what he could do for Ceylon to repay her thoughtfulness. She didn't hesitate a moment with her answer.

"Sing for me, Martin."

Martin froze for a second, then gave Ceylon a sardonic look. "Oh, you think I won't do it, huh? Come on," he said, extending his hand. "I've got something for you."

They went into the living room and Martin retrieved an acoustic guitar from the array of stringed instruments displayed on the wall. Ceylon sat on one of the big leather sofas while Martin sat across from her, checking the tuning of the instrument. After a few preliminary chords, he began to play and sing. His song of choice was the classic "I Love You Just the Way You Are," immortalized by Billy Joel.

Ceylon's eyes widened in amusement at his the song he'd chosen—talk about ironic! However, her heart absolutely melted at the rich timbre of his voice. He continued to play and sing, this time choosing one of Ceylon's absolute favorites, a Portuguese love song called "Dindi." She was lost in the song of the lovely lyrics interpreted in Martin's deep, rich voice. After the song completed, she applauded sincerely and appreciatively.

"Lover, that was beautiful! Your voice is wonderful, Martin, just amazing! How is it that you and Malcolm and Marcus can sing but Clay can't?" she wanted to know.

Martin put the guitar aside and snorted. "Honey, Clay can better than any of us, he just doesn't let anybody *know* that little fact. I'll bet even Bennie doesn't know Clay can carry a tune," he said with amusement.

The phone rang and Martin reached for the cordless that was on the end table nearest him. He answered the phone and did more listening than talking for a few moments. After disconnecting the call, he changed sofas so that he was sitting next to Ceylon with his arm around her.

He looked at her for a long moment before speaking. "It's all over, Butter. They got Duane."

Chapter Fifteen

Bump looked at Ceylon, who gave every indication of being lost in her own little world. She sat perfectly still, staring at nothing in particular with a completely blank look on her face. They were nearing the end of another productive session of recording the music that would become the *Idlewild* sound track. While Bump was playing around with a new arrangement, Ceylon had wandered off into her thoughts, so much so that when she looked up, the studio was empty. She sat on a high stool in the recording booth, and Bump was seated at the control panel looking at her quizzically. She blushed, embarrassed at being caught daydreaming, then hastily left the booth to join her mentor. Sitting next to Bump at the console, she leaned her head on his shoulder and issued a sigh from a place deep within.

Bump immediately put his around her and gave her a fatherly squeeze. "What's troubling you, little girl? Things seem to be looking up for you these days, so why the long face?"

"You're absolutely right, Bump. Even after all that drama with the IRS and the Treasury department, my money is in the bank, thank you very much, and I don't owe anybody so much as a red cent. If I wanted to I could go out and buy a candy apple red Ferrari for cash, not that I want one," she added hastily. "But I do like knowing that I could. I can also buy a house of my very own. A place that's all mine with my stuff in it, in every single room from top to bottom, if that's what I want to do. But I don't think I'm going to do that, at least not yet. Martin's surgery is in two weeks and I'm going to keep staying with him until he's all healed," she said artlessly, and then blushed again, as she didn't want to flaunt her live-in status in front of Bump who was, after all, old enough to be her father.

He chuckled at seeing her reaction. "Look-a-here, y'all are grown folks. What you do and when and how you do it, that's your business. You'll be getting married anyway, so what's the difference. That's why you don't want to buy a house, you know where you'll be living pretty soon," he teased her.

Ceylon gave him an impish smile. "Well," she drawled, "he hasn't asked me yet, so I guess I'm going to have to pop the question myself if he doesn't get a move on. But you're right. I chased that man for almost five years; he'd *better* know we're gettin' hitched. If I had a daddy he'd be comin' after him with a gun," she laughed.

"So," Bump said, administering a small shake to Ceylon's shoulders, "what's bothering you?"

She was actually happy to unburden herself. Rising from the bench on which they sat, Ceylon idly paced around the floor as she told him the whole story of Duane's capture.

"This Titus Argonne, the investigator friend of Martin's, had set up a scam to lure Duane in. He had an associate pretend to be a con man and *he* pretended to be a Treasury agent trying to stop the scam. He promised Duane this big reward and of course Duane went for it. It all involved him coming to Miami to have these bogus funds transferred into an American bank, then transferred back to the Caymans in a different account. These two other employees of Titus Argonne's would pretend to arrest the guy who was playing the con artist, and when the smoke cleared, there'd be Duane thinking he had one point five million dollars in his Cayman account along with my money, when in actuality he had nothing. Zip, zero, zilch."

Ceylon looked up at Bump to make sure he was following the story. At his nod of affirmation, she continued. "That was as far as Titus was supposed to take it. I told him I didn't want Duane arrested; let the Lord take care of his punishment. I just wanted what was owed me, period."

At the look on Bump's face, Ceylon made a face of her own. "I know, I got the same lecture from Martin. But I had to go with my heart and I just didn't have it in me to be somebody's prosecutor," she said emphatically. "God, however, must have made His own decision about the situation because Duane got arrested big time, right there in Miami and it had nothing whatsoever to do with me. The nincompoop was involved with all kinds of dirty dealings, including a little money laundering, and the real Feds were waiting to pick him up on grand larceny and about a hundred other charges. Plus the fact that his organized crime connections are hot on his heels; there's several little things they'd like to discuss with him regarding certain financial matters. Word around the campfire is that Big Brother might be doing some hard time in the big house, or even go into the Witness Protection program. All of which is poetic justice, which was not caused by anything sanctioned by me. It took longer to get my funds back due to some unintentional red tape, but I'm free of that burden at last," she sighed. "Martin and I had a little tug of war when it came to paying for Titus Argonne's services, but I won that round. I paid for the man's services. It only seemed right," she said with satisfaction.

Bump, however, wasn't satisfied with her explanation, detailed though it was. He looked at her pointedly while he ticked off pointed on his long fingers. "The soundtrack is coming along beautifully. We're gonna have a big hit on our hand, believe me. You have some gigs coming up, including the Detroit Jazz Festival next week, your voice is better than ever, the fish are jumping, and the cotton is high, so what's troubling you, little girl?" Bump repeated in frustration. "You're telling me everything that's going right in your life but you're sitting around looking like somebody stole your dolly. Talk to me, child!"

Ceylon finally stopped wandering around the spacious studio and faced Bump. Making a droll little face she said in a barely audible voice, "My sister called me last night."

Hearing her sister Olivia's voice on the telephone had been nothing short of earth shattering for Ceylon. Since Duane's act of perfidy had cost her everything, she never heard from her sisters Olivia and Rochelle, or from her brother Kenneth. It was as though she served no purpose in their lives other than a checkbook, so when the source of their largesse was stolen, so did their use for her as a money source. When they stopped communicating with her it was a relief. How ironic that the phone would start ringing as soon as she got her finances back in order. That was her first thought upon hearing her sister's voice. Actually, that was the second thought; the first was how she'd managed to get Martin's private number. She wasted no time in asking Olivia that very question.

"Ceylon, honey, I work for the student loan people! They can track down anybody in the free world, trust me. I can get anybody's number if I put my mind to it, it's the nature of my job," she laughed. "Of course, I don't abuse that ability, it wouldn't be ethical."

"Excuse me, did you say you *work*?" Ceylon asked bluntly. The last time she'd seen Olivia, she was raising two truly bratty children sans father and living off the state in Section Eight housing. Ceylon realized how harsh she sounded and started to beg Olivia's pardon but to her shock, Olivia laughed.

"Yes, that's right, the original welfare queen is a working

woman. You know I had some college credits from here and there, I'd been to every C.C. in southeastern Michigan; Wayne County Community College, Macomb County Community College, you name a Community College, I had some classes there. I finally got tired of handouts, Ceylon. I wanted my children to be proud of me like they're proud of their Auntie Ceylon. I wanted them to see me get up and go to work every morning, so they would understand how to take care of themselves. After what Duane did to you, I felt so bad that I had to take a good hard look at myself and my life, and I didn't like what I saw. So I did something about it. I took all those ragtag credits and went to a private college that has a really good program of business administration. I went to school three nights a week and in eighteen months I had my bachelor's degree. I got financial aid to pay for it, plus I was able to work at the school part-time. And now I have a good job with benefits, I live in a nice little house that I'm buying, and my girls are as proud of me as they are of you," she finished. She had a smile in her voice that could not be disguised.

By now Ceylon's mind was reeling. This conversation was beyond unbelievable; it was like something off of one of those sappy made-for-television melodramas. This couldn't be real; Olivia had to be up to something. Before she could say something along those lines, Olivia went on:

"Look, Ceylon, Kenneth and I have been doing a lot of talking and we want to see you, if you're willing. I know you're going to be in Detroit for the Jazz Festival. We'd like to get together then, if you can put the bad feelings aside for an evening," she said humbly.

At this point, Ceylon took a deep breath and stopped meandering around in circles. She sank down into a chair and stared at Bump.

"Are you done," he asked with one thick eyebrow raised. "You're through walking in circles? 'Cause I have to tell you, you were making me dizzy, girl."

Ceylon smiled wanly.

"Come over here, Ceylon," Bump said and held out a hand to her. She sat down next to him and he put an arm around her. "Now look, you don't have to see these people if it's going to make you uncomfortable. Maybe everything she's saying is true, maybe she's exaggerating, maybe it's a big pile of . . . junk," he said, obviously struggling not to use a more pungent word. "But you won't know unless you go. And you don't have to go alone," he pointed out. " Lillian and I will be there, you know she won't let me out of her sight. Renee and Andrew are right there in Detroit. She'd be happy to run interference for you, if you like. She'll be glad to get out of the house from all those screaming little girls of hers. And I'm at least ninety-nine percent sure that Martin is going to the festival with you. It's not like he can let you out of his sight for more than thirty minutes. I'm surprised the man can go to work, the way he hovers all over you."

Having elicited the desired laughter from Ceylon, he continued in a more serious vein. "I didn't have the same experiences with my family that you did, Ceylon. I was real close with my brothers and sisters, and still am. They'll be here in about a month worrying the heck out of me like they do every year," he said in mock irritation. "But I don't know that I'd trade in a single one of them. Especially Elizabeth. She's my pet, always has been. And please don't tell the rest of 'em that. I'd never hear the end of it!" Bump rolled his eyes.

"What I'm trying to say, my dear child, in what my wife unfairly refers to as my rambling fashion, is that family does matter. If you can find it in your heart to make a relationship with them, it will make your life even sweeter," he said, giving her a hug and a kiss on the forehead. Of course, being Bump, he had to end on a comic note.

"Unless they try to steal, too. Then we'd just have to lock 'em up, put 'em in cement, and drop them in the Chattahoochee River, I don't know. Set 'em on fire or somethin', what do you think?"

Ceylon's only response was a burst of laughter. When all else failed, Bump could always make her feel better.

What Bump had to show Ceylon did more than cheer her up, however, it made her cry with joy.

"I've got something for you," Bump said quietly. "When I did this, I didn't know how and when I would return them to you, because of all that other mess. But I knew that this was something that shouldn't go out of your possession, you worked too hard for them."

With that he drew Ceylon across the room and opened a cupboard to reveal all of Ceylon's awards that had been confiscated and sold when the IRS seized her possessions. They were all there, her Grammys, her People's Choice Awards, her American Music Awards, everything. Ceylon was speechless, except for a soft sound of surprise.

"You worked too hard for these, Ceylon. I wasn't about to let them be taken from you," Bump said.

Those were the last words he spoke for a few minutes as Ceylon's arms went around his neck and she started thanking him for all she was worth.

"Oh, Bump, how can I ever thank you for this? This is the most wonderful thing anyone's ever done for me! Thank you a million times, Bump! I can never repay you for this, never," Ceylon wept.

"You don't have to pay me back, I did it because I wanted to," protested Bump. "And you can thank me by not crying all over my shirt, I swear you're just like my sister. Elizabeth will drown you in tears at the drop of a hat. If she's happy she's crying, if she's sad she's crying, if she's mad, well, if she's mad she'll hit you. You're not going to hit me if you get mad at me are you?"

Ceylon shook her head and continued to enjoy the happy tears. "I'm never going to get mad at you, Bump. Never in this world."

*   *   *

Right up until the evening before her departure, Ceylon had deeply conflicted feelings about going to Detroit. She wasn't exactly dreading the trip; she loved her hometown and looked forward to every opportunity to visit there. She was certainly looking forward to performing; every artist loves to get a chance to come home and put on a great show for people who knew them when. She was elated that she'd be performing with Bump; she loved nothing better than being onstage with him and his band. And traveling with Martin was something she anticipated greatly. They were going to stay in the Atheneum Hotel, the beautiful Greektown establishment that pampered its guests beyond comparison. No, the only thing that Ceylon was nervous about was the prospect of meeting with Kenneth and Olivia. Like Bump, Martin tried to convince her that she wasn't obligated to go. But her curiosity, plus the fact that she'd already agreed to do it, made it a moot point. She certainly appreciated his support, however, something she reminded him of the night before they left Atlanta for the trip to Detroit.

They were in the living room of Martin's home, listening to music and enjoying each other's company, snuggled together on one of the big leather sofas. Ceylon took a sip of the glass of Shiraz they were sharing and passed the glass back to Martin. As he took a swallow of the rich red wine, she stared at his profile, enjoying the little shiver that still stirred her whenever she looked at him. The smile of contentment on her face was so complete it made Martin comment.

"You look awfully happy," he observed. "What's putting that pretty smile on your face?"

"You are," she answered demurely. "Your love for me makes me extremely happy. To know that you're on my side no matter what, that makes me happy. To know that you'll take time out of your extremely busy schedule to be with me when I need the moral support, that just elates me. I'm more than happy; I'm content and fulfilled, and I feel very, very blessed that you're in my life, Martin. Thank you for loving me," she said and leaned into him for a kiss.

Martin returned her kiss, softly and tenderly, stroking her cheek and looking deeply into her eyes before speaking. "Don't ever thank me for loving you, Ceylon. I should be down on my knees every day thanking God that you came into my life. I was pretty much a mess before I met you Ceylon. I had a lot of bitterness in my heart, a lot of misery. And ever since the first time you danced with me, the first time I held you in my arms, there hasn't been any room for pain," he said slowly. "I was afraid to admit it for a long time, but from the first time I saw you, I knew you were someone special. I never told you this before, but every time I touched you, I felt warm all over. There was just something about your touch; it was like you were thawing me out. There was nothing but ice inside me, Ceylon, until you brought me back to life." As he continued, he wiped away the tears that were slipping from Ceylon's eyes with his thumb. He kissed away the moisture, and then touched her lips in a brief, warm caress before continuing. He brushed an errant curl from her forehead, then stood up to his full height and smiled down at her.

"Ceylon Simmons, you are the most vibrant, the most loving, most exciting woman I've ever known. Your beauty starts on the inside and radiates all around you until everything is more beautiful just because you're in the world. You're the only woman who's ever loved the person she knew was inside me, the only woman who's ever loved me just because I'm me. Ceylon, you're the only woman I've ever truly loved," he said solemnly.

Kneeling in front of her, he reached into the pocket of his slacks and pulled out a small black velvet box. "I can't even think about one day of the rest of my life without you, Ceylon. Will you marry me? Be my love for the rest of our lives?"

By this time the tears were running freely down Ceylon's

face. "Yes, Martin. It will be my pleasure to be your wife," she said through the tears. She placed her hands on his shoulders and kissed him tenderly, a kiss that deepened as her arms wrapped around his neck. They held each other tightly for several minutes before Martin realized that Ceylon hadn't seen her ring.

"Umm, Butter, I think I was supposed to show you this before you accepted," he said with a smile. "You might change your mind when you see it."

Ceylon released him from her embrace with great reluctance. She looked at the small box, then at Martin. "Open it, Martin! I can't wait," she admitted. The look on her face was one Martin would treasure for the rest of his life. He knew he'd never forget the look of absolute delight that transformed her visage. Ceylon's eyes were enormous, her mouth formed a perfect 'O' as she stared at the ring—a square, cushion-cut six carat blue white diamond surrounded by a double row of smaller stones in a deep topaz color, all set in magnificent platinum and eighteen karat gold setting.

Martin took the ring out the box and slid it on her finger. "Those are chocolate diamonds, Butter. It just seemed appropriate for you. Something new and exciting and rare, just like you," he said softly.

Ceylon sighed with happiness and slid off the sofa to join Martin on the floor. After adjusting his position so that she was sitting in his lap, he held her tightly as they both admired the ring's beauty.

"Martin, I had no idea I could feel like this," she murmured. Turning to look at him, she traced his jaw line with one finger and smiled. "I'm going to make you very, very happy, you know that, don't you?"

Martin grasped her hand in his and kissed her fingers. "Aw baby, you already do. You just don't know how much."

* * *

The first people to learn of Martin and Ceylon's engagement were Marcus and Angelique. Marcus was coming to
collect his nephew, as he irreverently referred to Satchel,
and Angelique was just along for the ride. Martin didn't like
leaving Satchel in a kennel when he was traveling; he hated
it as much as Satchel despised being there. With the aid of
much bribery, he was usually able to get Marcus to care for
Satchel when he was on the road. When Martin answered
Marcus's ring of the doorbell, he was pleased to see the two
of them. He was suddenly dying to tell everyone in the world
the news about him and Ceylon.

Ceylon was putting Satchel's favorite toys and his special
water and food dishes into a canvas tote bag when Martin
beckoned her come out of the pantry to join him and his siblings. The radiant look on her face told the whole story;
Angelique blurted it out before either of them could say a
word.

"You're engaged, aren't you?" she said, making it sound
more like an accusation than a cause for celebration.

Marcus immediately kissed Ceylon and hugged her
tightly, then pounded his brother on the back. He insisted on
champagne for a toast and he and Martin went to the refrig-
erated wine closet to find some. Angelique, in the meantime,
flounced off to the atrium. Ceylon uttered a brief prayer for
guidance and followed her.

Angelique's back was to her as she entered the room.
Ceylon said her name softly and to her utter shock, Angelique
turned around and gave her a tight hug. Her long lashes were
starred with tears, but she was actually happy, that was un-
deniable.

"I know everybody thinks I'm a bad-ass," Angelique
sniffed, "but I really do love my family. Martin needed
somebody *real* in his life, Ceylon, and I'm glad you never
gave up on him. I always knew you liked him, but I knew
you were the right person for him because of the way you

looked at him. You always just lit up whenever he came in the room; you still do, for that matter," she said in a teary voice.

"That hag he was with before, well, let's not even go there. You and Martin belong together. Just be happy, Ceylon. And have a couple of babies soon, please, my nieces and nephews are getting too grown." Angelique looked at Ceylon and burst out laughing. "You thought I was gonna tear your head off, didn't you? Thought I was gonna make one of my well-known scenes and say something really ugly, huh? Just goes to show you, you don't know everything about me," she teased.

While Ceylon went into a mild form of shock at Angelique's rather touching reaction to the news, Martin and Marcus were having a slightly different conversation in the kitchen, having fetched the champagne.

Martin watched his younger brother expertly work the cork out of the bottle with a minimum of noise; Marcus had been taught from his youth how to select wine, pour wine and how to uncork champagne properly. His older brothers had taken it upon themselves to teach him how to be a man of distinction with the correct social aptitude, as well as a serious code of conduct. After their father's death, the older Deveraux men took their role as guardians quite seriously. Marcus poured a small amount of the sparkling wine into two flutes and the two men raised their glasses in a salute.

"Congratulations, Martin. Ceylon is going to be a beautiful wife for you, man. You two are perfect together. She's a wonderful woman. I'm just amazed you had the sense to propose, I thought she was gonna have to rope you and drag you down the aisle kicking and screaming," he joked.

Martin shook his head. "Come on, man. Of course I was going to ask her to marry me. Do you think I'm completely crazy? Don't answer that," he said as he could see his brother's eyes light up with glee. "It was really special, Marcus. Scary, oh hell yeah, but it was nice. I was shaking like a leaf, which I hope she didn't notice. I made a beautiful speech, I gave her my heart and a very expensive ring and that's that. The wedding ceremony, that's a formality. I feel like we're married already," he said with satisfaction.

Marcus raised both brows in reaction to the unusual show of emotion from the normally reserved Martin. Martin laughed at the expression on his face.

"When you take the plunge, you'll know what I mean. Speaking of which, when are you gonna settle down? You're not getting any younger," he reminded him.

"Negro, please! I've just entering my prime, I've got plenty of time for that, if I choose to get married, which I do not," he emphasized. "There's only one woman in the world I'd ever want to marry and she's not available," he said with surprising fervor.

At Martin's inquiring look, Marcus sighed deeply and confessed. "Oprah won't return my phone calls," he said forlornly.

The two men collapsed in laughter, which is how Angelique and Ceylon found them when they entered the kitchen. Angelique looked at Ceylon and suggested she might want to reconsider. "Everybody in my family is nuts. Are you sure you want to do this?"

Ceylon went to Martin's side and accepted his embrace. "Oh, honey, nothing on earth could keep me away from this man," she vowed. The room suddenly seemed to be lit with a rosy glow from the reflected beauty of the smiles she and Martin bestowed on each other.

Chapter Sixteen

"There's nothing like being back home," Ceylon said with a contented sigh. So far the weekend held nothing but promise. The suite she and Martin shared at the Atheneum hotel in Greektown was world class. They'd turned down a gracious invitation from Renee and Andrew to stay in the Outhouse, the family name for the apartment over the garage of their Indian Village home. Lillian and Bump were more than happy to occupy the charming rooms, though. Andrew and Renee lived in the home that Bennie had owned before her marriage to Clay, although it was apparent they would have to seek larger quarters soon as their family was still growing. At the moment, Ceylon was in the big master bedroom of the house, chatting with Renee.

Renee Kemp Cochran looked much the same as she had before her marriage to Andrew with the addition of a serenity that had previously not been a part of her makeup. Having the calm, handsome Andrew as a mate seemed to bring out a side of Renee no one knew existed; that, plus the presence of her four little girls, three of whom were triplets. She didn't even have the decency to have put on weight after giving birth to four babies in two pregnancies, something Ceylon pointed out.

Renee just laughed it off, commenting that chasing after her lively daughters was enough to keep her in shape. "Honey, when you have a four-year-old and three in the terrible twos you keep busy! Valerie is managing Urban Oasis for me, and I'm seriously thinking about selling it to her."

She smiled at the incredulous expression on Ceylon's face. "Yes, I really mean it. Urban Oasis used to be my baby, but I got me some *real* babies now. My priorities have completely changed since I've become a wife and mother. I am more than happy to put my career on hold for a while," she admitted. "There's way too much to do around here."

This idea was underscored by the appearance of a tiny, winsome brown girl clad in charmingly feminine cotton underwear, dragging a party dress in one hand.

"This dress, Mommy. Not shorts, *this* dress," she said urgently.

Renee smiled patiently and ran her hand over little Stephanie's wildly curling mass of hair. "Sweetie, we're all going to wear play clothes today. Your pretty dress is for church, you know that. You and your sisters are all wearing shorts today, remember?" She turned back to Ceylon. "Before I forget, you didn't tell me how the fabulous Angelique reacted to the news that one of her precious brothers is getting married. Did she have another side door fit like she did with Bennie and Clay?"

Ceylon was happy to inform Renee that the change in Angelique over the past few years was remarkable. "Girl, she's like a different person now! She has a job for a change, she's working at The Deveraux Group as a photographer's assistant. She's really calmed down and matured. I swear, I think it's Bump that caused the change in her. She really acts like he's her father. Ever since he and Lillian got married, he's had a huge influence on her," Ceylon told her.

"Well shoot, wonders never do cease, do they? I was

ready to give that little heifer a good ol' Cleveland beat down when Bennie and Clay were engaged. What a piece of work she was!" Renee shuddered delicately, remembering the old Angelique. She stopped Stephanie from festooning herself with a long strand of freshwater pearls. "Wait a minute, sweetie. You see if Auntie Ceylon will comb your hair while I go get your outfit," she said as she left the room.

Ceylon held out her arms to the child who obligingly came to her and got settled on her lap while Ceylon began the process of gently combing the soft but extremely abundant hair. Renee returned shortly with a more appropriate outfit.

"All I can tell you, girl, is if you have more than one at a time, get a helper. Mrs. Madison is a Godsend, a retired nurse with more patience than Job," she said. Turning her full attention to Ceylon, Renee reminded her that she hadn't heard the entire story of the reunion with Kenneth and Olivia. "Well, how did it go? Don't keep me waiting, I don't often get to hear stories that don't involve princesses and fairies and talking cats and whatnot," she said with a laugh.

"I a princess," little Stephanie intoned.

"I *am* a princess," corrected Renee.

"No you not, you Mommie!" Stephanie squealed with delight.

Ceylon hugged the little girl and kissed her before beginning to speak.

"Well, it wasn't like anything I expected, Renee. Kenneth and Olivia came up to our suite at the Atheneum and we just stood there looking at each other for a minute or two, then Olivia and I broke down and started crying for some reason, then Kenneth got into the act, and we all just bawled for a while. Martin was really thrilled with this, as you can well imagine!

"Then Kenneth started talking. He apologized for all the times they mistreated me when we were kids, for the way they used to abuse me, basically. Then he apologized for the

214   *Melanie Schuster*

way they treated me as adults, about how they used to borrow money and expect me to do things for them just because I could. And they both admitted that a large part of it was Louise's influence," she added.

At Renee's quizzical look, Ceylon elaborated. "Louise is my mother's name. Louise Simmons Carter. I'm a Simmons because that's her maiden name and I was legally adopted by my grandparents," she reminded her. "Since I became an adult I can't think of her as anything but Louise. That's what I call her, too. It would be just too hypocritical for me to try to call her by any of the names you'd normally call a mother."

Ceylon had continued to brush and comb little Stephanie's hair and it was now an adorable arrangement of a big pouf on either side of a part down the center. Renee dressed her in the proper attire of a pink T-shirt and yellow and pink printed shorts with matching pink socks and yellow canvas sneakers, just minutes before an identically clad duo wandered into the room.

The other little girls came into the bedroom. One was named Benita for her aunt and the other was named Ceylon. After many kisses from the children, Ceylon tackled another head of hair while continuing the story.

"Renee, I have no idea what Louise's problem is, but I learned a few things. Such as, Olivia and Kenneth and Rochelle didn't fare any better than I did, really. For some reason, Duane was the only child for whom Louise had any love. She used to play the others against him, and certainly played them all against me. She used to lie to them that I hated them, that I laughed at them behind their backs and bragged that I had more than they did, which is why they were determined to destroy everything I had on the few occasions we were together," she said shaking her head sadly.

"And the big reason they never got in touch with me after Duane stole everything was that dear Louise informed them I wanted nothing to do with them. Just part of her full service . . . *witchery*," Ceylon laughed bitterly.

Renee combed little Ceylon's hair, trying to discourage Stephanie's help while listening to the tale.

"The thing is, Renee, both of them really have changed their lives. They don't see Rochelle too often; she's still out there living the life of a kept woman, apparently. She's hooked up with some big time crack dealer or something equally unsavory. But according to Olivia, seeing how I just kept on going after Duane took everything I owned made them both stop and examine what they were doing with their lives, and they both came to the conclusion that they needed to do better.

"Olivia is finished with school and has a good job and a nice home, and her girls have changed one hundred percent. They used to be the worst children in the world; I was actually scared of them, no lie! The little thug-ettes, they were Satan's handmaidens for real. Used to be bratty, loudmouthed, horribly behaved children! Now they're polite, low-key, well-behaved little ladies. Olivia and Kenneth both go to church every Sunday and participate fully in the activities, and honey, it's like talking to two different people! Kenneth is about to finish his student teaching, girl. My big brother is going to be a teacher!"

Ceylon's delight in the change in her siblings was evident. "Anyway, we had a big cookout at Olivia's house that night and it was just wonderful. Kenneth has a lovely girlfriend, who has two children of her own, and he now has partial custody of his two from that girlfriend of his, the 'babymama' he never got around to marrying. And Olivia has a nice boyfriend, I mean a *really* nice guy. A big, handsome guy named Jimmy, he works at Rouge Steel. Smart, too; Olivia says he's working on a master's degree for when he retires. He wants to teach history."

Finishing little Benita's hair, Ceylon beamed at her, and then gave her and her sisters more big kisses.

"Bump was absolutely right, Renee. I really did owe it to myself to meet with them; it surpassed anything I could have imagined. Just think, I have family again. Not that you and Bennie and everybody aren't my family—it's not that. But to think that I can actually have a relationship with my brother and sister, that's kind of overwhelming. Martin is very happy, too. I think he really enjoyed himself at the cookout."

Renee's oldest, Andrea, made an appearance then, fully dressed in a yellow T-shirt with little pink overall shorts that were sprinkled with white daisies. Mrs. Madison had combed her thick black hair, which was arrayed in two long twisted ponytails on either side of her winsome, dark face, identical to her mother's, right down to her large golden eyes.

"Look, Aunt Ceylon! Look what I did!" she exclaimed.

Sashaying behind her were the true divas of the household, the little black terriers, Patti and Chaka, adorable tiny dogs that Andrew had given Renee while they were dating. One was adorned with a big pink bow around her neck; the other was wearing an equally large yellow one.

"Well, Andie, they look . . . lovely," Ceylon said. "Do they like wearing those things?" she asked, concerned for their comfort.

Renee sighed and shook her head. "Those two will let her get away with anything. They seem to feel like the girls are their puppies or something. Okay, is everybody ready?"

The little girls were indeed spanking clean, beautifully attired and coiffed and ready to greet their public.

"Oh, you ladies look lovely!" Ceylon wished she had a camera to capture their charm.

"Yes, and it only took three grown women, two dogs, and two and a half hours to get them into that condition," Renee laughed. She looked at Ceylon with a smile. "Try to have them one at a time, honey; you'll get more done that way. Okay girls, let's go," she urged as they started down the stairs.

Babies . . . Martin's babies. Ceylon's eyes widened and it hit her for the first time that by this time next year, she could have a baby or two of her own, since twins ran in Martin's family. *But not in mine, thank goodness! I don't know if I can handle two-fers.*

While Ceylon and Renee caught up on the latest events of their lives, Martin and Andrew were sequestered in Andrew's study. Partly to talk about all that had happened most recently, and partly so that Andrew could give Martin's scar a good going over. The surgery would take place the next week and Andrew wanted to make sure that Martin was fully prepared for what would transpire.

"So, Martin, how do you really feel about the family reunion? I know Ceylon was all excited, but are you okay with it?" Andrew asked.

Martin was both surprised by Andrew's perception and relieved to be able to express himself to a fairly neutral party. "Well, it's like this. I pride myself on having a good nose for BS, and I have to say they seemed completely sincere. It was like something off that women's cable network, a lot of crying and I'm sorry and we were wrong, blah-blah-blah. I will say that compared to the way they *were* living, both her brother and sister have cleaned up their acts. The important thing is that Ceylon absolutely believes in their sincerity, which is what I pointed out to Kenneth when he and I had a moment or two alone," Martin gave a lethal smile as he recalled the conversation.

He and Kenneth had been minding the grill when Martin, noticing that they were alone in the spacious yard, pointed something out to Kenneth. "Your sister, my fiancée, is the most important person in my life. There is never going to be a time that anyone is going to hurt her as long as I'm alive, you understand?"

Kenneth looked Martin directly in the eye, something Martin appreciated. "Look, you obviously don't know anymore about me than the man in the moon," Kenneth had said quietly. "For that matter, Ceylon doesn't really know me and

Olivia, not since we gave it up to God and started living our lives right. We did that girl a lot of wrong in her life, and we're truly grateful for the opportunity to be part of her family again. There's no way we would ever try to harm her in any way. You have my word on it."

He stopped speaking for a moment, then took another swallow of Faygo's RedPop, the soda of choice for backyard barbecues throughout Detroit and the strongest beverage he now consumed. He then looked Martin full in the face yet again. "But Martin, we're not the enemy. *Louise's* the one you need to watch out for."

Martin stopped in his reverie, distracted by the sounds of feminine invasion. Andrew immediately went to work, commenting that they would all be leaving for brunch at his father's house momentarily. He gestured to Martin to sit in a wing chair near the window, and turned on a small table lamp with a high intensity halogen bulb. Angling the lamp so that he could get an unobstructed view of Martin's face, Andrew gently and thoroughly examined the scarring. When he was done, he turned off the lamp and nodded.

"Martin, I told you that David Whitney is one of the best plastic surgeons in the country, and he is, besides being a good man and a good friend. This is going to be a textbook case for him. You don't keloid, the scarring from the second-degree burns isn't deep enough to require excision and your skin is fair enough that you're not going to have a permanent discoloration to replace the scar. Plan on taking a few days off from work because there will probably be some redness and seeping after the procedure. Just take it easy and let Ceylon wait on you for a few days. I'm sure it'll be a real hardship, but you can handle it," Andrew said with a laugh. "I think you'll be pleased with the results, Martin. The procedure should make the scar all be undetectable."

Just then the door to the study entered and the dark, satiny smooth face of Renee looked in. "Okay, the caravan is loading up, are you gentlemen ready?" she asked gaily.

Andrew immediately answered in the negative. "You haven't given me my morning kiss," he reminded her. "I don't leave the house without one, you know that."

"Oh. Well maybe I can remedy that," she smiled.

Martin beat a discreet retreat and went in search of a kiss of his own. He found Ceylon on the deck in conversation with Bump and Lillian with two of the triplets on her lap and little Andrea leaning on the arm of her chair. Martin smiled as he realized that this time next year her lap could be full of their baby. *Better yet, babies, plural . . . maybe that twin thing will work for us,* he thought with glee.

Ceylon's performance at the legendary Detroit Jazz Festival was the hit of the entire show. Hart Plaza is home to the many music and ethnic festivals that take place from late spring to early fall in Downtown Detroit, and the Jazz festival is definitely one of the most popular. Detroit's reputation as a musical city is well earned; during the summer it's possible to enjoy everything from true Detroit techno, gut bucket blues, country, hip-hop, R&B, and jazz from some of the biggest headliners in the business. And when the performers had roots in Detroit, the crowds are always extra appreciative, showing the homefolks all kinds of love. It was no exception when Ceylon took the stage. In fact, the audience's reaction to seeing their homegirl verged on hysteria.

Ceylon took the stage wearing a vibrant red dress created just for her. It was supple silk jersey and deceptively simple, a long sleeved confection that was off the shoulder with a complex design of shoulder straps that intersected at unusual angles. The dress flared out from a formfitting midriff and flowed into the asymmetrical hem that was so courant. Dangerously high red open toed shoes accompanied it, although they would find themselves discarded by the end of her set. Like the legendary Patti Labelle, Ceylon would come out of her shoes in a heartbeat. Her short, glistening brown hair was styled off the face in deference to the fact that she would certainly perspire before all was said and done. Her makeup was applied at a minimum as usual, although she wore black false eyelashes and her favorite red MAC lipstick. Big gold hoops adorned her ears, but the only other jewelry she wore was her fantastic engagement ring and the diamond pendant that never left her neck.

"Hello, Detroit, it's good to be home!" Ceylon waved to the crowd as she took the mike from its stand. She then treated the audience to a solid ninety minutes of music, ranging from blues-accented jazz like "At Last," to the sweet and sentimental like "My One and Only Love." She and Bump sang a couple of numbers together and she generously shared the spotlight with the backup singers. Watching from backstage, Martin experienced a swell of pride like nothing he'd ever felt before. The energy and passion she put into her act was nothing short of amazing. Even more amazing was the fact that she still had energy after the set. Martin had to practically sit on her to get her to go back to the hotel to relax; she had some crazy idea about finding an all night place for breakfast or even going to the casinos to wind down.

"C'mon, Butter, you know we've got a lot to do for the dinner. You're not tired now, but you will be in the morning if you down slow down. Besides," he said, lowering his voice, "I haven't been alone with you for two minutes today. I was hoping to spend a little time with my fiancée tonight." That did it. They were back at the hotel in next to no time, thanks to Martin's last statement.

The dinner to which he referred was something Ceylon had insisted upon; she wanted to treat everyone to dinner at Sweet Georgia Brown, the Greektown establishment generally considered to be one of the best restaurants in the city. Sweet Georgia Brown had only been open a couple of years, but its reputation for fine dining and top-notch service was without peer. That meant something in a city with as many fine restaurants as Detroit. She and Martin struggled quite a bit as to who was actually hosting the party, since he flatly refused to allow her to pay for anything. Despite the fact that her funds were intact and she could certainly afford to pay for an elaborate party, Martin wasn't having it; to his mind, that was something a husband did, and since all that separated him from that status were a few words, he was claiming his husbandly rights.

Ceylon finally threw up her hands to concede his victory. "Fine, Martin! You win this one, are you happy?" she asked in mock outrage.

Martin stretched lazily in the suite's king-sized bed and yawned sleepily. "If you come over here and get in this bed with me, I'll be perfectly happy, baby," he said in a sexy voice. "Forget the party, let's talk about how astonishing you were tonight. Damn, Ceylon you were amazing. I've never been so proud in my life."

Ceylon promptly forgot their disagreement and immediately removed her long peach colored silk robe and slid into Martin's waiting arms.

"Thank you for saying that, Martin. I hope you know that every note I sang tonight was all about you. Especially that one song," she said with a small yawn. She was suddenly exhausted from her energetic performance and the pace they'd been keeping on this trip.

Martin pulled her closer into his embrace and wrapped one long leg around her, savoring the sweet warmth they shared. "What song, Butter?"

Ceylon sighed deeply, abandoning herself to the intimate embrace. "You know, that one song . . . 'My One and Only Love.' Because you are," she yawned and fell asleep.

Touched to his very heart, Martin followed her into slumber.

The gathering at Sweet Georgia Brown was everything Ceylon hoped it would be; almost everyone she cared about in one place, smiling, enjoying the sublime cuisine, adding congratulations and best wishes to the newly engaged couple. Sweet Georgia Brown had only been open a couple of years, but its reputation for fine dining and top-notch service was without peer. That meant something in a city with as many fine restaurants as Detroit. The ambiance was remarkable, from the exceptional service to the carpet with fiber optics in it to the see-through floor with the underground river that meandered under the dining room. Sweet Georgia Brown was as fantastic a restaurant as Ceylon was an entertainer. Bump and Lillian, Renee and Andrew, Andrew's father, the indomitable Big Benny Cochran, and his charming bride Martha were all present. In addition, Andrew's twin brothers Andre and Alan were there with their wives, Tina and Faye, ranged about the tables. Another Cochran brother, Adam, was in attendance with his best friend and business partner, Alicia Fuentes. The youngest Cochran brother, Adonis, nicknamed Donnie, was there without a date for a change.

Ceylon noticed him looking around the room as if searching for someone. She immediately zeroed in on it and teased him unmercifully. "Sorry, Donnie, Angelique isn't here. I see you came stag and I think I know why. Sorry to disappoint you," she said with a laugh.

Donnie gave an exaggerated shudder. "Praise Allah that she stayed in Georgia, or wherever she is! You know how Evilene and I feel about each other," he said fervently.

Ceylon cocked her head and smiled smugly. It was true; Donnie and Angelique did not get along, they never did. But she also remembered how Andrew and Renee had battled for years and now look at them. She was kind enough not to mention that fact, though. *Let them figure it out for themselves*, she thought.

Kenneth was there, nicely attired in a smart dark suit, accompanied by Margaret Jones, the buxom, pretty woman he'd met in church and who had captured his heart. Olivia and Jimmy were also in attendance, both of them wreathed in smiles.

Renee looked at Ceylon's siblings with great interest and commented to Andrew that they didn't resemble their sister in the least, which was true. Ceylon was tall and full-figured, with beautiful brown skin that shimmered with a gold undertone, silky brown hair, and amazing hazel eyes. Kenneth and Olivia were different kettles of fish entirely, both slender to the point of wiriness, both a much lighter color than their sister, with dark brown eyes and jet black hair. Olivia was quite petite, actually, only about five foot two and Kenneth was of a decidedly medium height for a man, a compact five feet ten inches, a mere inch taller than Ceylon. They certainly looked alike, but not like Ceylon.

Andrew shrugged. "Part of the fun of being black, honey. You never know how we're gonna come out, there was so much race mixing during slavery. I'm just glad our daughters take after you and my sister so they'll be just as beautiful when they grow up," he said, caressing her face with his eyes.

The evening was warm and festive, made more so by the complimentary champagne sent by the restaurant's owner. He was a big, handsome man with a lively personality, who stopped by the table to greet everyone personally and make sure everyone was enjoying the meal.

Ceylon gave him one of her best smiles and told him she'd perform one night gratis if he'd give her the recipe for the sweet potato bisque. A roar of laughter was her only answer.

"I guess that means no," she said to no one in particular. She contented herself with another spoonful of the peach ice cream made especially for the restaurant that accompanied the legendary peach cobbler. Sighing with sheer happiness, she turned to Martin.

"You are the most wonderful man in the world, Martin.

Thank you for everything, my love," she said in a voice full of adoration.

"Ceylon, you're entirely welcome, but if you want to thank me," he leaned in closer to her ear, "let's get out of here and put that big jacuzzi to some extremely creative use. And when we get home, remind me to have one put into the atrium." He licked the special spot right beneath her ear. Ceylon shivered right down to her toes and sighed in anticipation. They were back in the Atheneum in an indecently short time, with Ceylon fretting that she hadn't said goodbye the way she wanted. Martin promised that no one noticed what she felt was an abrupt end to the party, but swore he'd make it up at the wedding.

"In the meantime, the jacuzzi is in there," he said indicating the bathroom "and we're in here, fully clothed, I might add. So how are we going to fix that?"

Ceylon gave him a sultry smile as she began to unbutton his shirt. "Oh, I think we can find a way to remedy that in just a moment or two," she purred.

Martin covered her mouth with his and swept her up into his arms, carrying her across the room into the bathroom where another kind of bliss awaited them.

Chapter Seventeen

Of all the people in the pre-op suite, Martin was by far the most relaxed. Ceylon was there, of course, along with Lillian and Angelique. Malcolm had come, too, but had already left for a critical meeting. Lillian insisted on coming to give Ceylon moral support, and Angelique came to keep her mother from driving Ceylon crazy, as she put it. Martin was fine with the arrangements, as he'd be sound asleep during it all. He would stay overnight in a private room at Piedmont Hospital and spend the next few days with his lovely fiancée fussing over him. A piece of cake as far as he was concerned, nothing to get riled up about. He had the utmost confidence in his surgeon and he knew beyond a doubt that no matter what the outcome of the surgery, Ceylon would love him anyway. It was a win-win situation for Martin.

Angelique finally persuaded Lillian to leave Martin and Ceylon alone for a moment so they could have a moment or two before the surgery. Martin's stay in pre-op was a bit long, but it couldn't be helped: the previous patient was taking a lot longer than planned. It was chilly in the room, at least according to Ceylon. "Do you want another blanket, sweetie? The nurse said you could have one if you like," she reminded him.

Martin smiled lazily at Ceylon. "What I want is the one thing I can't have, Butter, and that's some of your extra juicy kisses," he drawled.

It was true, Martin had already been prepped for surgery and Ceylon couldn't touch anything above his waist, something that was driving her crazy; she wanted to kiss him so badly!

"Don't remind me. Well, it'll all be over in a few hours and tomorrow you'll be at home so we can cater to your every whim for a few days," she told him with a smile.

Martin grinned at her words. "Yeah, and I plan to milk it for all it's worth, too. I'm gonna need all kinds of special attention, Ceylon, especially late at night. All night, as a matter of fact," he added with a wink.

Ceylon had to laugh with relief, Martin could still make sexual innuendoes even while laying on a cold hard gurney in a chilly pre-op room. And he could still look sexy, even with his moustache shaved for the surgery, his hair covered by a dorky looking surgical cap, and his left side protected by a gauze patch, as they'd removed the prosthetic eye for the surgery. Ceylon couldn't reply, as the surgical team came to fetch him just then. He looked at her carefully to make sure there were no tears in her eyes.

"I'll be back in a few, Butter. Love you," were the last words he said to her before disappearing through the double doors as the orderly pushed his gurney into the operating room.

"I love you, too," she whispered.

The wait seemed to take forever. Angelique tried to keep her mother and Ceylon entertained with several bridal magazines she'd purchased in the gift shop, but it wasn't working too well. She pointed out to Ceylon that they'd have to start planning the wedding sooner or later, and now was as good time as any, but her only response was an absent nod. Sighing, Angelique gave up on Ceylon and bullied her mother into going to the cafeteria for coffee.

When the two women left, Ceylon folded her hands in her lap and quietly prayed for Martin's safety in the operating room. She had no idea, no conception of how much of her heart was in the operating room with him, not until the reality of it set in when they wheeled him through those double doors. The only way she was going to get through the next four hours until he was out of recovery and in his private room was to concentrate on a higher power. Just about then, Angelique and Lillian returned from the cafeteria, and Angelique took charge again, sending Ceylon off for something to drink.

"It's practically deserted down there. You can sit by the windows and think," she said quietly.

Ceylon, grateful for the suggestion, took off at once. Even though she wasn't feeling it, she looked her very best in a charming peach chemise style dress with a matching long jacket. Martin loved her in dresses because he liked looking at her legs. Ceylon varied from her usual habit by putting a Constant Comment tea bag in her customary hot water, taking the styrofoam cup to an empty table by the window. Like many people, Ceylon disliked hospitals intensely. Her thoughts always went back to her grandparent's last days and the endless hours she'd spent in waiting rooms, conferring with doctors, trying to sleep on the uncomfortable chairs in their rooms, and the stealthy, inexorable progression of their deaths. Ceylon sipped the hot tea slowly, trying to derive some comfort from its fragrant essence. The day was thick with gray clouds and a steady spattering of cool rain dotted the window. She sat without moving, trying to will the peace she always got from rain to invade her body. She'd almost made it to a place of calm and serenity when a painfully familiar voice broke into her meditation.

"Well, well, well. Something going wrong for the golden girl at last, hmm? Well, it's no more than you deserve. This is what they call poetic justice, you selfish bitch."

Ceylon turned slowly to face the source of the hateful words.

"How did you get here, Louise?"

She looked into the face of the woman who had given birth to her, the woman she would always refer to as Louise and nothing else. The years had been kind to her in an odd way. Louise had been a real beauty once, but the truth of her personality now showed too clearly for her to appear beautiful. Her face, once soft and feminine, was now sharp and harsh, although unlined. The jet black hair, now courtesy of Dark and Lovely permanent blue black, drained the color from her ochre skin, leaving it a pasty pinkish yellow that looked haggard. The once lustrous hair now looked painted, lacquered into a hard, immobile French roll that made her look even more severe.

She was still a fabulous dresser, though, wearing a killer three piece navy and cream suit that screamed Adele St. John. It could have been bought off the rack from Nordstrom's or off the street from a booster. One never knew with Louise. She followed one rule and one rule only: Whatever Louise wants Louise gets, regardless of the cost to anyone else. Her very presence in the hospital cafeteria made this abundantly clear. Obviously someone Ceylon cared about was having some kind of problem, but it wasn't about to stop Louise from getting what she wanted, whatever it might have been.

In her typical fashion, she took a seat across from Ceylon without waiting for an invitation. "Since you don't have the manners of a dog to ask your mother to be seated, or stand up while she does so, I guess I have to help myself," she said with a clenched jaw.

Ceylon repeated her earlier question. "How did you find me?" she asked dully.

Louise's eyes glittered with malice. "How did I find

you?" she mocked. "Like you're so damned special that you can't be touched." She leaned forward on the small table and stared at Ceylon with absolute hatred. "Do you think you're the only one who can hire a detective? Is that supposed to be your exclusive province or something? It was remarkably easy to find out exactly where you were and what you're doing."

She spoke in a low, intense voice rich with venom. "Yes, I know all about you and that scarred-up boyfriend of yours. You think you're stepping in high cotton, don't you? You think you can just treat my son any way you want and not have it come back to you, is that it? You're wrong about that, girl, just as wrong as you can be."

Ceylon's uneasiness began to mount as she watched the metamorphosis across the table. Louise began to look more than haggard; she started to look a bit unhinged.

"I begged you to leave my son alone. *Begged* you, came to you on my knees and asked you to walk away. Duane made a mistake," she said in a voice shaky with emotion. "A mistake, Ceylon, that's all it was. I asked you to forgive his error in judgment. I told you the money would be returned to you. I told your greedy ass it would be returned; it was just going to take some time for him to get things organized so it could be repaid." She stopped to clear her throat and rummaged in her big Gucci bag for a tissue.

The anger Ceylon had tamped down for years finally broke through. "That's really rich, Louise. *Return* the money to me? He took it out of the country and stashed it where it couldn't be found. Those aren't exactly the actions of someone trying to atone for a wrong, now are they? Duane had no intentions of returning one single dime of my money. And *you* had no intention of seeing that any of it was returned to me. You know it and I know it," Ceylon said, looking at her mother as though she were a complete stranger, which in many ways she was. "So after waiting around for almost three years, after working like a slave to pay back money that was stolen from me by your precious son, I came to my senses and did something about it."

"Now as far as Duane being in jail, that's nothing to do with me. I wasn't the only injured party, Louise. Duane did many evil things to many people and *they* are the ones who had him arrested. If you have a problem with that, go see the Justice Department, the Treasury Department, and the Federal Bureau of Investigation, because it seems that your darling Duane was stepping in some pretty high cotton himself. And that, Louise, is what they call criminal justice," she said, deriving a certain satisfaction out of seeing the woman's pale face turn the color of cold grits.

"I do have to ask you one thing and then I'm through with this mess forever. What I want to know is *why* you're like this. Why in the world do you hate me so much? And why do you love Duane so much? More than any of your other children? How does that work? How does a woman who gave birth to five children worship one of them, manipulate three of them, and try to kill one? Please explain it to me and we can go our separate ways and be through with this," she said calmly. And to her own surprise, she *was* calm, much more rational than she ever thought she'd be when asking the question that had haunted her for much of her life.

Oddly, Louise looked happy to answer Ceylon's questions; excited might have been a better word. Sure enough her words bore out that impression. "I'm really glad you asked that question, girl, I've been waiting long enough to tell you this," she said with a ugly grimace that was supposed to be a smile. "You're right, I do love Duane, more than the rest of you pickaninnies put together. None of you is worth his big toe as far as I'm concerned, and that's because his father was the finest man who ever drew a breath on this planet. Duane's father was my first husband, Richard. He was tall, with dark brown skin and good hair, beautiful straight hair. My Richard had hair like a white man." She sighed in apparent bliss at the memory. "He was so good to me. He treated me like a queen, you understand? Richard loved my dirty drawers; there was nothing he wouldn't do for me. Anything he thought I wanted, he got for me. Richard took care of me like nobody else in this world ever did," she said softly, with something like pain in her eyes. Those eyes suddenly turned as hard as flints.

"Then he died, and I was left alone, all alone except for my baby. Duane was the spittin' image of his daddy, and had all of his ways, too. He was Richard reborn; my Richard came back to me in the form of my Duane. He was all I had left of Richard," she said in an oddly hoarse voice.

Ceylon was riveted despite herself. She knew the wise thing was to get up and walk away, but the practical part of her knew that Louise would follow her wherever she went. This was going to be ended today.

"So you loved Duane the best because you loved his father more than my father," she said dispassionately. "At least that part's clear, or somewhat clear. I mean, you married my father, Thomas Carter, and he was good to you, too, at least he seemed to be. He adopted Duane and gave him his name, he gave you more children—Kenneth, Rochelle, Olivia, and me. He worked every day and didn't fool around, and he was pretty good looking as I recall. I didn't get to see much of him," Ceylon said with irony. "I'm not going to try and figure out why your marriage went bad, but I do have to ask one thing, why did you despise me so much, Louise?"

This time there was no mistaking the expression on Louise's face; it was pure hatred. She leaned even closer to Ceylon with a maniacal sneer and spat the words at her. "You stupid cow. Thomas Carter is not your father. I thought you were smart. You never figured that one out, did you?"

Ceylon felt nothing but ice from the top of her head to the bottom of her feet. She was so constricted with shock she couldn't move. She wanted nothing more than to bolt from the table, to run as far away from the deranged woman as possible.

"Yes, that's right, you're a bastard. The stinking little bastard who ruined my life. I tried to get rid of you, but you wouldn't go. Then I tried to dump you, but my meddling mother wasn't having it. So I was stuck with you, stuck with the little bastard who eventually broke up my marriage. Thomas wasn't stupid, even if you were. He knew you weren't his child. I think he knew it from the get-go, which is why he didn't say a mumbling word when I left your squalling ass in the hospital," she said with great satisfaction at the look of horror on Ceylon's face.

"I'll tell you something else, girl: he knew about the abortion and he didn't try to stop me. Nobody wanted you, you little bastard. You should have died. You should have died and none of this would have happened. It's all your fault, you little . . ."

Ceylon reacted more quickly than Louise would have thought she could. She grabbed the hand coming up to slap her face and dug into the bony wrist with her fingernails.

"Oh, I don't think so, *Mother*," she said, enunciating each syllable with all the disgust she was feeling. "I've had about all I'm going to take from you today and for the rest of my life. So you break your marriage vows and I'm the result and it's somehow *my* fault? The mere fact that I was born is the reason your beloved child, the angel of your heart, is in jail? How long did it take you to come up with that theory? I'm no more responsible for your marriage breaking up than I'm the reason for Duane being a thief and a liar. You need to look in the mirror to find that person. Take responsibility for your own actions, because I am not the one, honey. Not today, not ever," she said, at last loosing her grip on the other woman's wrist. "Just stay the hell away from me, Louise, away from me and my family. You've done me enough harm in my lifetime and you're not going to do me any more. Stay away from me. I'm not going to tell you again," Ceylon said with unmistakable steel in her voice.

"Oh but you're wrong, bastard," hissed Louise as she nursed her wrist with exaggerated care. "I'm going to ruin you, girl. You don't know who the hell your father is, but I'm going to make sure the whole world knows you're a bastard and just whose bastard you are. You're going to be ruined, just like Duane; no, *worse* than Duane because you'll not only look like a fool all over again, but people will see you for what you really are. A dirty little bastard whelp who should have died in the womb. I'm going to tell everything, girl, unless . . ." her voice trailed off and she looked at Ceylon expectantly. When Ceylon remained mute, with no expression on her face, Louise went on: "Either you get those charges dropped, or I put this story out for the whole world to know. Get my Duane out of jail in the next forty-eight hours or I go to the press with this," she ended triumphantly.

Ceylon stared at Louise blankly for a few moments and began to feel pity for the shell of a woman. She had truly gone round the bend. She hadn't listened to a thing Ceylon said. "Louise, you don't get it. I can't do anything to help Duane because I'm not the one who pressed the charges. These are Federal charges, government charges. There's nothing I can do. And to be honest, I wouldn't if I could. As far as telling the whole world, knock yourself out. Who do you think is going to care that I'm illegitimate? As many people that have babies out of wedlock these days? No one's going to be shocked, no one's going to care. If you can find someone who's interested in the story, tell it. It won't make any difference to me."

She gave Louise one more pitying look and rose to leave. Louise grabbed at her arm, making Ceylon jerk away from her.

"You think that fancy society man will still want your mongrel ass after he knows the truth? You think his fancy momma will still stand the sight of you? Just wait, little bastard, just wait. This is justice, girl, plain and simple. You did unto me and I'm going to do unto you," she said to Ceylon's back.

Ceylon got out of the cafeteria as quickly as possible. Incredibly, the entire ugly scene had only taken about fifteen minutes to enact. If she stopped now and rinsed her face with cold water, she could slip upstairs and rejoin Lillian and Angelique with no one the wiser. Increasing her speed, she planned to do just that, then stopped when she saw a door marked Chapel. Opening the door, she entered and sat down in the dimly lit room. The peace for which she'd been searching surrounded her. Slipping down onto her knees, she let the solace of faith comfort her.

Bennie looked across the table at her old friend and knew that something was amiss. Martin had been home from the hospital for two days, and here Ceylon was obviously seeking refuge in her kitchen. Under ordinary circumstances Bennie doubted that she would have left his side for a minute, but she'd arrived about fifteen minutes before, looking pale and unhappy. Ceylon seemed to sense what Bennie was thinking, and gave her a wan imitation of her usual smile.

"I know I look bad, but I haven't been sleeping too much," she admitted. "Lillian is at the house with Martin and while he was taking a nap, I ran out on the pretext of picking up a prescription for him. I just had to talk to someone, Bennie," she said with a pleading note in her voice.

Bennie immediately reached over and squeezed Ceylon's free hand. The other hand cuddled one of Bennie's twin sons, little Martin, who chattered happily to her. "Honey, you sound dangerously close to apologizing to me for being my friend! Don't even think about going there. Let me get these guys busy doing something else and we can talk freely," she said.

She rose gracefully from her chair and took Martin from Ceylon, thwarted his brother Malcolm from his quest to remove all the pots from the cupboard in which he was rummaging, and called little Clay away from whatever mischief he was contemplating. In short order, she had the boys occupied with crayons and paper on the big kitchen table. She and Ceylon seated themselves in the adjoining solarium that had been added the previous year to the rambling house.

Ceylon was drawn up in a corner of the comfortable rattan sofa upholstered in a vintage print of palm trees, looking miserable. She once again rubbed the bridge of her nose with her index finger. Bennie couldn't stand it any longer; she made Ceylon stand up so she could give her a big hug. "Come on and get it off your chest," she urged. "Something is obviously wrong, so tell me about it."

Ceylon sighed, started to pace, and then stopped abruptly, rejoining Bennie on the sofa. She looked at her friend for a moment before she began speaking. "Louise came to visit while Martin was in the operating room," she said finally. Nodding briefly at Bennie's shocked expression, she told the whole sorry tale of Louise's hateful diatribe with an eerie lack of emotion.

"It's so simple, now that I have all the pieces," Ceylon said thoughtfully. "Of course she didn't want me. I was living proof that she'd had an affair. She had to get rid of me, or try to; it was the only way she could preserve her marriage. It actually makes sense, in a Medea kind of way."

Bennie covered her mouth with her hand, visibly distressed by what she was hearing. "Ceylon, no! What she said, that's horrible! What kind of sick, twisted wench would tell her own child that?"

Ceylon waved her hand almost idly. "Bennie, don't stress yourself. *You* would never do anything like that because you're a normal, loving woman with normal emotions. Louise . . . well, she's a different breed of cat. Sick as it may sound, she did what's normal for her. I'm not saying that her normal is most people's reality; she's got her own agenda, that's for sure."

She moved her head slowly from side to side, rubbing her thumb across her lower lip as she did so. "But you know what, Bennie? I keep thinking how much better off I was not growing up with that woman! Look at what she did to my brothers and sisters! If you could have heard her talking about Duane's father and Duane . . . there's definitely something unhealthy about that kind of attachment, truly there is." She suddenly laughed, alarming Bennie greatly.

Ceylon explained, "She kept going on and on about Richard's beautiful 'white man's hair'. Duane sho' didn't get *that* in his so-called reincarnation! I wonder how she felt about those nappy naps of his," she said with a chuckle.

Before Bennie had to think of a suitable answer, Ceylon stood up. "So, once again my life is an open book. She swears she's going to tell the whole world that I'm her little bastard child and who the sperm donor was. Like that's supposed to just ruin my life or something, the mere fact that the mailman or the garbage man or the numbers man left a little package for a cheating wife. Yeah, whatever," she said defiantly.

"I just hope it's not somebody like Idi Amin or Osama bin Laden," she said with painful bravado. "That could be a problem, you know? That could definitely keep me off the A-list. No, on second thought, it would get me *on* the A-list; you know how Hollywood is," she said with a snap of her fingers.

Seeing the look on Bennie's face, she relented. "Okay, I'm acting like it doesn't matter, and in some ways it doesn't. I meant some of what I said, like being glad I wasn't raised by her, and the reasons behind my abandonment make sense to me now. It really does explain a lot, Bennie. As depraved as we might think she is, she was acting in a way that's perfectly logical to her. It might be sick and wrong for the rest of the world, but she has a whole different reality, which is why I'm not really worried about her making some big announcement concerning my paternity. I'm way past being embarrassed about anything. And I'm yesterday's news as far as the tabloids go. They have much bigger fish to fry. That's the one thing you can count on in this world; somebody's always doing stupid and somebody else wants to read all about it. She can't hurt me. She has no power over me," Ceylon said firmly, then hesitated.

"The only thing I'm worried about, really, is telling Martin, because he may go off on my behalf and he needs to stay calm and relaxed. So I've been mousing around trying to pretend like everything is okay when I've got this little time bomb under my skirt. Ughhh!" she moaned in frustration.

She looked around the room, selected a chaise longue, and flung herself back on it with the back of one hand over her forehead, the very picture of diva angst. Looking at Bennie out of the corner of one eye, she said in a little girl voice, "I'll give you five dollars if you tell Martin for me. No, wait—five dollars, a gallon of Blue Moon ice cream, and a bag of Better Made potato chips. How's that?" She just knew the mention of some of Detroit's favorite fun foods would make Bennie laugh, but it didn't.

Bennie wasn't fooled by Ceylon's antics a bit. "Ceylon . . . look, I can't tell you how to think or how to feel about this, obviously I can't. But I know you, Ceylon, and I know that despite the brave front you're putting on, this has to hurt on a lot of levels. It's not going to be easy to deal with, not for you and anyone who cares about you, and there are a lot of us. And you're absolutely right, Martin may very well hit the roof, but the longer you put it off, the worse it's going to be. Deveraux men . . . well, I don't have to tell you what they're like. Paternalistic, territorial, protective and aggressive, every single one of them," she said wryly. "Those aren't *bad* things, as long as you stand your ground and don't let them baby you too much, but those are the facts. If somebody messes with you, Ceylon, they have Martin to deal with and for that matter, Clay and Malcolm and Marcus, too."

Instead of comforting her, Bennie's words made Ceylon distinctly uneasy. "So how do you deal with it, Bennie?"

Bennie's familiar, radiant smile lit up her face. "Oh honey, I had years of practice. The Deveraux men are exactly like the Cochrans. You know that houseful of he-men I grew up with, don't you? Years and years of practice," she repeated. "After a year or two of marriage, you'll be able to handle it, too. You just have to remember one thing. These men mate for life and the one thing they want over and above everything else is the happiness and comfort of those they love starting with their mate.

"The only thing they're guilty of is loving deeply, very, *very* deeply, like a wolf protecting his den. Underneath it all, they really are kittens," she said.

Chapter Eighteen

Ceylon had the dubious pleasure, that very afternoon, of seeing her own kitten turn into a raging lion when he heard what had transpired at the hospital. The fact that his anger was on her behalf was of little consolation; Ceylon had never seen a human get so very angry so fast. They had been relaxing in Martin's living room, listening to music. Martin was playing the guitar very quietly while Ceylon appeared to listen intently.

Ceylon noticed again how well Martin's face was faring after the surgery. The redness was still there, but the seepage was at a minimum. There was even reason to believe that smooth, unmarked skin would be the end result. Ceylon also enjoyed looking at the thick gold chain around his neck. It had been a present from Ceylon, along with the Citizen watch on his wrist with the mother-of-pearl face. Martin had protested at first, but Ceylon so wanted to show him how much he meant to her than he had finally demurred and accepted the gifts graciously. She was stalling, trying to figure out the best way to tell Martin, when he spoke.

"Butter, what's on your mind, baby? I can tell something's

bothering you, what is it?" he asked in a voice full of concern.

Ceylon moved uneasily and tried to bluff. "Now, why would you say that? I'm, umm . . ." she swallowed hard, and then gave up the pretense. "Okay, Martin here goes.

It took her surprisingly few minutes to tell how Louise had accosted her in the hospital cafeteria and the sordid tale she'd told. Before she finished speaking, Martin's fury was evident. His nostrils thinned, his face turned a bright puce, and rage emanated from every pore. When he could speak, his words were harsh and measured.

"That woman," he spat the word, "is diseased. What kind of sick, sorry excuse for a human being could do that to their own child? How dare she try to threaten you, of all people?" he ground out through his tightly clenched jaw. He rose and started pacing the room, running his hand over his head in agitation. "If that sick bitch thinks she's ever coming within one hundred yards of you again, she'll find herself in a world of trouble. And if she dares to slander or libel you I will personally see to it that she spends time behind bars, the miserable . . ." his words died out as he finally focused on Ceylon.

He took one good look at her curled in the corner of the sofa and his anger dissipated immediately. She looked absolutely miserable, huddled in the corner of the sofa clutched a throw pillow. Her eyes were huge with pain and fright, and Martin knew that his histrionics helped put the look there. He stopped his pacing and sat next to her on the couch; drawing her into his lap so he could hold her and comfort her.

"Ceylon, sweetheart, I'm so sorry. I'm sorry I frightened you, baby. I'm sorry you had to go through this, too. What can I do for you, Ceylon? What do you need from me right now?" he asked tenderly.

Ceylon took a deep, tearful breath. "There isn't anything I need from you except for this. Your love and support are all I need," she said softly. She pulled away from him a bit to look him directly in the face. "The next few weeks are bound to be a circus, Martin. When she makes good on her threat about going to the media, I'm liable to end up everybody's favorite topic of gossip yet again. It's not going to be easy to deal with," she warned him. "And this time your family will be involved, too, because we're engaged. Are you sure you can handle this? Because the last thing I'd ever want to do is hurt you or your family. I don't want to drag you through the mud with me, and with Louise there's bound to be lots of it." she said.

Martin had to work very hard to keep his simmering rage from erupting at her words, spoken so matter-of-factly. He chose his next statement very carefully, as he didn't want to upset Ceylon further, but this was something that needed to be said.

"Ceylon, you are my heart," he said slowly. "Just like I couldn't live without my physical heart pumping blood through my body, I couldn't possibly live without you. You're a part of me, the most essential part of me. You're my family, my home, my treasure and no one is ever going to come between us. My family loves you as much as I do. What makes you think we could be inconvenienced or embarrassed by a bunch of lies about you?" He leaned over and kissed her trembling lips. "You belong to me, Ceylon. Just like I belong to you and always will. Nothing's ever going to change that. Nothing."

Ceylon was so touched by Martin's words that the tears filling her eyes miraculously eased away. She smiled, tremulously at first, and then the first real one of the past few days broke through.

"Martin, that was so beautiful," she said, kissing him gently. "I love you so much, you and your family. I would die before I let any harm come to any of you. But Martin, this is Louise we're talking about. There's no telling what she might say or do. And you and I know it doesn't have to be true for the tabloid papers and the sleazy TV shows to jump on it. I couldn't stand to bring shame onto your family name," she said sadly.

Amazingly enough, Martin began to laugh. It started as a chuckle and turned into a deep belly laugh. "Butter, you sound like a Gothic novel—'bring shame upon your family name.' There's no way in the world you could ever embarrass me or my family. Besides, you forget what we do for a living. We are the media, honey. Newspapers, magazines, TV and since the merger with Cochran Communications, radio. If we know how to do anything, it's put a spin on something. If it comes to it, don't worry, we can take care of our own."

Ceylon allowed herself to be comforted for the moment. Martin made her feel safe, protected, and loved, and she needed to feel that way. But there were some practical matters to deal with, too, as she told Martin.

"I need to call Shelley and let him know that there are storm clouds on the horizon. And I need to talk to Bump and your mother, and get a statement ready for the press," she said thoughtfully. At Martin's inquiring look, she explained. "For when Louise jumps crazy, and she will. I've never known her to not go through with a threat," Ceylon said with a shrug of her shoulders.

Martin didn't say anything for a moment; he just continued to hold onto Ceylon, loving the feel of her in his arms. Protecting her was all he wanted right now, keeping her away from Louise's evil intentions. Suddenly something occurred to him.

"Ceylon, what if she's lying?" he asked.

"Honey, I told you, I've never known her to back down from anything. If she says she going to do something, it's as good as done. As soon as she can find someone who wants to hear that I'm illegitimate, she'll be spreading the news like fertilizer on a field of collard greens," she said with finality.

"No, baby, that's not what I mean. Suppose she made up the stuff about you being the product of a one-night stand. Suppose she's bluffing?"

Ceylon tilted her head slightly and considered Martin's question. Finally she shook her head in disagreement. "I can see your point, but I think she's telling the truth. It explains why she tried to abort me, it explains why she abandoned me, it explains a lot of things. I was a constant reminder of her stupidity. Not her *sin*. I don't think she thinks in those terms. In fact, I know she doesn't. But I *was* a permanent reminder that she'd messed up, that she'd miscalculated, and that would really get to her. Louise hates to be wrong and hates being in a vulnerable position of any kind. She never bothered to tell me the circumstances of my birth before this because she couldn't exploit me with it. I was giving generously to her and my brothers and sisters, so she didn't need a lever to pry it out of me. Now she does and she's not going to stop until she's done everything she can to hurt me. I'm telling you, Martin, the woman is a juggernaut."

At that, Martin gave another of his lethal grins. "That's a coincidence. So am I."

The only good thing to come out of the next few days, as far as Ceylon was concerned, was an increased closeness to Martin and his family. They seemed to go out of their way to make her feel special, so much so that she brought it up to Lillian. Bump and Lillian had come over for dinner and just finished the lovely meal that Ceylon had prepared with Martin's help. Due to the fact that there were still no dining room chairs, they ate in the atrium, which had a great ambience anyway. They had finished the pecan-crusted chicken breasts, fresh green beans and spinach salad and were about to have dessert and coffee. Martin cleared the table and he and Bump were in the kitchen making the coffee and preparing the dessert tray, leaving Lillian and Ceylon alone in the atrium.

Lillian commented on the various specimens of plants and once again expressed her amazement that Martin had created all this beauty. "If I asked him to weed the garden you'd have thought he was dying! I never saw a child who hated yard work worse than Martin. Except for Marcus. Now he . . . Ceylon, dear, what's the matter?" Lillian caught the look Ceylon was giving her and stopped in mid sentence.

Ceylon blushed along her cheekbones and looked away for a moment. She took a deep breath and started speaking rapidly. "Lillian, I just want you to know how much I appreciate you and Bump being on my side. I know this has to be uncomfortable for you, and I'm terribly sorry about it," she said quietly.

Lillian drew back as if she'd been slapped. The two women sat at a circular glass topped table and Ceylon was close enough for Lillian to touch, which she did. She brought her chair closer to the table and put one hand on Ceylon's shoulder and with the fingers of her other hand she turned Ceylon to face her. She looked both tender and fierce, like she wasn't about to tolerate any nonsense. Her words emphasized that.

"Listen here, my dear. That is going to be the last time you apologize to me for anything, do you understand? How can you think that Bill and I would be anywhere other than on your side? You're like family to us, Ceylon! Bill couldn't love you any more if you were his own daughter, and as for me, I've always cared about you and you know it! From the first time I met you at Big Bennie's retirement party I've thought you were a wonderful, sweet, talented woman. And when I realized how much you cared for my son. I prayed that he would find his way to you. Anything that happens to you happens to us, Ceylon, and don't you forget it. Apologize to me? You better not, girl," the older woman admonished her fondly. She and Ceylon embraced tightly, laughing and sniffling at the same time.

In the kitchen, Bump and Martin were deep in their own conversation. Bump looked unusually serious as he questioned Martin.

"So how is Ceylon handling all this? I have to tell you, I've heard a lot of sorry tales, but this one really stands out. That mother of hers is a piece of work," he said bitterly.

Martin nodded his agreement as he took cream out of the refrigerator for the coffee. "She's a miserable cow, no doubt. Ceylon's . . . well, she's Ceylon, that's all I can tell you. She's trying to be brave about it, but I know the whole thing freaks her out. Her memories of that part of her childhood were rough enough; now they're unbearable. It was bad enough to be abandoned and mistreated by the woman who gave you life, but to suddenly find out that your father wasn't the man you believed him to be, that's deep. She's trying not to let it get to her, but I know Ceylon, and I know that it bothers her," he said glumly.

"At first, she took the line that it didn't matter who fathered her. Her grandfather raised her and as far as she was concerned, that was the end of it; he was her father. But a couple of days later she let her guard down a little, because she brought it up again. She said something about not knowing if the man was alive or dead, if he was a decent Christian or a convicted felon. It was the not knowing that really bugged her, she said."

Bump looked even more somber. "The whole thing is truly sad. That woman, that Louise, she needs to be horsewhipped. The idea that she could treat her own flesh and blood like that, it just passes all understanding. You know, I never had children, Martin. My Anna and I, well, we had a baby and lost it shortly afterwards. Crib death. She was never able to have anymore and it was, well, those are the cards you're dealt. But to have a beautiful child like that and just throw her away, that makes no sense to me. How a woman like Ceylon came from a critter like that just amazes me."

"Who is this woman and where did she come from, anyway?" Bump demanded. He fixed an unwavering eye on

Martin and pointed with his index finger. "Don't lie to me, 'cause I know you got that detective friend of yours on the case already."

Martin first looked dumbfounded, then sheepish before answering. "Okay, you're right, Titus is doing some checking. He hasn't found out too much, just that she was one of three children; she has a younger sister still in Michigan. The brother apparently died some years ago. She's very intelligent, worked as an executive secretary at a brokerage firm. Never did anything of a criminal nature, never really did anything out of the ordinary that Titus could find. She always had a liking for high rollers, though. She used to like to hang out a lot and party with the big ballers. That first husband of hers, the one she claims was so crazy about her, now he was a trip. He had a rap sheet a mile long with petty larceny, racketeering, the whole nine yards. Whatever she says about him now sounds like a fairy tale. Get this; the guy died in a knife fight in the county lock up! Doesn't sound like the love of a lifetime to me, but what do I know?" He laughed bitterly. "Her second husband was just an average Joe, worked at one of the automotive plants, no bad habits except playing the numbers. Just went to work and came home and tolerated what was no doubt a tense marriage. I just get the feeling that Louise thought she was settling for crumbs after being with the pretty boy."

Bump rubbed the bridge of his nose with his forefinger. "Listen, just pour me a cup of hot water, man. If I drink coffee this late I'll keep your mother up all night walking around in circles, running my mouth and watching television. I'm too old to have her taking a switch to me, which is what she'd try to do," he said morosely. When Martin started laughing, he pretended to take great offense. "You have no idea how your mother can be once she gets started," he protested. "That woman rules me with a rod of iron."

Lillian overheard his last words as she and Ceylon had come to find out what was taking so long.

"I don't rule you, dearest. I just know what's best for you," she said demurely. She didn't look the least ashamed of herself; she just smiled warmly and embraced her tall, handsome husband. Bump's face was also smiling as he added a kiss to her hug.

"If you knew what was best for me, you wouldn't let my relatives come here," he grumbled. "They're all swooping over here like hawks in the next couple of days. She knows they drive me out of my feeble mind."

"Bill, hush! You know you look forward to seeing them every year. You have more fun than anyone at these little gatherings. Besides, it's our turn to host. We went to Louisiana the last two times," she reminded him.

The normalcy of the scene was just what Ceylon needed to end her day. Standing there in the kitchen with her future in-laws and the man who would love her forever made Louise's vicious threats drift away like smoke in the wind.

Against Martin's better judgment, Ceylon was on her way to Los Angeles. She had to take a couple of meetings with Shelley and talk about some proposals with a couple of studio bigwigs. Plus, she had to be ready for anything that Louise might throw her way. It had been almost a month since their confrontation in the hospital, but the threat of Louise selling a story to the media was always present. As Ceylon tried to explain to Martin, it was critical that she appear like a competent, well-balanced person to potential producers and directors, and not like some strung-out, issue-laden diva.

"Like it or not, Martin, image is everything in this business," she said frankly as she continued to pack for the trip. They were in the master bedroom. Martin lay on his stomach, watching Ceylon fill a large suitcase that was on the bed next to him.

"The quickest way to sabotage your career is to start having a lot of drama, start missing concert dates, holding up productions, that kind of thing. My name has been in the paper once too often and I can't afford to have people not consider me for a project because they think I'm flaky. I need to let people see me and see for themselves that I'm in my right mind," she added with a saucy smile.

Martin didn't buy that reasoning and said so. "Any body who knows you already knows that," he groused. "You didn't fall into a nervous breakdown when you woke up broke. You went to work every single day and turned all that money over to pay for something you didn't do. You broke your back out there, Ceylon, and nobody had better say you didn't. In your right mind? Hell, you're the most levelheaded person I know. You don't have to prove anything to those Hollywood hot- shots," he grumbled.

He finally stopped complaining and entertained himself by taking something out of the suitcase every time she turned to the closet. She caught him at it and fixed him with a steely glare. "Stop it! I'm going to be gone two days! Two measly days, is that too much to ask?"

He didn't look in the least contrite. He merely sighed and rolled over on his back and stared at the slowly rotating ceil- ing fans. "A lot can happen in two days, Ceylon."

She finally took pity on him as she put the last item into the suitcase. Closing the lid, she snapped the clasps and spun the little built in combination locks to secure it. She walked around to his side of the bed and leaned over for a long, soft, wet kiss.

"Martin, I'll be back before you know it. Those two days will go by so fast you won't even know I'm gone," she pre- dicted.

The next morning, Ceylon prepared to leave the house for the airport. She insisted that Martin go to the office as he usually did; he had a harrowing series of negotiations for acquisitions and she saw no reason to be, as she put it, "taken to her gate like a five-year-old." Airport good-byes were not something she found romantic in any case. The car Martin arranged to take her to Hartsfield International wasn't due for another ninety minutes, so she was relaxed with a fragrant cup of coffee. The phone rang and she smiled, thinking it was Martin. Putting on her sultriest voice, she picked up the receiver.

"Hello," she said breathily.

"Oh, you can save that, girl. I'm not your rich man. I suggest you turn on your television, though. You might find the Jackie Rivers show very informative," Louise sneered.

Before Ceylon could say another word, the line went dead. Ceylon stared blankly for a moment, then felt her stomach capsize. This was it. This was what she'd been dreading all along. She found the remote control for the 13-inch TV mounted under the kitchen cupboard and frantically tried to locate the right channel for the Jackie Rivers show. It was the kind of sleazoid television Ceylon never watched, the kind with exposés of disgusting family secrets, loud, profane fights between unhappy wives and cheating husbands; in short, the perfect venue for what Louise wanted to do to Ceylon.

Finally she found the channel, and sat transfixed in horror. There sat Louise, all dolled up and looking like the world's most perfect mother. The harsh blackness of her hair had been toned down greatly, and the sharp, unflattering lines of her face had been softened with makeup so that she looked vulnerable and dignified. Before Ceylon could fully process this shock, she was caught up in the words issuing from Louise's mouth.

"Yes, I was happily married when it all happened," she said, bowing her head in shame. "And my marriage ended because of it. I was left with four children to raise, barely able to put food on the table, all because of that man." She issued a soft sigh and raised a trembling hand to her eye.

Jackie Rivers immediately whipped out a linen handkerchief and pressed it into her hand. She looked up and valiantly mouthed a silent thank you.

Jackie Rivers was sleaze personified, with his fluffy blond hair, gold-rimmed glasses, and expensively tailored suits. He thrived on scouring the underbelly of society and nothing seemed to bring him more joy than broadsiding some schmuck. His special stock in trade was breaking stories of great scandal and standing aside with faux innocence on his conniving face as some poor sap tried to deal with the fact that his wife just confessed to being pregnant with his brother's child, or something equally shameful.

Ceylon tried to brace herself for what was coming; she knew that any second they would announce the name of her biological father and that he would be saunter out from behind the curtain to join her sniveling mother onstage. Her adrenaline flow increased, her mouth got dry, and her palms sweated. Her heart started beating at a much faster rate than normal. Sure enough, she didn't have long to wait. Jackie Rivers paraded across the stage with one of his typical, long-winded summations.

"So, Mrs. Carter, may I call you Louise?"

Louise bravely waved the now-sodden handkerchief to indicate she'd welcome the intimacy. The studio audience made sympathetic noises at this show of ladylike composure.

"Louise, you've not had an easy life. Your marriage was ended, your youngest child taken away from you, and you were doomed to a life of poverty, all because of what happened one night over thirty years ago. Your youngest daughter was taken out of your custody and raised by her grandmother because you couldn't care for her. And that daughter grew up to be Ceylon Simmons, the world-famous singer and actress, did she not?"

Louise nodded humbly, and looked, amazingly, proud that Ceylon was her daughter, something that the studio audience apparently agreed with as they clapped and cheered at the mention of Ceylon's name. Jackie, seeming to feel it was time for the kill, stopped strutting about the stage and sank into a chair next to Louise's.

"You've never told anyone what you're about to tell me, have you?"

Louise managed a whispered response. "I never told a soul. I was too . . . ashamed," she confided.

Jackie leaned in closer, and took her hand for effect. "Can you tell us now, Louise? Can you share with us the name of the man who destroyed your life?"

Louise took a deep breath, and tightened her grip on Jackie's hand, as well as the ill-fated handkerchief. She looked out at the studio audience, then into Jackie's beady eyes, so full of concern.

"The man's name is . . . Bill Williams," she said in a surprisingly strong voice for a poor helpless woman.

Jerry gave one of his patented I'm-so-shocked facial expressions and immediately elaborated on her reply.

"Are you speaking of jazz musician extraordinaire Bill 'Bump' Williams? The man who is largely responsible for your daughter's career in music?"

"Yes, that's the man," Louise said defiantly, this time facing the cameras. "That's the man who destroyed my life,"

The studio audience in Chicago went wild with boos and hisses and shouting and screeching. The audience of one in a sunny kitchen in the Piedmont area of Atlanta was remarkably silent. Her only response, other than silent tears, was three words: "It can't be."

Chapter Nineteen

Reactions to the news varied, but there was no doubt that it was news of the front-page variety. The wire services immediately picked up on the story. E!, MTV, BET, CNN and every other cable news network went into high gear on it. Naturally, it was all over The Deveraux Group with the speed of light. Clay and Marcus walked into Martin's office and closed the door behind them, both looking unusually serious.

"Turn on the television, Martin," Clay instructed.

Without question, Martin flicked the remote and stared at the split screen picture of Ceylon and Bump as the anchor repeated the top story of the entertainment news.

"Once again, it was revealed on the Jackie Rivers show that Bill 'Bump' Williams, legendary jazz pianist and orchestra leader, is the father of Ceylon Simmons, the singer-actress who, for all intents and purposes, owes her career to him."

The screen then switched to a replay of the scene of Louise choking out the name of the man that she claimed ruined her.

"Mr. Williams is not returning any calls at this point, his

publicist says he'll be releasing a statement shortly. Ms. Simmons is not available for comment. More on this as the story develops,"

Martin immediately hurled the remote control at the flat screen television, only to have Marcus expertly intercept it. "That's not going to get you anywhere, bro. There are three people we need to be talking to now, and they are Mom and Bump and Ceylon. Where is Ceylon, by the way?"

Martin was so angry he could barely answer, but he managed to get the words out. "She's on her way to California to meet with Shelley. God, I hope those vultures don't pounce on her when she gets off the plane," he said harshly.

He had no way of knowing that she was, at that moment, taking steps to assure that wouldn't happen.

Ceylon had gotten through the morning on autopilot. She got into the hired car and went to Hartsfield International as scheduled. She picked up her ticket and was preparing to go to the gate when something inside her just shut down. She tried to ignore what she'd heard, tried to pretend like it hadn't happened, but it had. Louise had announced that Bump Williams, her mentor, her sponsor, her staunchest ally and dear, dear friend was her father. It just wasn't possible. And if it was, how could she live with the consequences?

Staring blindly ahead, she walked slowly in the direction of the gate indicated on her ticket, then excused herself vaguely as she bumped into someone.

"Ceylon, it's me. You look way off in the clouds somewhere. Are you alright?" a deep male voice asked.

She blinked, and looked into the dark, compelling eyes of Tank Jackson, the Falcons star and Vera Jackson's husband.

"Tank, I'm sorry, I just have a lot on my mind," she said dully.

"So where are you headed?" he asked.

"Los Angeles. I'm on my way to California," she answered slowly.

Tank made a sound of envy. "Dang, that's where I'm supposed to be heading, but I can't get a flight for four more hours; everything is booked. I've got a meeting that I'm going to have to cancel, too."

Ceylon really focused on him for the first time. "You need to leave on this flight? Come with me, let's see what we can do," she said decisively.

Handing him the handle to her wheeled bag, she led the way back to the ticket counter.

The main conference room of The Deveraux Group held an unusual assortment of occupants that day. In attendance were all of the Deveraux brothers, Clay, Malcolm, Martin, and Marcus. Also present was their mother Lillian and their stepfather, Bill Williams, as well as Vera Jackson. Martin was about to leave to go to his mother's house when she and Bump turned up in the reception area by his office.

Lillian took command, informing him that it seemed the most expedient way of everyone getting on the same page. "Bill has tried to explain things to me, but I told him it was better if we all heard it at once, since we're obviously going to need to know what to say to the press," she said with an air of perfect serenity. Whatever she and Bump had discussed on the way to the office complex, it obviously hadn't shaken her in any way.

The massive double doors of the conference room opened and Bennie and Selena entered together, both having been invited to sit in. The reason for the meeting was fairly obvious. Bump had gathered everyone who mattered in one room to get the whole story told quickly and to figure out what needed to happen next. The only person who was missing was Angelique; she was out of town with some friends and this news was too critical to wait for her return.

To no one's surprise, Bump and Lillian sat next to each other at the head of the oversized conference table, their hands joined in a show of unity. Bump looked around the table to include everyone present in his remarks, but he was plainly directing them to Lillian more than anyone else.

"The first thing I want to say is that there is a ninety-nine percent chance that I am indeed Ceylon's father. The events of this morning, seeing that woman on television, brought something back to me I had all but forgotten. I want my wife to know what happened and I want all of you to know how I came to break my marriage vows with that woman," he said quietly.

"First of all, you should know that Lillian was my first love, my true love. We've known each other since we were toddlers, practically. I always had it in my head that she and I would get married when we grew up. I never put much practical thought into *how* it would happen. I just knew it would. She was my girl and that was it. Everything changed when I went into the Army, though. I was in basic training and Big Clay Deveraux came along and swept her off her feet. I'm not going to say I was happy about it, because I wasn't. But that's not the issue here, not at all," he said in the same quiet tone of voice.

"I got married when I left the service. She was also a girl from my hometown, Anna May Thibodaux. She was a pretty little thing, quiet and sweet and docile. One of those innocent little girls you just want to protect: you know what I mean. Well, we got married and things were going along nicely. We were very happy, at least I thought we were. I was starting to get some serious bookings and she traveled with me. We were having a great time and then she got pregnant. Man, we were the two happiest people on earth. Me, I was just over the moon, I was so elated. I was going to be a father. I thought it was the greatest thing on earth, me being a daddy."

Bump paused to gather his thoughts and Marcus immediately got up to pour him a glass of water from the thermal pitcher on the credenza against the far wall. Nodding his thanks, Bump continued.

"It wasn't an easy pregnancy for her, although I supposed no pregnancy really is. Anna seemed to have morning sickness for the entire nine months, never did gain a lot of weight, never had cravings or anything. I think she was still wearing her regular clothes when she went to deliver the baby. Anyway, we had a son, Bill, Jr. Pretty little baby, looked just like his mother, had a head full of jet-black hair and these big black eyes that could look right through you. Anna had a difficult delivery, even though the baby was kind of small at birth. She was still listless and tired for weeks after he was born.

"I had somebody to come in and take care of Billy and Anna whenever I had to be gone. I tried not to be on the road at all, but this was the only income we had, and we had to eat," he said tiredly. The strain of getting the story out seemed to be mounting, and his voice trailed off. Lillian tightened her grip on his hand and smiled at him encouragingly, even seemed to give him the motivation to continue.

"One night Miles Davis was playing in town and the boys in the band wanted to go hang out for a few minutes, just to listen to one set. They called me up and I begged off as always, saying I had to stay home with Anna and Billy. If I wasn't working, that's exactly what I did. There was no place else I really wanted to be, you know? I loved my wife and that baby." Bump's eyes grew misty with remembered emotion.

"Well, Anna heard me on the phone and insisted that I go. She said she was tired of me hovering over her all the time like she was helpless, that she could take care of Billy for one evening on her own. She was so adamant about it that I felt like I'd been depriving her of a chance to be a real mother. So I went with the boys and hung out for a couple of sets. When I got home, the first thing I did was go check on Billy. He was dead," Bump said in a flat, dull voice.

He downed some more water, and looked down at Lillian's hand before speaking.

"Anna was sound asleep. She didn't move when I called her, didn't hear me at all. Billy was already cold, so cold that he must have been like that for hours. I called 911 immediately and when they got there I was shaking her over and over asking what had happened. All she could do was cry and scream that she didn't know, she didn't know. My God, what a nightmare that night was. They worked over the baby and worked over him, but it was too late. The funeral home came and took his body away, but the ambulance left with his mother. She had a complete mental breakdown.

"Back then they didn't know nearly as much about Sudden Infant Death Syndrome as they do now," he said. "They basically just handed out a lot of platitudes about it being God's will or something. I don't think they even routinely autopsied the babies back then; I requested it and Anna went crazy. She couldn't stand the thought of her baby being cut up, she said. The very thought of it sent her into a worse mental state, something she never really recovered from, as a matter of fact."

Bump turned to look at Lillian fully then, and never took his eyes from her face. "From that day until she died, Anna and I were never man and wife. We were married, of course, but it was like having a sister. Sometimes it was like having a child. Some days would be good; she would be lucid and we'd have nice conversations, maybe even go out to dinner or to a movie. Some days she'd be a total mute, not saying a word, not moving, not responding to anyone. And sometimes she'd completely out of control, ranting and raving and screaming down the house. I had her in one home after another, institution to institution and nothing helped.

"The only thing that seemed to work was to keep her at home with a round-the-clock nurse. We were living in California then; we had moved there right after we got married. She seemed happy in that house, for the most part.

After a while, she never wanted to leave. Going out of the house for any reason filled her with fear, so she basically stayed home. Having company was out of the question. Once, we were having dinner with my sister and her husband who were visiting and she excused herself and came back in the dining room butt naked except for a strand of pearls. She was giggling like a little girl, like a two year old who was playing a trick on her parents. That was pretty much the end of any social life," he said without any show of emotion.

He released Lillian's hand and cupped her face, kissing her briefly. Taking both hands in his, he spoke directly to her. "What I've told you doesn't excuse what I'm about to reveal to you, but I hope it explains it. I was never unfaithful to Anna. I couldn't do it. I always felt like maybe it was my fault that she had the breakdown. If I hadn't been gone when Billy died, if I had just been there for her, maybe none of it would have happened. All I know is that I was pretty much dead inside. I had my music and that was it, outside of trying to take care of Anna the best I could.

"I was playing in Detroit one time, at a place called Baker's Keyboard Lounge, a real hip spot for jazz back in the day. It's still open and thriving if I'm not mistaken. Anyway, there was a real nice looking lady in the audience, not a glamour girl, not a knockout like you, she just looked like someone who would be nice to talk to. By then I was so lonely I thought *I* was going to have a breakdown. I didn't see any harm in chatting with another human being for a while. I sent drinks over to her table and she invited me to join her between the sets.

"Her name was Betty, and I believe she was a schoolteacher. But she and I didn't really get to have our chat because of her friend Louise. I'm still not sure that was the name she used. I think she said her name was Charlotte or something, I'm almost sure she didn't use her real name. But I *am* sure that this was the woman who flirted with me, fondled me under the table, and helped me get tipsy enough that

I forgot all about her little schoolteacher friend. I'm sure, beyond a shadow of a doubt, that Louise was the woman who came to my hotel room that night. And that's one of the reasons I'm sure Ceylon is my child," he said quietly.

He finally stopped speaking and waited for Lillian to respond. She stared at him through the tears in her eyes and let go of his hands so she could embrace him. "Oh Bill, my Bill. Oh, what you had to go through," she whispered to him.

They eventually stopped hugging long enough for Bump to look around the table at each face. Some, like Bennie, Vera, and Selena, wiped tears from their eyes. The men looked concerned and caring, except for Martin, who was a bit preoccupied. The thing that was on his mind was obvious. This would be wonderful news for Ceylon, if they could just find her to tell her about it. Martin spoke his thoughts aloud and let the others know he was going to call Shelley Brillstein to find out where Ceylon was at that precise moment. Not for the first time, he cursed her aversion to cell phones; she had one that she refused to use, claiming that they were rude and bordered on total lack of civilization. He went back to his office to get Shelley's number and when he returned everyone was gathered at Bump's end of the conference table.

Bump beckoned for Martin to come and look at what was spread out on the tabletop. "Here's the other reason I'm sure Ceylon is mine. I don't know why I never noticed this before, but take a look for yourself."

There were several old photographs on the table. One was of Bump's mother, some of his sisters, and one in particular of his youngest sister, his pet, Elizabeth. All were plump and even in the black and white photos the warmth of their brown skin, so much like Ceylon's, was evident. The capper, though, was the picture of Elizabeth when she was Ceylon's age. Her bright smile was identical to Ceylon's, right down to the dimples. And as this was a color picture, her long lashed hazel eyes, so much like Ceylon's, were there for all to see.

Martin was thunderstruck. The resemblance to the women in Bump's family was indeed compelling, making the need to talk to Ceylon even more pressing. Before Martin could dial Shelley's number, though, his cell phone started ringing. He answered it immediately, hoping it was his beloved.

It was Shelley, however. Martin listened rather than spoke and in seconds it was apparent that the words he was hearing weren't good. He turned a sickening pasty white and dropped the phone as his long legs folded under him when collapsed into a nearby chair.

"My God, son, what is it," implored Lillian.

"Ceylon. Ceylon's plane is missing," Martin said hoarsely.

Chapter Twenty

After Ceylon turned in her ticket to California so that Tank Jackson could use her seat, she decided she needed time to think and a place in which to do it. She rented a car at the airport and drove around for a while formulating a plan. She simply selected a nice motel from the many that populated the area near the airport and checked in, leaving a "do not disturb" at the front desk and placing the sign with the same message on the door handle of the room. She didn't turn on the television or radio, she needed absolute silence in which to think, to plan. Everything in her world had once again come crashing down around her, only this time she was taking down everyone she loved, too.

She drew the heavy draperies shut, turned on the bedside lamp, and took off her clothes. Laying across the bed in her lingerie, she stared up at the ceiling. How could this be happening? Louise had to be lying, she had to. Bump had been married when Ceylon was conceived. It was highly unlikely that he'd cheated on his wife. Louise had probably said that because she knew it would make him look bad to the public. Bump had always enjoyed a spotless reputation without a hint of scandal; Louise would take extreme pleasure in making him look despicable.

This will make Bump look like a total heel. That must be why she said it, Ceylon thought angrily. The depth of Louise's hatred shook her to her foundations. *How can she hate me enough to want to destroy other people's lives like this?*

Ceylon couldn't imagine what Bump and Lillian must be going through right at that moment. They were gracious, sophisticated people with innate dignity and charm. Who knew what they were going to go through when the news became public knowledge? And Martin . . . was he ever going to look at her the same way after he was responsible for his family being held up to ridicule? Bennie, Selena, Vera, Marcus, Malcolm, would any of them look at her the same way? And she didn't even want to think what Angelique would have to say. Ceylon turned over onto her stomach and groaned aloud.

The worst part she had to acknowledge was the bitter feeling of wanting it to be true. God help her, she wanted Bump to be her father so badly she could taste it. He was kind, sweet, and patient and he had always believed in her. Bump had guided her career, given her lessons, and taught her things that many musicians would never, ever know. And he'd done it all because he cared about her as a person, loved her unselfishly and genuinely, the way her grandparents had, the way Martin did. Yes, Bump would be the perfect father for her, she thought. Just like Martin would be the perfect husband. In minutes, she drifted off to sleep.

Hours later, Ceylon awoke, feeling heavy and lethargic instead of well rested. She looked at the digital clock on the dresser and gasped. She'd slept away the entire day! She scrambled to a sitting position and shook her head to clear it.

This is ridiculous. Here you are hiding out like a bandit and you haven't done anything wrong. You'd better get in that shower and get yourself dressed, girl, and get back to

your man if you know what's good for you. Ceylon couldn't
have said for sure if the thoughts were her own or if it was
her granny's voice chiding her, but she did as she was bid.
She leapt off the bed and unpacked enough clothes to make
a quick change. She took a thorough shower with tepid water
so she could shake off the last vestiges of sleep. When she
emerged from the shower she was wide awake and ready for
action.

She applied a minimum of makeup and let her hair air dry
as she packed the clothes she'd removed earlier. Thanking
God for credit cards, she checked out by telephone; she didn't
even have to go to the front desk, although she would have
liked some help with the big suitcase. She made it back to
the rental car and before starting the engine, she inserted a
favorite CD and sang along all the way back to Martin's
house. Leaving the bag in the car, she hastened to the front
door. Here it was ten o'clock at night and she'd been AWOL
all day. *I hope he hasn't been worried*, she fretted.

Martin sat in the dimly lit living room, his face a reflection of his misery. Marcus was with him, afraid to let him
out of his sight. Martin's reaction on hearing that Ceylon's
plane was missing was frightening in the sheer anguish that
ripped him in two. It was left to the other Deveraux brothers
to try and gather information about the missing jet and the
search process that was taking place, Martin was almost
catatonic. Equally heartrending were the reactions of Bump
and Lillian. Lillian started crying immediately and Bump
turned into an old man right in front of everyone's faces. He,
too, sank into a chair, saying over and over, "not again, not
again."

Marcus vainly tried to think of something to say to Martin.
Conversation seemed futile and ridiculous at a time like this.
Satchel suddenly jumped from his post next to Martin and
ran to the front door expectantly, his tail happily wagging.

Marcus followed the big dog curiously. "Do you have to
go out, Satch? Ready for a walk?"

Satchel's only answer was to paw the front door anxiously. Marcus opened it to find Ceylon about to put her key in the lock. He shouted with joy and grabbed Ceylon so hard she feared he was going to rupture something. His cry brought Martin out of his stupor and he immediately came into the foyer, the dark circles under his eyes attesting to the kind of day he'd had. All his anguish was forgotten when he saw Ceylon standing there. Without a word he wrapped his arms around her and held her as if he could never let her go. When he finally released his hold on her, it was to kiss her with all the pent up desire and longing in his heart. He kissed her like a man who'd been given a second chance to live. When he finally stopped, it was to utter her name with such adoration that Ceylon had difficulty breathing.

"Martin, darling what is it? What's wrong?" she asked anxiously.

Martin was too spent to speak, so Marcus explained. "Sis, we've been looking for you all day. Shelley called Martin and told him your plane had disappeared. It's been all over the news all day . . ." he paused as it was evident that Ceylon had suffered a shock.

"The plane. I gave Tank Jackson my seat on that plane. Oh Marcus, Tank was on that plane," she cried.

Marcus took about thirty seconds to register a reaction. "Vera. Oh God, Vera has no idea," he mumbled and was out the door.

Ceylon and Martin clung to each other and walked over to one of the sofas in the living room. She sat in his lap and kissed his face over and over again while they clung to each other. "Martin, I'm so sorry, so sorry, baby. I suppose you know about those lies Louise told on TV this morning. Well, they got me so upset I think I just slipped a cog for a while. I checked into a hotel to think and I fell asleep, that's all. I had no idea all this was going on, I really didn't. I wasn't trying to cause more trouble. I was trying to think of a way to get out of the trouble Louise caused," she said ruefully.

By now Martin's breathing had returned to normal and he had processed the idea that his beloved fiancée was in his arms, not smashed to bits on the side of a mountain or something worse. He was finally able to get out some coherent sentences, ones that made perfect sense to him, but Ceylon had trouble understanding.

"Ceylon, baby, it's okay. Bump knows he's your father and he's very, very happy about it. In fact, we're going over there right now," he said.

The big circular driveway at Bump and Lillian's was so full of cars it was hard for Martin and Ceylon to make their way in. They had to park at the very end of the driveway and walk up to the house. Luckily, all the activity was confined to the back of the house and no one saw them approach. Ceylon was still fretting mentally over the idea that they were just going to barge in the door without calling first, but Martin saw no point in a long phone conversation. "He'd be just as shocked if you called, believe me. Don't worry so much, Butter. He's going to be so glad to see his daughter that nothing else will matter," Martin advised.

When they reached the house, Martin opened the front door with his key. He was hoping to be able to get Bump alone to present Ceylon, but this was even better. Lillian and Bump were sitting together in the living room talking quietly. Martin spoke softly, so as not to alarm them. "Mom, Pop, I brought you something," he said, choking back the emotion in his voice.

Ceylon walked hesitantly into the living room and before she could utter a sound Bump was on his feet and had her in his arms. "Thank you Lord, thank you," he said fervently.

He hugged Ceylon tightly and kissed her cheek several times. Not bothering to hide the tears running down his face, he started cracking jokes as always. "Don't you try anything like this again, young lady. You're not too old to have a curfew, you know," he said with an attempt at his usual laugh.

By now Lillian was on her feet to get her share of hugs and kisses from Ceylon. "Oh, baby, you have no idea what this means to Bill, just none," she whispered.

Before any more conversation could commence, the people in the kitchen and back yard began to flow into the living room. It was Bump's family from Louisiana, as well as Bennie and Clay, with Malcolm and Selena. Ceylon was surrounded by the people she loved and who loved her and it was almost too much for her to take. She scanned the crowd for Martin's face and the relief on hers was visible when he made his way to her side. He stayed there as Ceylon was introduced to relative after relative, many of whom she resembled, especially the fabulous Elizabeth. They looked enough alike to be mother and daughter, from their glossy hair down to their deep dimples and charming smiles. Elizabeth just opened her arms and Ceylon walked right into them for a long, heartfelt hug.

"Welcome to the family, puddin'," Elizabeth said softly. "We're so happy to have you belong to us."

Ceylon again felt happy tears moisten her eyes. "Are you sure?" she asked humbly. "This is a lot for your family to take in, I know," she said.

Elizabeth just laughed. "Oh honey, please. My brother hasn't been this happy since Lillian said she'd marry him. Look at him now, Ceylon, doesn't he look happy?"

Ceylon leaned against Martin who had resumed standing behind her with his arms wrapped around her waist. She looked over at Bump, who was regaling his family with one of his stories, and she had to admit that he looked totally in his element and completely happy. As if he could read her mind, he looked into her eyes at just that moment and smiled broadly.

"That's my baby," he said proudly to no one in particular.

* * *

The celebration went on into the wee hours, until Martin and Ceylon were extremely weary. The only pall on the evening was the fact that Vera's husband was on the missing plane and was very likely dead. Bennie and Clay left early to be with Vera, although Marcus was still with her. When they were finally able to tear themselves away from the family, they got home in record time and immediately headed for the bed. Late as it was, and as weary as he had been, Martin took a shower and was ready to show Ceylon how much he'd thought he'd lost when she was presumed to be missing.

Martin came out of the bathroom naked except for a towel and he soon divested himself of that. Ceylon waited for him in the big bed, completely naked. They reached for each other and let the tension of the day be replaced by passion, raw, unbridled passion, as they lost themselves in their lovemaking. It was fierce and hot, unlike anything they'd ever shared before. Neither of them spoke. They gave into their hunger for each other and renewed their love in the most physical way possible. As the last tremors of pleasure left their spent bodies, Martin pulled Ceylon onto him and held her tight.

"I thought I'd lost you today, Ceylon. I can't tell you what that felt like. It must be what dying feels like. I couldn't move, couldn't speak, I could barely breathe. I know I'd be dead without you, baby. Don't ever think about leaving me, because I couldn't let you go," he said quietly.

"I could never leave you Martin. Not for anything in this world or the next," she assured him. "I can only imagine what you went through today and I'll spend the rest of my life making it up to you, I promise. Your love for me is what got me through this. It's what made me stop acting crazy and come home to you. No matter what anybody said or did, I knew you'd be waiting for me. That's what made me come to my senses," she said softly, kissing his chest afterwards.

"Martin, can we get married right away? I don't want a big ceremony, I don't want a lot of fuss, I just want to be your wife as soon as possible. With my daddy to walk me down the aisle," she added with awe in her voice.

Martin laughed at the wonder of her words. "It's hard to believe, isn't it, baby? No matter what havoc Louise was trying to wreak, she only succeeded in bringing together two people who deserve love more than anyone else. Aw, Butter, if you could have seen Bump this afternoon, it would have torn your heart out," he admitted. He had told Ceylon everything that went on in the conference room and she had been moved to tears.

"The thing was, Ceylon, he was so happy you're his daughter. He was so proud, we all felt it. And don't you worry about the press on this one. We've got the exclusive on this and it's going to be done right. You'll be proud of the coverage and so will he. And the rest of your family, too," he added sleepily.

"Olivia. And Kenneth, don't forget we have to call them tomorrow," she yawned.

"Okay, baby, whatever you say," Martin sighed and in seconds they were both sound asleep.

The next morning, Ceylon and Bump had some time alone. She and Martin had gone over to Bump and Lillian's first thing in the morning before going to see Vera. Ceylon and Bump were alone in the studio. At first they said very little; they just stared at each other with huge smiles on their faces. Finally, Ceylon spoke.

"I think we should have a blood test done," she said firmly. "I think we should know once and for all that we are father and daughter." She spoke quietly, but there was an earnestness about her tone that could not be mistaken. To her relief, Bump started laughing.

Bump immediately answered the question that was in Ceylon's eyes. "I told Lillian last night that you were going to want some kind of blood test or DNA sample or something. I told her you were going to want to have it on paper that I really, truly am your father. And it's fine with me, sweetheart. I already made an appointment for us to go have the tests done. But you have to understand this, Ceylon; I already know in my heart that you're my daughter, my baby girl, my own flesh and blood, and I couldn't be happier. I couldn't have asked God for a more wonderful surprise in my life, and I'll spend the rest of my life thanking him for you," he said.

Ceylon brushed away the tears that were falling from her eyes and hugged her father hard. They embraced tightly and then Ceylon pulled back slightly and looked up at Bump with a mischievous smile. "Do I get to call you Daddy now?"

"You better believe it, kiddo. Of course, I get to call you Babygirl whenever I feel like it, so get ready for it," he warned.

Ceylon smiled hugely in reply. "It will be my true pleasure to answer to that, Daddy."

The weeks that followed were crazy and hectic, as Ceylon had predicted, but it was a different kind of activity. Much of the time was spent preparing for the wedding, which was going to take place almost as soon as Ceylon liked, but on a much bigger scale, unfortunately. There were just too many people to invite and too many participants for it to be a small-scale affair. Ceylon was surprised at how easily she adjusted to the idea. The only pall on the whole affair was the fact that the ill-fated plane had indeed gone down with no survivors. With her love for Vera and her exaggerated sense of responsibility, Ceylon found it very difficult to control the guilt she felt over her part in the situation.

"If only I'd kept the ticket," she moaned. "If only I hadn't let him take that seat, he'd still be alive." It took a lot of talking on Martin's part to get her to believe otherwise, punctuated with similar talks from Bennie, Clay, and Bump. It was

Bennie, in fact, who suggested that Ceylon consider having a chat with John Flores, a wonderful psychiatrist and counselor who'd helped her and Clay get over the trauma of losing their first child when Bennie was in a car accident. They had evolved a deep friendship and had stayed in touch over the years.

"John called me last week and he's going to be coming here for a conference next week," Bennie had told Ceylon the week after the fatal crash. "In fact, he's going to be here for a while, he's going to be a guest lecturer at Emory University Medical School. You remember John, don't you? From California? Just think about it, Ceylon."

Ceylon did indeed remember John Flores. She also remembered the way he used to look at Bennie with longing and love in his eyes but she didn't bring that up. She thought she'd be able to handle things on her own. She'd even coped when Angelique arrived and pitched the fit she'd been warned about time and again. Two days after the story broke about Bump being her father, Angelique showed up out of nowhere, breathing fire.

She accused Ceylon of dragging the family name through the dirt, of using Bump to bolster her flagging career, of trying to grab the spotlight and any other ridiculous thing she could think of. Ceylon was at a loss as to what brought this on, until Angelique turned to leave.

"You just had to have him, too, didn't you? Nobody thought about me, about how I would feel, but then again, nobody ever does. You had to have everything and you took him from me. And I thought we were friends. It just goes to show that you can't trust anybody," she spat as she stormed out of the house as quickly as she'd burst in.

Ceylon's hands flew to her face in dismay as she realized why Angelique was so upset. She had begun to feel secure in her position as Bump's daughter and the revelation about Ceylon had pulled the rug out from under her, leaving her rootless and feeling displaced yet again. Ceylon told Martin about it that evening, cautioning him to be very gentle with his only sister. "She's feeling really lost right now, Martin. We have to make her know how important she is to all of us," Ceylon cautioned.

Martin was, as always, touched by her concern for Angelique. Assuring her that he would do his very best to make this adjustment easy for her, he kissed her hard.

"What was that for?" she asked sweetly. "I'll do it again, just to get another one of those from you."

"It was because I love you so much," he answered honestly. "And because I can't wait until next week so we can be man and wife. And because I'm really happy that Bump has twins in his family, too," he added with a wicked grin. "I can't wait for you to get pregnant, Ceylon. I hope we have about six children. Or eight, or twelve. I can't wait to start our family," he said dreamily. He was so caught up in his fantasy of little Ceylons running all over the house that he didn't notice the fact that Ceylon hadn't uttered a word.

The day of the wedding finally arrived, a warm, clear fall day full of sunlight and promise. It was the perfect day to get married, right down to the brief morning shower to bless the bride and groom. Rain on the wedding day was considered good luck, for some reason. Ceylon was the picture of radiant serenity as everyone fussed over her. No one knew what a debt she owed to John Flores, or that he was the reason the wedding was taking place on schedule.

After Martin talked about having children, Ceylon found herself in a place of panic, a dark, dire hole from which she thought there was no escape. The thought of her having a baby made her think of Louise, the poster child for rotten mothers. Suppose she turned out the same way? Life held no guarantees, after all, and Louise's blood ran through her veins, like it or not. She could turn out to be the same kind of unbalanced, selfish witch that her mother was, how could she possibly contemplate giving birth?

Her fear of ending up like Louise was what sent her to John. Actually, John came to her as they met at Bennie's house. The first thing that Ceylon noticed was that John still reminded her of Bennie's younger brother, Adam. In fact, he was a dead ringer for the other man; it was uncanny how they resembled each other. The next thing she noticed was that John still looked at Bennie with a poignant sort of yearning, as if he couldn't get enough of her beauty. Ceylon let a brief uncharitable thought race through her mind and then berated herself for it. *My Lord, if Clay ever saw him looking at Bennie like that he'd be carrying his head home in a sack.*

She and John sat in the sunny solarium with a large pitcher of iced tea at hand. John encouraged Ceylon to talk about the things that were on her mind and talk she did, starting with her childhood. She talked about her first marriage, how she went to cosmetology school, then became an instructor, when she met Bennie and Renee and became friends, and when Bennie introduced her to Bump, which was the beginning of her career.

She shared with him her devastation when her grandparents passed away, her strained relationships with her siblings, and how Duane had spirited her money away, including the fact that she didn't try to prosecute him because of her mother's intercession on his behalf. Ceylon also explained the mad crush she'd had on Martin for years and how they wound up on St. Simon's Island together, which led directly to their engagement.

John listened attentively, not taking notes, just watching Ceylon's animated face and making quiet comments and asking questions from time to time. Ceylon finally arrived at the juncture that had brought her to John in the first place. Taking a deep breath, she blurted out her deepest fear.

"Martin wants to have children. A lot of them. I always

wanted children, John, but now I'm scared. How can I possibly hope to be a decent mother when I had Louise for a role model? I know she didn't raise me, but her blood runs in my veins, John. What if I start acting just like her? What if the same thing that makes her as loony as a fruit bat makes me that way, too? I'm so frightened of turning out like her I can't sleep at night. I keep thinking, like mother like daughter, over and over until I make myself sick," she admitted.

John looked at Ceylon's unhappy face for a long moment before speaking. "Ceylon, I'm not trying to make light of your fears, but I do want you to be able to keep your concerns in perspective. I hope, in fact, that you'll be able to dismiss them entirely because I believe them to be groundless. They are real for you at the moment, but I honestly don't think they have any merit.

"From speaking with you I know you to be a deeply compassionate woman who has strong emotions for the people she loves. It was your compassion that led you to accede to Louise's wishes in the situation with Duane. Would Louise have done something like that? When she threatened to expose your natural father to the world, your concern was for Martin and his family, not for yourself. Could Louise share that kind of concern for someone else?" John probed gently.

"Time after time, Ceylon, you demonstrate that you're a completely different sort of person than your biological mother. You were raised with love and compassion by your grandparents and shows in every act of your heart. The mere fact that you are concerned about the kind of mother you'll be indicates your inner strength and the fact that you will undoubtedly be a warm, adoring mother who raises healthy well-adjusted children with the help of a doting mate. I've seen the way you and Martin are together and I have every reason to believe you'll be as happy as Bennie and Clay," he said with assurance.

Ceylon beamed at John. "Is that your professional opinion, Doctor?" she asked.

"No, Ceylon. It's the carefully considered observation of a friend. The things I've told you today are common sense, not psychobabble. If I thought you needed counseling, I'd be glad to refer you to someone. I think what you needed was a neutral party as a sounding board. Frankly, Ceylon with all you've been through in the past months it's a wonder you're handling things so well. A lesser woman would have broken under the strain. The things you're feeling and thinking, well, they're perfectly normal under the circumstances. I'm glad I was able to talk you through them as a friend," he said with a smile.

That talk was all Ceylon needed to put her world to rights. She sat quietly, the picture of composure while Renee and Bennie fussed with her hair and makeup, and Olivia adjusted her dress. They and Lillian were already in the sublime silk crepe gowns they would wear as bridesmaids, all in a heavenly shade of violet. Amariee, Jilleyin, and Jasmine served as junior bridesmaids, along with Olivia's two daughters and a young cousin of Ceylon's from Bump's side of the family. These young ladies all wore hyacinth dresses. The flower girl was Renee's oldest daughter Andrea, in a fantastic lilac frock that was much coveted by her little sisters who were deemed too young to participate. They were mollified somewhat by being able to wear matching dresses to the ceremony. With Bennie and Clay's oldest son, Trey, as ring bearer, the wedding party was huge, but Ceylon didn't care.

All she cared about was the fact that her father was about to escort her down the aisle to the man she loved. The weather was perfect for the outdoor ceremony and the flowers in shades of purple from creamy lavender to deepest royal purple, were amazing. Vera had done most of the planning for the wedding, although she wasn't feeling up to being a bridesmaid. As she explained to Ceylon, keeping busy was the best thing for her while she grieved for her husband. The love and effort she put forth on behalf of the wedding was something Ceylon would never forget. The men stood at the flower-bedecked altar looking handsome and dignified in their black tuxedoes with the hyacinth vests and white band collared shirts, setting off Martin, who wore a violet vest. Even wearing what he referred to as a sissy color didn't make him any the less gorgeous in Ceylon's eyes. She looked him the way she always did, as if he were the most wonderful sight she'd ever witnessed in her life.

It was a look Martin returned with even more fervor as he watched Bump and Ceylon walk down the white runner to the altar where they would become one. Ceylon wore a stunning off the shoulder dress of silk georgette with long sheer sleeves and a tight bodice that flared out into a full skirt with three overlays of georgette very lightly tinted with shades of violet. She chose not to wear a veil, but had tucked a flower or two into her shining hair. As Bump delivered her into Martin's hands, he muttered under his breath. "This is *not* a loan, got me?"

Ceylon turned to her father and kissed him on the cheek before turning to the man she adored, the man who would love her forever.

Hand in hand they recited the vows they'd both taken before, but this time it was forever.

"You're mine, Ceylon. Now and forever," Martin whispered to her after they were pronounced man and wife.

"And you're mine, my beautiful Martin," she answered. "My one and only love." She smiled through tears of joy.

Epilogue

A cheery *knock-knock* from the kitchen made Lillian stop what she was doing in the pantry and come out to greet her guests. "Well, it's about time you got here! I was beginning to think you were trying to skip out on us." Lillian's chiding words held no meaning as her face was wreathed in a smile. "Let me have that little one. Come to Grammy, darling," she cooed as she held out her arms for little Elizabeth Mercier Deveraux, the newest member of the Deveraux family. Elizabeth was, at one year of age, a beauty who resembled both her mother and her father. She had the dimples and sparkling hazel eyes of her mother, and the golden coloring, thick black hair and implacable will of her father. She also had the entire family under her thumb, something of which Ceylon despaired.

"Lillian, I'm so glad I'm pregnant again! I want Elizabeth to have brothers and sisters so she won't be totally spoiled. Between Daddy and Martin, I can only imagine what she'll be like when she grows up," Ceylon said with a mock shudder.

Lillian pretended outrage as she took the little girl off to see her grandfather. "Spoiled? This precious girl? Oh, I don't think so! We won't let her daddy spoil her, no sir!"

Martin entered the sunny kitchen in time to hear those last words. "Hey, I'm not spoiling her. I'm just giving her the attention she needs for proper development," he protested.

Ceylon sighed deeply. "Since when do diamond studs from Tiffany's constitute proper development? Even though I'm not letting her have her ears pierced until she's ten, you went right out and bought them, didn't you?"

Martin smiled down at his dearly loved wife. "Yes, but I bought you some too, remember? If anything I'm spoiling you both," he whispered in her ear as he kissed the soft fragrant skin of her neck.

Marcus entered the kitchen then, shaking his head at the sight of Martin and Ceylon kissing. "Don't y'all ever come up for air? This is where those babies come from, you know this, right?" He proceeded to go into the refrigerator and pour a large glass of iced tea.

Martin laughed and said, "Your turn is coming, Marcus. One of these days you're going to be in this exact same position, so crazy about your woman you won't be able to see straight and trying to pop out as many babies as possible. Trust me."

Marcus snorted. "Not in this lifetime, bro. I told you there's only one woman in the entire world I'd ever marry." He stopped to take a long swallow of tea before continuing. "And since Oprah won't return my calls, I guess I'm married to the company."

The family had gathered at Bump and Lillian's to celebrate another milestone, the official launch of the music division of The Deveraux Group. Martin would head this division and the first artist signed was of course, Ceylon Simmons Deveraux, followed by Bump Williams. The new division meant that with Clay handling TV and film production, Malcolm handling the financial and development end and Martin the music, it fell to Marcus to head the company.

No one was really surprised when the decision was made to name Marcus CEO; this had been his dream since he was ten years old.

Ceylon laughed along with the two men, but her eyes followed Marcus as he went out into the backyard where the festivities were taking place. "I don't really believe him, do you?" she murmured to Martin.

"Who, Marcus? No, I think he just hasn't found the right woman. When he does, he'll fall like a ton of bricks, just the way the rest of us did. But I really don't want to talk about Marcus," he said softly.

He led Ceylon over to the breakfast bar and seated her on one of the tall stools. "I want to talk about you and how you're feeling, Butter. Are you sure this isn't too much for you?" he said with concern in his voice.

Ceylon pulled him in to her embrace, and they hugged tightly for a long moment. "Baby, I'm fine. I feel wonderful. Once the daily morning sickness has made its appearance, I'm good to go, you know that. Besides I need to stay active because I don't want to gain too much weight."

Martin kissed her long and sweet before replying. "You'll be fine, Butter. You gained just the right amount with Elizabeth and you took it off quite nicely," he said with a touch of chagrin.

Ceylon laughed at his tone of voice. "I didn't lose those last seven pounds and you know it. You're just sounding sad because you like me big! Well, you may get your wish this time because there's no telling what two babies will do to this figure," she said quietly.

Martin was too absorbed in kissing Ceylon's temple, her ear and her neck to let the words sink in at first, finally it hit him.

"Two babies? *Two?* At once?"

"Yes, darling. Twins. I found out this morning but I thought it would be nice to tell everyone today. Do you mind?"

"Not in the least, baby. In fact, I'll go tell them now," Martin said with a smile.

Ceylon looked at her big handsome husband and sighed with contentment. "If you're real nice to me, I'll tell you if they're boys or girls," she said.

Martin paused for a moment, then smiled. "Well, I'll always be nice to you because I love you more than anything. But there have to be a few surprises in life, so don't tell me. I want to find out the old-fashioned way," he said as took his one and only love's hand.

And in the very old-fashioned way, he found out a few months later that the babies were strong, healthy boys.

To My Readers:

I hope you all enjoyed Martin and Ceylon's story. It was a story I wanted to write both to satisfy the many readers who wanted to see the reclusive Martin find happiness, and because I really believed in the power of Martin and Ceylon's love to enable them to build a new life together. As Ceylon already knew and Martin found out, there are scars on the inside that can wound more deeply that the ones on the outside, but love and understanding go a long way to making the scars a thing of the past.

I can't thank you enough for your continued support. The lovely letters and e-mails I've received again humble me. Thank you all for taking the time to write. And a special thank you to all my friends in Florida; I hope to visit there soon!

Next March will bring the story of Vera Clark Jackson who so tragically lost her husband in a plane crash. It's two years after his death and everyone seems to think it's time for Vera to love again, especially someone who has loved her for years. But is she ready to trust in love again? You'll find out in *Let It Be Me*!

Until then, be blessed!

Melanie
I Chronicles 4:10

MelanieAuthor@aol.com
P.O. Box 5176
Saginaw, Michigan 48603

ABOUT THE AUTHOR

Melanie Woods Schuster currently lives in Saginaw, where she works in sales for the largest telecommunications company in the state. She attended Ohio University. Her occupations indicate her interests in life; Melanie has worked as a costume designer, a makeup artist, an admissions counselor at a private college and in marketing. She is also an artist, a calligrapher, and she makes jewelry and designs clothing. Writing has always been her true passion, however, and she looks forward to creating more compelling stories of love and passion in the years to come.

The Arabesque At Your Service Series

Four superb romances with engaging characters and dynamic story lines featuring heroes whose destiny is intertwined with women of equal courage who confront their passionate—and unpredictable—futures.

__TOP-SECRET RENDEZVOUS
by Linda Hudson-Smith   1-58314-397-1 $6.99US/$9.99CAN

Sparks fly when officer Hailey Douglas meets Air Force Major Zurich Kingdom. Military code forbids fraternization between an officer and an NCO, so the pair find themselves involved in a top-secret rendezvous.

__COURAGE UNDER FIRE
by Candice Poarch   1-58314-350-5 $6.99US/$9.99CAN

Nurse Arlene Taft is assigned to care for the seriously injured Colonel Neal Allen. She remembers him as an obnoxious young neighbor at her father's military base, but now he looks nothing like she remembers. Will time give them courage under fire?

__THE GLORY OF LOVE
by Kim Louise   1-58314-411-0 $6.99US/$9.99CAN

When pilot Roxanne Allgood is kidnapped, Navy Seal Col. Haughton Storm sets out on a mission to find the only person who has ever mattered to him—a lost love he hasn't seen in ten years.

__FLYING HIGH
by Gwynne Forster   1-58314-427-7 $6.99US/$9.99CAN

Colonel Nelson Wainwright must recover from his injuries if he is to attain his goal of becoming a four-star general. Audrey Powers, a specialist in sports medicine, enters his world to get him back on track. Will their love find a way to endure his rise to the top?